Erewhon

SAMUEL BUTLER

EREWHON

or Over the Range

COLLIER BOOKS
NEW YORK, N.Y.

Collier Books is a division of The Crowell-Collier Publishing
Company.

First Collier Books Edition 1961

Contents

PREFACE TO REVISED EDITION vii

PREFACE TO SECOND EDITION xi

PREFACE TO FIRST EDITION xv

1 Waste Lands 17

2 In the Wool-Shed 21

3 Up the River 25

4 The Saddle 29

5 The River and the Range 35

6 Into Erewhon 42

7 First Impressions 48

8 In Prison 53

9 To the Metropolis 59

10 Current Opinions 67

11 Some Erewhonian Trials 75

12 Malcontents 81

13 The Views of the Erewhonians Concerning Death 86

14 Mahaina 92

15 The Musical Banks 95

16	Arowhena	104
17	Ydgrun and the Ydgrunites	110
18	Birth Formulae	115
19	The World of the Unborn	119
20	What They Mean by It	125
21	The Colleges of Unreason	130
22	The Colleges of Unreason—(*continued*)	136
23	The Book of the Machines	143
24	The Book of the Machines—(*continued*)	148
25	The Book of the Machines—(*concluded*)	155
26	The Views of an Erewhonian Prophet Concerning the Rights of Animals	165
27	The Views of an Erewhonian Philosopher Concerning the Rights of Vegetables	171
28	Escape	178
29	Conclusion	186

Preface to the Revised Edition

MY PUBLISHER wishes me to say a few words about the genesis of the work, a revised and enlarged edition of which he is herewith laying before the public. I therefore place on record as much as I can remember on this head after a lapse of more than thirty years.

The first part of *Erewhon* written was an article headed "Darwin among the Machines," and signed Cellarius. It was written in the Upper Rangitata district of the Canterbury Province (as it then was) of New Zealand, and appeared at Christchurch in *The Press* newspaper, 13th June, 1863. A copy of this article is indexed under my books in the British Museum catalogue. In passing, I may say that the opening chapters of *Erewhon* were also drawn from the Upper Rangitata district, with such modifications as I found convenient.

In 1865 I rewrote and enlarged "Darwin among the Machines" for *The Reasoner,* a paper published in London by Mr. G. J. Holyoake. It appeared 1st July, 1865 under the heading "The Mechanical Creation," and can be seen in the British Museum. I again rewrote and enlarged it, till it assumed the form in which it appeared in the first edition of *Erewhon.*

The next part of *Erewhon* that I wrote was "The World of the Unborn," a preliminary form of which was sent to Mr. Holyoake's paper, but as I cannot find it among those copies of *The Reasoner* that are in the British Museum, I conclude that it was not accepted. I have, however, rather a strong fancy that it appeared in some London paper of the same character as *The Reasoner,* not very long after 1st July, 1865, but I have no copy.

I also wrote about this time the substance of what ultimately became "The Musical Banks," and the trial of a man for being in a consumption. These four detached papers were, I believe, all that was written of *Erewhon* before 1870. Between 1865 and 1870 I wrote hardly anything, being hopeful of attaining that success as a painter which it has not been vouchsafed me to attain, but in the autumn of 1870, just as I was beginning to get occasionally hung at Royal Academy exhibitions, my friend, the late Sir F. N. (then Mr.) Broome, suggested to me that I should add somewhat to the articles I had already written, and string them together into a book. I was rather fired by the idea, but as I only worked at the MS. on Sundays it was some months before I had completed it.

I see from my second Preface that I took the book to Messrs. Chapman and Hall 1st May, 1871, and on their rejection of it, under the advice of one who has attained the highest rank among living writers, I let it sleep, till I took it to Mr. Trübner early in 1872. As regards its rejection by Messrs. Chapman and Hall, I believe their reader advised them quite wisely. They told me he reported that it was a philosophical work, little likely to be popular with a large circle of readers. I hope that if I had been their reader, and the book had been submitted to myself, I should have advised them to the same effect.

Erewhon appeared with the last day or two of March 1872. I attribute its unlooked-for success mainly to two early favourable reviews—the first in *The Pall Mall Gazette* of 12th April, and the second in *The Spectator* of 20th April. There was also another cause. I was complaining once to a friend that though *Erewhon* had met with such a warm reception, my subsequent books had been all of them practically still-born. He said, "You forget one charm that *Erewhon* had, but which none of your other books can have." I asked what? and was answered, "The sound of a new voice, and of an unknown voice."

The first edition of *Erewhon* sold in about three weeks; I had not taken moulds, and as the demand was strong, it was set up again immediately. I made a few unimportant alterations and additions, and added a Preface, of which I cannot say that I am particularly proud, but an inexperienced writer with a head somewhat turned by unexpected success is not to be trusted with a preface. I made a few further very trifling alterations before moulds were taken, but since the summer of 1872, as new editions were from time to time wanted, they have been printed from stereos then made.

Having now, I fear, at too great length done what I was asked to do, I should like to add a few words on my own account. I am still fairly well satisfied with those parts of *Erewhon* that were repeatedly rewritten, but from those that had only a single writing I would gladly cut out some forty or fifty pages if I could.

This, however, may not be, for the copyright will probably expire in a little over twelve years. It was necessary, therefore, to revise the book throughout for literary inelegancies—of which I found many more than I had expected—and also to make such substantial additions as should secure a new lease of life—at any rate for the copyright. If, then, instead of cutting out, say fifty pages, I have been compelled to add about sixty *invita Minerva*—the blame rests neither with my publisher nor with me, but with the copyright laws. Nevertheless I can assure the reader that, though I have found it an irksome task to take up work which I thought I had got rid of thirty years ago, and much of which I am ashamed of, I have done my best to make the new matter savour so much of the better portions of the old that none but the best critics shall perceive at what places the gaps of between thirty and forty years occur.

Lastly, if my readers note a considerable difference between the literary technique of *Erewhon* and that of *Erewhon Revisited* I would remind them that, as I have just shown, *Erewhon* took something like ten years in writing, and even so was written with great difficulty, while *Erewhon Revisited* was written easily between November 1900 and the end of April 1901. There is no central idea underlying *Erewhon,* whereas the attempt to realize the effect of a single supposed great miracle dominates the whole of its successor. In *Erewhon* there was hardly any story, and little attempt to give life and individuality to the characters; I hope that in *Erewhon Revisited* both these defects have been in great measure avoided. *Erewhon* was not an organic whole, *Erewhon Revisited* may fairly claim to be one. Nevertheless, though in literary workmanship I do not doubt that this last-named book is an improvement on the first, I shall be agreeably surprised if I am not told that *Erewhon,* with all its faults, is the better reading of the two.

Samuel Butler.

7th August, 1901.

Preface to the Second Edition

HAVING BEEN enabled by the kindness of the public to get through an unusually large edition of *Erewhon* in a very short time, I have taken the opportunity of a second edition to make some necessary corrections, and to add a few passages where it struck me that they would be appropriately introduced; the passages are few, and it is my fixed intention never to touch the work again.

I may perhaps be allowed to say a word or two here in reference to *The Coming Race,* to the success of which book *Erewhon* has been very generally set down as due. This is a mistake, though a perfectly natural one. The fact is that *Erewhon* was finished, with the exception of the last twenty pages and a sentence or two inserted from time to time here and there throughout the book, before the first advertisement of *The Coming Race* appeared. A friend having called my attention to one of the first of these advertisements, and suggesting that it probably referred to a work of similar character to my own, I took *Erewhon* to a well-known firm of publishers on the 1st May 1871, and left it in their hands for consideration. I then went abroad, and on learning that the publishers alluded to declined the MS., I let it alone for six or seven months, and, being in an out-of-the-way part of Italy, never saw a single review of *The Coming Race,* nor a copy of the work. On my return, I purposely avoided looking into it until I had sent back my last revises to the printer. Then I had much pleasure in reading it, but was indeed surprised at the many little points of similarity between the two books, in spite of their entire independence of one another.

I regret that reviewers have in some cases been inclined to treat the chapters on Machines as an attempt to reduce Mr. Darwin's theory to an absurdity. Nothing could be further from my intention, and few things would be more distasteful to me than any attempt to laugh at Mr. Darwin; but I must own that I have myself to thank for the misconception, for I felt sure that my intention would be missed, but preferred not to weaken the chapters by explanation, and knew very well that Mr. Darwin's theory would take no harm. The only question in my mind was how far I could afford to be misrepresented as laughing at that for which I have the most profound admiration. I am surprised, however, that the book at which such an example of the specious misuse of analogy would seem most naturally levelled should have occurred to no reviewer; neither shall I mention the name of the book here, though I should fancy that the hint given will suffice.

I have been held by some whose opinions I respect to have denied men's responsibility for their actions. He who does this in an enemy who deserves no quarter. I should have imagined that I had been sufficiently explicit, but have made a few additions to the chapter on Malcontents, which will, I think, serve to render further mistake impossible.

An anonymous correspondent (by the handwriting presumably a clergyman) tells me that in quoting from the Latin grammar I should at any rate have done so correctly, and that I should have written "agricolas" instead of "agricolae." He added something about any boy in the fourth form, etc., etc., which I shall not quote, but which made me very uncomfortable. It may be said that I must have misquoted from design, from ignorance, or by a slip of the pen; but surely in these days it will be recognized as harsh to assign limits to the all-embracing boundlessness of truth, and it will be more reasonably assumed that *each* of the three possible causes of misquotation must have had its share in the apparent blunder. The art of writing things that shall sound right and yet be wrong has made so many reputations, and affords comfort to such a large number of readers, that I could not venture to neglect it; the Latin grammar, however, is a subject on which some of the younger members of the community feel strongly, so I have now written "agricolas." I have also parted with the word "infortuniam" (though not without regret), but have not dared to meddle with other similar inaccuracies.

For the inconsistencies in the book, and I am aware that there are not a few, I must ask the indulgence of the reader. The blame, however, lies chiefly with the Erewhonians themselves, for they were really a very difficult people to understand. The most glaring anomalies seemed to afford them no intellectual inconvenience; neither, provided they did not actually see the money dropping out of their pockets, nor suffer immediate physical pain, would they listen to any arguments as to the waste of money and happiness which their folly caused them. But this had an effect of which I have little reason to complain, for I was allowed almost to call them lifelong self-deceivers to their faces, and they said it was quite true, but that it did not matter.

I must not conclude without expressing my most sincere thanks to my critics and to the public for the leniency and consideration with which they have treated my adventures.

9th June, 1872.

Preface to the First Edition

THE AUTHOR wishes it to be understood that Erewhon is pronounced as a word of three syllables, all short—thus, E-re-whon.

Chapter 1

Waste Lands

IF THE reader will excuse me, I will say nothing of my ante-
cedents, nor of the circumstances which led me to leave my
native country; the narrative would be tedious to him and
painful to myself. Suffice it, that when I left home it was with
the intention of going to some new colony, and either finding,
or even perhaps purchasing, waste crown land suitable for
cattle or sheep farming, by which means I thought that I could
better my fortunes more rapidly than in England.

It will be seen that I did not succeed in my design, and that
however much I may have met with that was new and strange,
I have been unable to reap any pecuniary advantage.

It is true, I imagine myself to have made a discovery which,
if I can be the first to profit by it, will bring me a recompense
beyond all money computation, and secure me a position such
as has not been attained by more than some fifteen or sixteen
persons, since the creation of the universe. But to this end I
must possess myself of a considerable sum of money: neither
do I know how to get it, except by interesting the public in my
story, and inducing the charitable to come forward and assist
me. With this hope I now publish my adventures; but I do
so with great reluctance, for I fear that my story will be
doubted unless I tell the whole of it; and yet I dare not do so,
lest others with more means than mine should get the start
of me. I prefer the risk of being doubted to that of being anticipated, and have therefore concealed my destination on leaving
England, as also the point from which I began my more serious
and difficult journey.

My chief consolation lies in the fact that truth bears its own
impress, and that my story will carry conviction by reason of
the internal evidences for its accuracy. No one who is himself
honest will doubt my being so.

I reached my destination in one of the last months of 1868,
but I dare not mention the season, lest the reader should gather
in which hemisphere I was. The colony was one which had
not been opened up even to the most adventurous settlers for
more than eight or nine years, having been previously unin-
habited, save by a few tribes of savages who frequented the

17

seaboard. The part known to Europeans consisted of a coast-line about eight hundred miles in length (affording three or four good harbours), and a tract of country extending inland for a space varying from two to three hundred miles, until it reached the offshoots of an exceedingly lofty range of moun-tains, which could be seen from far out upon the plains, and were covered with perpetual snow. The coast was perfectly well known both north and south of the tract to which I have alluded, but in neither direction was there a single harbour for five hundred miles, and the mountains, which descended al-most into the sea, were covered with thick timber, so that none would think of settling.

With this bay of land, however, the case was different. The harbours were sufficient; the country was timbered, but not too heavily; it was admirably suited for agriculture; it also contained millions on millions of acres of the most beautifully grassed country in the world, and of the best suited for all manner of sheep and cattle. The climate was temperate, and very healthy; there were no wild animals, nor were the natives dangerous, being few in number and of an intelligent tractable disposition.

It may be readily understood that when once Europeans set foot upon this territory they were not slow to take advan-tage of its capabilities. Sheep and cattle were introduced, and bred with extreme rapidity; men took up their 50,000 or 100,000 acres of country, going inland one behind the other, till in a few years there was not an acre between the sea and the front ranges which was not taken up, and stations either for sheep or cattle were spotted about at intervals of some twenty or thirty miles over the whole country. The front ranges stopped the tide of squatters for some little time; it was thought that there was too much snow upon them for too many months in the year—that the sheep would get lost, the ground being too difficult for shepherding—that the expense of getting wool down to the ship's side would eat up the farmer's profits—and that the grass was too rough and sour for sheep to thrive upon; but one after another determined to try the experiment, and it was wonderful how successfully it turned out. Men pushed farther and farther into the mountains, and found a very considerable tract inside the front range, between it and another which was loftier still, though even this was not the highest, the great snowy one which could be seen from out upon the plains. This second range, however, seemed to mark the extreme limits of pastoral country; and it was here, at a small and newly founded station, that I was received as a cadet, and soon regularly employed. I was then just twenty-two years old.

I was delighted with the country and the manner of life. It was my daily business to go up to the top of a certain high mountain, and down one of its spurs on to the flat, in order to make sure that no sheep had crossed their boundaries. I was to see the sheep, not necessarily close at hand, nor to get them in a single mob, but to see enough of them here and there to feel easy that nothing had gone wrong; this was no difficult matter, for there were not above eight hundred of them; and, being all breeding ewes, they were pretty quiet.

There were a good many sheep which I knew, as two or three black ewes, and a black lamb or two, and several others which had some distinguishing mark whereby I could tell them. I would try and see all these, and if they were all there, and the mob looked large enough, I might rest assured that all was well. It is surprising how soon the eye becomes accustomed to missing twenty sheep out of two or three hundred. I had a telescope and a dog, and would take bread and meat and tobacco with me. Starting with early dawn, it would be night before I could complete my round; for the mountain over which I had to go was very high. In winter it was covered with snow, and the sheep needed no watching from above. If I were to see sheep dung or tracks going down on to the other side of the mountain (where there was a valley with a stream —a mere *cul de sac*), I was to follow them, and look out for sheep; but I never saw any, the sheep always descending on to their own side, partly from habit, and partly because there was abundance of good sweet feed, which had been burnt in the early spring, just before I came, and was now deliciously green and rich, while that on the other side had never been burnt, and was rank and coarse.

It was a monotonous life, but it was very healthy; and one does not much mind anything when one is well. The country was the grandest that can be imagined. How often have I sat on the mountain side and watched the waving downs, with the two white specks of huts in the distance, and the little square of garden behind them; the paddock with a patch of bright green oats above the huts, and the yards and wool-sheds down on the flat below; all seen as through the wrong end of a telescope, so clear and brilliant was the air, or as upon a colossal model or map spread out beneath me. Beyond the downs was a plain, going down to a river of great size, on the farther side of which there were other high mountains, with the winter's snow still not quite melted; up the river, which

19

ran winding in many streams over a bed some two miles broad, I looked upon the second great chain, and could see a narrow gorge where the river retired and was lost. I knew that there was a range still farther back; but except from one place near the very top of my own mountain, no part of it was visible: from this point, however, I saw, whenever there were no clouds, a single snow-clad peak, many miles away, and I should think about as high as any mountain in the world. Never shall I forget the utter loneliness of the prospect—only the little far-away homestead giving sign of human handiwork; the vastness of mountain and plain, of river and sky; the marvellous atmospheric effects—sometimes black mountains against a white sky, and then again, after cold weather, white mountains against a black sky—sometimes seen through breaks and swirls of cloud—and sometimes, which was best of all, I went up my mountain in a fog, and then got above the mist; going higher and higher, I would look down upon a sea of whiteness, through which would be thrust innumerable mountain tops that looked like islands.

I am there now, as I write; I fancy that I can see the downs, the huts, the plain, and the river-bed—that torrent pathway of desolation, with its distant roar of waters. Oh, wonderful, wonderful! so lonely and so solemn, with the sad grey clouds above, and no sound save a lost lamb bleating upon the mountain side, as though its little heart were breaking. Then there comes some lean and withered old ewe, with deep gruff voice and unlovely aspect, trotting back from the seductive pasture; now she examines this gully, and now that, and now she stands listening with uplifted head, that she may hear the distant wailing and obey it. Aha! they see, and rush towards each other. Alas! they are both mistaken; the ewe is not the lamb's ewe, they are neither kin nor kind to one another, and part in coldness. Each must cry louder, and wander farther yet; may luck be with them both that they may find their own at nightfall. But this is mere dreaming, and I must proceed.

I could not help speculating upon what might lie farther up the river and behind the second range. I had no money, but if I could only find workable country, I might stock it with borrowed capital, and consider myself a made man. True, the range looked so vast, that there seemed little chance of getting a sufficient road through it or over it; but no one had yet explored it, and it is wonderful how one finds that one can make a path into all sorts of places (and even get a road for pack-horses), which from a distance appear inaccessible; the river was so great that it must drain an inner tract—at least I thought so; and though every one said it would be madness to attempt taking sheep farther inland, I knew that only three years ago the same cry had been raised against the country which my master's flock was now overrunning. I could not keep these thoughts out of my head as I would rest myself upon the mountain side; they haunted me as I went my daily rounds, and grew upon me from hour to hour, till I resolved that after shearing I would remain in doubt no longer, but saddle my horse, take as much provision with me as I could, and go and see for myself.

But over and above these thoughts came that of the great range itself. What was beyond it? Ah! who could say? There was no one in the whole world who had the smallest idea, save those who were themselves on the other side of it—if, indeed, there was any one at all. Could I hope to cross it? This would be the highest triumph that I could wish for; but it was too much to think of yet. I would try the nearer range, and see how far I could go. Even if I did not find country, might I not find gold, or diamonds, or copper, or silver? I would sometimes lie flat down to drink out of a stream, and could see little yellow specks among the sand; were these gold? People said no; but then people always said there was no gold until it was found to be abundant: there was plenty of slate and granite, which I had always understood to accompany gold; and even though it was not found in paying quantities here, it might be abundant in the main ranges. These thoughts filled my head, and I could not banish them.

Chapter 2

In the Wool-Shed

AT LAST shearing came; and with the shearers there was an old native, whom they had nicknamed Chowbok—though, I believe, his real name was Kahabuka. He was a sort of chief of the natives, could speak a little English, and was a great favourite with the missionaries. He did not do any regular work with the shearers, but pretended to help in the yards, his real aim being to get the grog, which is always more freely circulated at shearing-time: he did not get much, for he was apt to be dangerous when drunk; and very little would make him so: still he did get it occasionally, and if one wanted to

21

get anything out of him, it was the best bribe to offer him. I resolved to question him, and get as much information from him as I could. I did so. As long as I kept to questions about the nearer ranges, he was easy to get on with—he had never been there, but there were traditions among his tribe to the effect that there was no sheep-country, nothing, in fact, but stunted timber and a few river-bed flats. It was very difficult to reach; still there were passes: one of them up our own river, though not directly along the river-bed, the gorge of which was not practicable; he had never seen any one who had been there: was there not enough on this side? But when I came to the main range, his manner changed at once. He became uneasy, and began to prevaricate and shuffle. In a very few minutes I could see that of this too there existed traditions in his tribe; but no effort or coaxing could get a word from him about them. At last I hinted about grog, and presently he feigned consent: I gave it him; but as soon as he had drunk it he began shamming intoxication, and then went to sleep, or pretended to do so, letting me kick him pretty hard and never budging.

I was angry, for I had to go without my own grog and had got nothing out of him; so the next day I determined that he should tell me before I gave him any, or get none at all.

Accordingly, when night came and the shearers had knocked off work and had their supper, I got my share of rum in a tin pannikin and made a sign to Chowbok to follow me to the wool-shed, which he willingly did, slipping out after me, and no one taking any notice of either of us. When we got down to the wool-shed we lit a tallow candle, and having stuck it in an old bottle we sat down upon the wool bales and began to smoke. A wool-shed is a roomy place, built somewhat on the same plan as a cathedral, with aisles on either side full of pens for the sheep, a great nave, at the upper end of which the shearers work, and a further space for wool sorters and packers. It always refreshed me with a semblance of antiquity (precious in a new country), though I very well knew that the oldest wool-shed in the settlement was not more than seven years old, while this was only two. Chowbok pretended to expect his grog at once, though we both of us knew very well what the other was after, and that we were each playing against the other, the one for grog, the other for information.

We had a hard fight: for more than two hours he had tried to put me off with lies but had carried no conviction; during the whole time we had been morally wrestling with one another and had neither of us apparently gained the least advantage;

at length, however, I had become sure that he would give in ultimately, and that with a little further patience I should get his story out of him. As upon a cold day in winter, when one has churned (as I had often had to do), and churned in vain, and the butter makes no sign of coming, at last one tells by the sound that the cream has gone to sleep, and then upon a sudden the butter comes, so I had churned at Chowbok until I perceived that he had arrived, as it were, at the sleepy stage, and that with a continuance of steady quiet pressure the day was mine. On a sudden, without a word of warning, he rolled two bales of wool (his strength was very great) into the middle of the floor, and on the top of these he placed another crosswise; he snatched up an empty wool-pack, threw it like a mantle over his shoulders, jumped upon the uppermost bale, and sat upon it. In a moment his whole form was changed. His high shoulders dropped; he set his feet close together, heel to heel and toe to toe; he laid his arms and hands close alongside of his body, the palms following his thighs; he held his head high but quite straight, and his eyes stared right in front of him; but he frowned horribly, and assumed an expression of face that was positively fiendish. At the best of times Chowbok was very ugly, but he now exceeded all conceivable limits of the hideous. His mouth extended almost from ear to ear, grinning horribly and showing all his teeth; his eyes glared, though they remained quite fixed, and his forehead was contracted with a most malevolent scowl.

I am afraid my description will have conveyed only the ridiculous side of his appearance; but the ridiculous and the sublime are near, and the grotesque fiendishness of Chowbok's face approached this last, if it did not reach it. I tried to be amused, but I felt a sort of creeping at the roots of my hair and over my whole body, as I looked and wondered what he could possibly be intending to signify. He continued thus for about a minute, sitting bolt upright, as stiff as a stone, and making this fearful face. Then there came from his lips a low moaning like the wind, rising and falling by infinitely small gradations till it became almost a shriek, from which it descended and died away; after that, he jumped down from the bale and held up the extended fingers of both his hands as one who should say "Ten," though I did not then understand him.

For myself I was open-mouthed with astonishment. Chowbok rolled the bales rapidly into their place, and stood before me shuddering as in great fear; horror was written upon his face—this time quite involuntarily—as though the natural panic of one who had committed an awful crime against unknown and superhuman agencies. He nodded his head and gibbered, and pointed repeatedly to the mountains. He would not touch the grog, but, after a few seconds he made a run through the wool-shed door into the moonlight; nor did he reappear till next day at dinner-time, when he turned up, looking very sheepish and abject in his civility towards myself.

Of his meaning I had no conception. How could I? All I could feel sure of was, that he had a meaning which was true and awful to himself. It was enough for me that I believed him to have given me the best he had and all he had. This kindled my imagination more than if he had told me intelligible stories by the hour together. I knew not what the great snowy ranges might conceal, but I could no longer doubt that it would be something well worth discovering.

I kept aloof from Chowbok for the next few days, and showed no desire to question him further; when I spoke to him I called him Kahabuka, which gratified him greatly: he seemed to have become afraid of me, and acted as one who was in my power. Having therefore made up my mind that I would begin exploring as soon as shearing was over, I thought it would be a good thing to take Chowbok with me; so I told him that I meant going to the nearer ranges for a few days' prospecting, and that he was to come too. I made him promises of nightly grog, and held out the chances of finding gold. I said nothing about the main range, for I knew it would frighten him. I would get him as far up our own river as I could, and trace it if possible to its source. I would then either go on by myself, if I felt my courage equal to the attempt, or return with Chowbok. So, as soon as ever shearing was over and the wool sent off, I asked leave of absence, and obtained it. Also, I bought an old pack-horse and pack-saddle, so that I might take plenty of provisions, and blankets, and a small tent. I was to ride and find fords over the river; Chowbok was to follow and lead the pack-horse, which would also carry him over the fords. My master let me have tea and sugar, ship's biscuits, tobacco, and salt mutton, with two or three bottles of good brandy; for, as the wool was now sent down, abundance of provisions would come up with the empty drays.

Everything being now ready, all the hands on the station turned out to see us off, and we started on our journey, not very long after the summer solstice of 1870.

Chapter 3

Up the River

THE FIRST day we had an easy time, following up the great
flats by the river side, which had already been twice burned,
so that there was no dense undergrowth to check us, though
the ground was often rough, and we had to go a good deal
upon the river-bed. Towards nightfall we had made a matter
of some five-and-twenty miles, and camped at the point where
the river entered upon the gorge.

The weather was delightfully warm, considering that the
valley in which we were encamped must have been at least
two thousand feet above the level of the sea. The river-bed
was here about a mile and a half broad and entirely covered
with shingle over which the river ran in many winding channels, looking, when seen from above, like a tangled skein of
ribbon, and glistening in the sun. We knew that it was liable
to very sudden and heavy freshets; but even had we not known
it, we could have seen it by the snags of trees, which must
have been carried long distances, and by the mass of vegetable
and mineral *débris* which was banked against their lower side,
showing that at times the whole river-bed must be covered
with a roaring torrent many feet in depth and of ungovernable
fury. At present the river was low, there being but five or six
streams, too deep and rapid for even a strong man to ford on
foot, but to be crossed safely on horseback. On either side of
it there were still a few acres of flat, which grew wider and
wider down the river, till they became the large plains on which
we looked from my master's hut. Behind us rose the lowest
spurs of the second range, leading abruptly to the range itself;
and at a distance of half a mile began the gorge, where the
river narrowed and became boisterous and terrible. The beauty
of the scene cannot be conveyed in language. The one side
of the valley was blue with evening shadow, through which
loomed forest and precipice, hillside and mountain top; and
the other was still brilliant with the sunset gold. The wide and
wasteful river with its ceaseless rushing—the beautiful water-
birds too, which abounded upon the islets and were so tame
that we could come close up to them—the ineffable purity
of the air—the solemn peacefulness of the untrodden region—

25

could there be a more delightful and exhilarating combination?

We set about making our camp, close to some large bush which came down from the mountains on to the flat, and tethered out our horses upon ground as free as we could find it from anything round which they might wind the rope and get themselves tied up. We dared not let them run loose, lest they might stray down the river home again. We then gathered wood and lit the fire. We filled a tin pannikin with water and set it against the hot ashes to boil. When the water boiled we threw in two or three large pinches of tea and let them brew.

We had caught half a dozen young ducks in the course of the day—an easy matter, for the old birds made such a fuss in attempting to decoy us away from them, pretending to be badly hurt as they say the plover does, that we could always find them by going about in the opposite direction to the old bird till we heard the young ones crying: then we ran them down, for they could not fly though they were nearly full grown. Chowbok plucked them a little and singed them a good deal. Then we cut them up and boiled them in another pannikin, and this completed our preparations.

When we had done supper it was quite dark. The silence and freshness of the night, the occasional sharp cry of the wood-hen, the ruddy glow of the fire, the subdued rushing of the river, the sombre forest, and the immediate foreground of our saddles, packs, and blankets, made a picture worthy of a Salvator Rosa or a Nicolas Poussin. I call it to mind and delight in it now, but I did not notice it at the time. We next to never know when we are well off: but this cuts two ways, —for if we did, we should perhaps know better when we are ill off also; and I have sometimes thought that there are as many ignorant of the one as of the other. He who wrote, *"O fortunatos nimium sua si bona norint agricolas,"* might have written quite as truly, *"O infortunatos nimium sua si mala norint";* and there are few of us who are not protected from the keenest pain by our inability to see what it is that we have done, what we are suffering, and what we truly are. Let us be grateful to the mirror for revealing to us our appearance only.

We found as soft a piece of ground as we could—though it was all stony—and having collected grass and so disposed of ourselves that we had a little hollow for our hip-bones, we strapped our blankets round us and went to sleep. Waking in the night I saw the stars overhead and the moonlight bright upon the mountains. The river was ever rushing; I heard one of our horses neigh to its companion, and was assured that they were still at hand; I had no care of mind or body, save that I had doubtless many difficulties to overcome; there came upon me a delicious sense of peace, a fulness of contentment which I do not believe can be felt by any but those who have spent days consecutively on horseback, or at any rate in the open air.

Next morning we found our last night's tea-leaves frozen at the bottom of the pannikins, though it was not nearly the beginning of autumn; we breakfasted as we had supped, and were on our way by six o'clock. In half an hour we had entered the gorge, and turning round a corner we bade farewell to the last sight of my master's country.

The gorge was narrow and precipitous; the river was now only a few yards wide, and roared and thundered against rocks of many tons in weight; the sound was deafening, for there was a great volume of water. We were two hours in making less than a mile, and that with danger, sometimes in the river and sometimes on the rock. There was that damp black smell of rocks covered with slimy vegetation, as near some huge waterfall where spray is ever rising. The air was clammy and cold. I cannot conceive how our horses managed to keep their footing, especially the one with the pack, and I dreaded the having to return almost as much as going forward. I suppose this lasted three miles, but it was well midday when the gorge got a little wider, and a small stream came into it from a tributary valley. Farther progress up the main river was impossible, for the cliffs descended like walls; so we went up the side stream, Chowbok seeming to think that here must be the pass of which reports existed among his people. We now incurred less of actual danger but more fatigue, and it was only after infinite trouble, owing to the rocks and tangled vegetation, that we got ourselves and our horses upon the saddle from which this small stream descended; by that time clouds had descended upon us, and it was raining heavily. Moreover, it was six o'clock and we were tired out, having made perhaps six miles in twelve hours.

On the saddle there was some coarse grass which was in full seed, and therefore very nourishing for the horses; also abundance of anise and sow-thistle, of which they are extravagantly fond, so we turned them loose and prepared to camp. Everything was soaking wet and we were half-perished with cold; indeed we were very uncomfortable. There was brushwood about, but we could get no fire till we had shaved off the wet outside of some dead branches and filled our pockets with the dry inside chips. Having done this we managed to start a fire, nor did we allow it to go out when we had once

27

started it; we pitched the tent and by nine o'clock were comparatively warm and dry. Next morning it was fine; we broke camp, and after advancing a short distance we found that, by descending over ground less difficult than yesterday's, we should come again upon the river-bed, which had opened out above the gorge; but it was plain at a glance that there was no available sheep country, nothing but a few flats covered with scrub on either side the river, and mountains which were perfectly worthless. But we could see the main range. There was no mistake about this. The glaciers were tumbling down the mountain sides like cataracts, and seemed actually to descend upon the river-bed; there could be no serious difficulty in reaching them by following up the river, which was wide and open; but it seemed rather an objectless thing to do, for the main range looked hopeless, and my curiosity about the nature of the country above the gorge was now quite satisfied; there was no money in it whatever, unless there should be minerals, of which I saw no more signs than lower down.

However, I resolved that I would follow the river up, and not return until I was compelled to do so. I would go up every branch as far as I could, and wash well for gold. Chowbok liked seeing me do this, but it never came to anything, for we did not even find the colour. His dislike of the main range appeared to have worn off, and he made no objections to approaching it. I think he thought there was no danger of my trying to cross it, and he was not afraid of anything on this side; besides, we might find gold. But the fact was that he had made up his mind what to do if he saw me getting too near it.

We passed three weeks in exploring, and never did I find time go more quickly. The weather was fine, though the nights got very cold. We followed every stream but one, and always found it led us to a glacier which was plainly impassable, at any rate without a larger party and ropes. One stream remained, which I should have followed up already, had not Chowbok said that he had risen early one morning while I was yet asleep, and after going up it for three or four miles, had seen that it was impossible to go farther. I had long ago discovered that he was a great liar, so I was bent on going up myself: in brief, I did so: so far from being impossible, it was quite easy travelling; and after five or six miles I saw a saddle at the end of it, which, though covered deep in snow, was not glaciered, and which did verily appear to be part of the main range itself. No words can express the intensity of my delight. My blood was all on fire with hope and elation;

28

but on looking round for Chowbok, who was behind me, I saw to my surprise and anger that he had turned back, and was going down the valley as hard as he could. He had left me.

Chapter 4

The Saddle

I COOEYED to him, but he would not hear. I ran after him, but he had got too good a start. Then I sat down on a stone and thought the matter carefully over. It was plain that Chowbok had designedly attempted to keep me from going up this valley, yet he had shown no unwillingness to follow me anywhere else. What could this mean, unless that I was now upon the route by which alone the mysteries of the great ranges could be revealed? What then should I do? Go back at the very moment when it had become plain that I was on the right scent? Hardly; yet to proceed alone would be both difficult and dangerous. It would be bad enough to return to my master's run, and pass through the rocky gorges, with no chance of help from another should I get into a difficulty; but to advance for any considerable distance without a companion would be next door to madness. Accidents which are slight when there is another at hand (as the spraining of an ankle, or the falling into some place whence escape would be easy by means of an outstretched hand and a bit of rope) may be fatal to one who is alone. The more I pondered the less I liked it; and yet, the less could I make up my mind to return when I looked at the saddle at the head of the valley, and noted the comparative ease with which its smooth sweep of snow might be surmounted: I seemed to see my way almost from my present position to the very top. After much thought, I resolved to go forward until I should come to some place which was really dangerous, but then to return. I should thus, I hoped, at any rate reach the top of the saddle, and satisfy myself as to what might be on the other side.

I had no time to lose, for it was now between ten and eleven in the morning. Fortunately I was well equipped, for on leaving the camp and the horses at the lower end of the valley I had provided myself (according to my custom) with everything that I was likely to want for four or five days. Chowbok had carried half, but had dropped his whole swag—I suppose, at the moment of his taking flight—for I came upon it when I ran after him. I had, therefore, his provisions as well as my own. Accordingly, I took as many biscuits as I thought I could carry, and also some tobacco, tea, and a few matches. I rolled all these things (together with a flask nearly full of brandy, which I had kept in my pocket for fear lest Chowbok should get hold of it) inside my blankets, and strapped them very tightly, making the whole into a long roll of some seven feet in length and six inches in diameter. Then I tied the two ends together, and put the whole round my neck and over one shoulder. This is the easiest way of carrying a heavy swag, for one can rest one's self by shifting the burden from one shoulder to the other. I strapped my pannikin and a small axe about my waist, and thus equipped began to ascend the valley, angry at having been misled by Chowbok, but determined not to return till I was compelled to do so.

I crossed and recrossed the stream several times without difficulty, for there were many good fords. At one o'clock I was at the foot of the saddle; for four hours I mounted, the last two on the snow, where the going was easier; by five, I was within ten minutes of the top, in a state of excitement greater, I think, than I had ever known before. Ten minutes more, and the cold air from the other side came rushing upon me.

A glance. I was *not* on the main range.

Another glance. There was an awful river, muddy and horribly angry, roaring over an immense river-bed, thousands of feet below me.

It went round to the westward, and I could see no farther up the valley, save that there were enormous glaciers which must extend round the source of the river, and from which it must spring.

Another glance, and then I remained motionless.

There was an easy pass in the mountains directly opposite to me, through which I caught a glimpse of an immeasurable extent of blue and distant plains.

Easy? Yes, perfectly easy; grassed nearly to the summit, which was, as it were, an open path between two glaciers, from which an inconsiderable stream came tumbling down over rough but very possible hillsides, till it got down to the level of the great river, and formed a flat where there was grass and a small bush of stunted timber.

Almost before I could believe my eyes, a cloud had come up from the valley on the other side, and the plains were hidden. What wonderful luck was mine! Had I arrived five minutes later, the cloud would have been over the pass, and

30

I should not have known of its existence. Now that the cloud was there, I began to doubt my memory, and to be uncertain whether it had been more than a blue line of distant vapour that had filled up the opening. I could only be certain of this much, namely, that the river in the valley below must be the one next to the northward of that which flowed past my master's station; of this there could be no doubt. Could I, however, imagine that my luck should have led me up a wrong river in search of a pass, and yet brought me to the spot where I could detect the one weak place in the fortifications of a more northern basin? This was too improbable. But even as I doubted there came a rent in the cloud opposite, and a second time I saw blue lines of heaving downs, growing gradually fainter, and retiring into a far space of plain. It was substantial; there had been no mistake whatsoever. I had hardly made myself perfectly sure of this, ere the rent in the clouds joined up again and I could see nothing more.

What, then, should I do? The night would be upon me shortly, and I was already chilled with standing still after the exertion of climbing. To stay where I was would be impossible; I must either go backwards or forwards. I found a rock which gave me shelter from the evening wind, and took a good pull at the brandy flask, which immediately warmed and encouraged me.

I asked myself, Could I descend upon the river-bed beneath me? It was impossible to say what precipices might prevent my doing so. If I were on the river-bed, dare I cross the river? I am an excellent swimmer, yet, once in that frightful rush of waters, I should be hurled whithersoever it willed, absolutely powerless. Moreover, there was my swag; I should perish of cold and hunger if I left it, but I should certainly be drowned if I attempted to carry it across the river. These were serious considerations, but the hope of finding an immense tract of available sheep country (which I was determined that I would monopolize as far as I possibly could) sufficed to outweigh them; and, in a few minutes, I felt resolved that, having made so important a discovery as a pass into a country which was probably as valuable as that on our own side of the ranges, I would follow it up and ascertain its value, even though I should pay the penalty of failure with life itself. The more I thought, the more determined I became either to win fame and perhaps fortune, by entering upon this unknown world, or give up life in the attempt. In fact, I felt that life would be no longer valuable if I were to have seen so great a prize and refused to grasp at the possible profits therefrom.

I had still an hour of good daylight during which I might begin my descent on to some suitable camping-ground, but there was not a moment to be lost. At first I got along rapidly, for I was on the snow, and sank into it enough to save me from falling, though I went forward straight down the mountain side as fast as I could; but there was less snow on this side than on the other, and I had soon done with it, getting on to a coomb of dangerous and very stony ground, where a slip might have given me a disastrous fall. But I was careful with all my speed, and got safely to the bottom, where there were patches of coarse grass, and an attempt here and there at brushwood: what was below this I could not see. I advanced a few hundred yards farther, and found that I was on the brink of a frightful precipice, which no one in his senses would attempt descending. I bethought me, however, to try the creek which drained the coomb, and see whether it might not have made itself a smoother way. In a few minutes I found myself at the upper end of a chasm in the rocks, something like Twll Dhu, only on a greatly larger scale; the creek had found its way into it, and had worn a deep channel through a material which appeared softer than that upon the other side of the mountain. I believe it must have been a different geological formation, though I regret to say that I cannot tell what it was.

I looked at this rift in great doubt; then I went a little way on either side of it, and found myself looking over the edge of horrible precipices on to the river, which roared some four or five thousand feet below me. I dared not think of getting down at all, unless I committed myself to the rift, of which I was hopeful when I reflected that the rock was soft, and that the water might have worn its channel tolerably evenly through the whole extent. The darkness was increasing with every minute, but I should have twilight for another half-hour, so I went into the chasm (though by no means without fear), and resolved to return and camp, and try some other path next day, should I come to any serious difficulty. In about five minutes I had completely lost my head; the side of the rift became hundreds of feet in height, and overhung so that I could not see the sky. It was full of rocks, and I had many falls and bruises. I was wet through from falling into the water, of which there was no great volume, but it had such force that I could do nothing against it; once I had to leap down a not inconsiderable waterfall into a deep pool below, and my swag was so heavy that I was very nearly drowned. I had indeed a hairbreadth escape; but, as luck would have it, Providence was on my side. Shortly afterwards I began to fancy that the rift was getting wider, and that there was more brushwood. Presently I found myself on an open grassy slope, and feeling my way a little farther along the stream, I came upon a flat place with wood, where I could camp comfortably; which was well, for it was now quite dark.

My first care was for my matches; were they dry? The outside of my swag had got completely wet; but, on undoing the blankets, I found things warm and dry within. How thankful I was! I lit a fire, and was grateful for its warmth and company. I made myself some tea and ate two of my biscuits; my brandy I did not touch, for I had little left, and might want it when my courage failed me. All that I did, I did almost mechanically, for I could not realize my situation to myself, beyond knowing that I was alone, and that return through the chasm which I had just descended would be impossible. It is a dreadful feeling, that of being cut off from all one's kind. I was still full of hope, and built golden castles for myself as soon as I was warmed with food and fire; but I do not believe that any man could long retain his reason in such solitude, unless he had the companionship of animals. One begins doubting one's own identity.

I remember deriving comfort even from the sight of my blankets, and the sound of my watch ticking—things which seemed to link me to other people; but the screaming of the wood-hens frightened me, as also a chattering bird which I had never heard before, and which seemed to laugh at me; though I soon got used to it, and before long could fancy that it was many years since I had first heard it.

I took off my clothes, and wrapped my inside blanket about me, till my things were dry. The night was very still, and I made a roaring fire; so I soon got warm, and at last could put my clothes on again. Then I strapped my blanket round me, and went to sleep as near the fire as I could.

I dreamed that there was an organ placed in my master's wool-shed: the wool-shed faded away, and the organ seemed to grow and grow amid a blaze of brilliant light, till it became like a golden city upon the side of a mountain, with rows upon rows of pipes set in cliffs and precipices, one above the other, and in mysterious caverns, like that of Fingal, within whose depths I could see the burnished pillars gleaming. In the front there was a flight of lofty terraces, at the top of which I could see a man with his head buried forward towards a keyboard, and his body swaying from side to side amid the storm of huge arpeggioed harmonies that came crashing overhead and round. Then there was one who touched me on the shoulder,

33

and said, "Do you not see? it is Handel"; but I had hardly apprehended, and was trying to scale the terraces, and get near him, when I awoke, dazzled with the vividness and distinctness of the dream.

A piece of wood had burned through, and the ends had fallen into the ashes with a blaze: this, I supposed, had both given me my dream and robbed me of it. I was bitterly disappointed, and sitting up on my elbow, came back to reality and my strange surroundings as best I could.

I was thoroughly aroused—moreover, I felt a foreshadowing as though my attention were arrested by something more than the dream, although no sense in particular was as yet appealed to. I held my breath and waited, and then I heard—was it fancy? Nay; I listened again and again, and I *did* hear a faint and extremely distant sound of music, like that of an Aeolian harp, borne upon the wind which was blowing fresh and chill from the opposite mountains.

The roots of my hair thrilled. I listened, but the wind had died; and, fancying that it must have been the wind itself—no; on a sudden I remembered the noise which Chowbok had made in the wool-shed. Yes; it was that.

Thank Heaven, whatever it was, it was over now. I reasoned with myself, and recovered my firmness. I became convinced that I had only been dreaming more vividly than usual. Soon I began even to laugh, and think what a fool I was to be frightened at nothing, reminding myself that even if I were to come to a bad end it would be no such dreadful matter after all. I said my prayers, a duty which I had too often neglected, and in a little time fell into a really refreshing sleep, which lasted till broad daylight, and restored me. I rose, and searching among the embers of my fire, I found a few live coals and soon had a blaze again. I got breakfast, and was delighted to have the company of several small birds, which hopped about me and perched on my boots and hands. I felt comparatively happy, but I can assure the reader that I had had a far worse time of it than I have told him; and I strongly recommend him to remain in Europe if he can; or, at any rate, in some country which has been explored and settled, rather than go into places where others have not been before him. Exploring is delightful to look forward to and back upon, but it is not comfortable at the time, unless it be of such an easy nature as not to deserve the name.

Chapter 5

The River and the Range

MY NEXT business was to descend upon the river. I had lost sight of the pass which I had seen from the saddle, but had made such notes of it that I could not fail to find it. I was bruised and stiff, and my boots had begun to give, for I had been going on rough ground for more than three weeks; but, as the day wore on, and I found myself descending without serious difficulty, I became easier. In a couple of hours I got among the pine forests where there was little undergrowth, and descended quickly till I reached the edge of another precipice, which gave me a great deal of trouble, though I eventually managed to avoid it. By about three or four o'clock I found myself on the river-bed.

From calculations which I made as to the height of the valley on the other side the saddle over which I had come, I concluded that the saddle itself could not be less than nine thousand feet high; and I should think that the river-bed, on to which I now descended, was three thousand feet above the sea-level. The water had a terrific current, with a fall of not less than forty to fifty feet per mile. It was certainly the river next to the northward of that which flowed past my master's run, and would have to go through an impassable gorge (as is commonly the case with the rivers of that country) before it came upon known parts. It was reckoned to be nearly two thousand feet above the sea-level where it came out of the gorge on to the plains.

As soon as I got to the river side I liked it even less than I thought I should. It was muddy, being near its parent glaciers. The stream was wide, rapid, and rough, and I could hear the smaller stones knocking against each other under the rage of the waters, as upon a seashore. Fording was out of the question. I could not swim and carry my swag, and I dared not leave my swag behind me. My only chance was to make a small raft; and that would be difficult to make, and not at all safe when it was made—not for one man in such a current.

As it was too late to do much that afternoon, I spent the rest of it in going up and down the river side, and seeing where I should find the most favourable crossing. Then I camped early, and had a quiet comfortable night with no more music, for which I was thankful, as it had haunted me all day, although I perfectly well knew that it had been nothing but my own fancy, brought on by the reminiscence of what I had heard from Chowbok and by the over-excitement of the preceding evening.

Next day I began gathering the dry bloom stalks of a kind of flag or iris-looking plant, which was abundant, and whose leaves, when torn into strips, were as strong as the strongest string. I brought them to the waterside, and fell to making myself a kind of rough platform, which should suffice for myself and my swag if I could only stick to it. The stalks were ten or twelve feet long, and very strong, but light and hollow. I made my raft entirely of them, binding bundles of them at right angles to each other, neatly and strongly, with strips from the leaves of the same plant, and tying other rods across. It took me all day till nearly four o'clock to finish the raft, but I had still enough daylight for crossing, and resolved on doing so at once.

I had selected a place where the river was broad and comparatively still, some seventy or eighty yards above a furious rapid. At this spot I had built my raft. I now launched it, made my swag fast to the middle, and got on to it myself, keeping in my hand one of the longest blossom stalks, so that I might punt myself across as long as the water was shallow enough to let me do so. I got on pretty well for twenty or thirty yards from the shore, but even in this short space I nearly upset my raft by shifting too rapidly from one side to the other. The water then became much deeper, and I leaned over so far in order to get the bloom rod to the bottom that I had to stay still, leaning on the rod for a few seconds. Then, when I lifted up the rod from the ground, the current was too much for me and I found myself being carried down the rapid. Everything in a second flew past me, and I had no more control over the raft; neither can I remember anything except hurry, and noise, and waters which in the end upset me. But it all came right, and I found myself near the shore, not more than up to my knees in water and pulling my raft to land, fortunately upon the left bank of the river, which was the one I wanted. When I had landed I found that I was about a mile, or perhaps a little less, below the point from which I started. My swag was wet upon the outside, and I was myself dripping; but I had gained my point, and knew that my difficulties were for a time over. I then lit my fire and dried myself; having done so I caught some of the young ducks and sea-gulls, which were abundant on and near the river-bed, so that I had not only a good meal, of which I was in great want, having had an insufficient diet from the time that Chowbok left me, but was also well provided for the morrow.

I thought of Chowbok, and felt how useful he had been to me, and in how many ways I was the loser by his absence, having now to do all sorts of things for myself which he had hitherto done for me, and could do infinitely better than I could. Moreover, I had set my heart upon making him a real convert to the Christian religion, which he had already embraced outwardly, though I cannot think that it had taken deep root in his impenetrably stupid nature. I used to catechize him by our camp fire, and explain to him the mysteries of the Trinity and of original sin, with which I was myself familiar, having been the grandson of an archdeacon by my mother's side, to say nothing of the fact that my father was a clergyman of the English Church. I was therefore sufficiently qualified for the task, and was the more inclined to it, over and above my real desire to save the unhappy creature from an eternity of torture, by recollecting the promise of St. James, that if any one converted a sinner (which Chowbok surely was) he should hide a multitude of sins. I reflected, therefore, that the conversion of Chowbok might in some degree compensate for irregularities and shortcomings in my own previous life, the remembrance of which had been more than once unpleasant to me during my recent experiences.

Indeed, on one occasion I had even gone so far as to baptize him, as well as I could, having ascertained that he had certainly not been both christened and baptized, and gathering (from his telling me that he had received the name William from the missionary) that it was probably the first-mentioned rite to which he had been subjected. I thought it great carelessness on the part of the missionary to have omitted the second, and certainly more important, ceremony which I have always understood precedes christening both in the case of infants and of adult converts; and when I thought of the risks we were both incurring I determined that there should be no further delay. Fortunately it was not yet twelve o'clock, so I baptized him at once from one of the pannikins (the only vessels I had) reverently, and, I trust, efficiently. I then set myself to work to instruct him in the deeper mysteries of our belief, and to make him, not only in name, but in heart a Christian.

It is true that I might not have succeeded, for Chowbok was very hard to teach. Indeed, on the evening of the same day that I baptized him he tried for the twentieth time to steal the brandy, which made be rather unhappy as to whether I could have baptized him rightly. He had a prayer-book—more than twenty years old—which had been given him by the missionaries, but the only thing in it which had taken any living hold upon him was the title of Adelaide, the Queen Dowager, which he would repeat whenever strongly moved or touched, and which did really seem to have some deep spiritual significance to him, though he could never completely separate her individuality from that of Mary Magdalene, whose name had also fascinated him, though in a less degree.

He was indeed stony ground, but by digging about him I might have at any rate deprived him of all faith in the religion of his tribe, which would have been half way towards making him a sincere Christian; and now all this was cut off from me, and I could neither be of further spiritual assistance to him nor he of bodily profit to myself: besides, any company was better than being quite alone.

I got very melancholy as these reflections crossed me, but when I had boiled the ducks and eaten them I was much better. I had a little tea left and about a pound of tobacco, which should last me for another fortnight with moderate smoking. I had also eight ship's biscuits, and, most precious of all, about six ounces of brandy, which I presently reduced to four, for the night was cold.

I rose with early dawn, and in an hour I was on my way, feeling strange, not to say weak, from the burden of solitude, but full of hope when I considered how many dangers I had overcome, and that this day should see me at the summit of the dividing range.

After a slow but steady climb of between three and four hours, during which I met with no serious hindrance, I found myself upon a tableland, and close to a glacier which I recognized as marking the summit of the pass. Above it towered a succession of rugged precipices and snowy mountain sides. The solitude was greater than I could bear; the mountain upon my master's sheep-run was a crowded thoroughfare in comparison with this sombre sullen place. The air, moreover, was dark and heavy, which made the loneliness even more oppressive. There was an inky gloom over all that was not covered with snow and ice. Grass there was none.

Each moment I felt increasing upon me that dreadful doubt as to my own identity—as to the continuity of my past and present existence—which is the first sign of that distraction which comes on those who have lost themselves in the bush. I had fought against this feeling hitherto, and had conquered it; but the intense silence and gloom of this rocky wilderness were too much for me, and I felt that my power of collecting myself was beginning to be impaired.

I rested for a little while, and then advanced over very rough ground, until I reached the lower end of the glacier. Then I saw another glacier, descending from the eastern side into a small lake. I passed along the western side of the lake, where the ground was easier, and when I had got about half way I expected that I should see the plains which I had already seen from the opposite mountains; but it was not to be so, for the clouds rolled up to the very summit of the pass, though they did not overlip it on to the side from which I had come. I therefore soon found myself enshrouded by a cold thin vapour, which prevented my seeing more than a very few yards in front of me. Then I came upon a large patch of old snow, in which I could distinctly trace the half-melted tracks of goats—and in one place, as it seemed to me, there had been a dog following them. Had I lighted upon a land of shepherds? The ground, where not covered with snow, was so poor and stony, and there was so little herbage, that I could see no sign of a path or regular sheep-track. But I could not help feeling rather uneasy as I wondered what sort of a reception I might meet with if I were to come suddenly upon inhabitants. I was thinking of this, and proceeding cautiously through the mist, when I began to fancy that I saw some objects darker than the cloud looming in front of me. A few steps brought me nearer, and a shudder of unutterable horror ran through me when I saw a circle of gigantic forms, many times higher than myself, upstanding grim and grey through the veil of cloud before me.

I suppose I must have fainted, for I found myself some time afterwards sitting upon the ground, sick and deadly cold. There were the figures, quite still and silent, seen vaguely through the thick gloom, but in human shape indisputably.

A sudden thought occurred to me, which would have doubtless struck me at once had I not been prepossessed with forebodings at the time that I first saw the figures, and had not the cloud concealed them from me—I mean that they were not living beings, but statues. I determined that I would count fifty slowly, and be sure that the objects were not alive if during that time I could detect no sign of motion.

How thankful was I when I came to the end of my fifty and there had been no movement!

I counted a second time—but again all was still.

I then advanced timidly forward, and in another moment I saw that my surmise was correct. I had come upon a sort of Stonehenge of rude and barbaric figures, seated as Chowbok had sat when I questioned him in the wool-shed, and with the same superhumanly malevolent expression upon their faces.

They had been all seated, but two had fallen. They were barbarous—neither Egyptian, nor Assyrian, nor Japanese—different from any of these, and yet akin to all. They were six or seven times larger than life, of great antiquity, worn and lichen grown. They were ten in number. There was snow upon their heads and wherever snow could lodge. Each statue had been built of four or five enormous blocks, but how these had been raised and put together is known to those alone who raised them. Each was terrible after a different kind. One was raging furiously, as in pain and great despair; another was lean and cadaverous with famine; another cruel and idiotic, but with the silliest simper that can be conceived—this one had fallen, and looked exquisitely ludicrous in his fall—the mouths of all were more or less open, and as I looked at them from behind, I saw that their heads had been hollowed.

I was sick and shivering with cold. Solitude had unmanned me already, and I was utterly unfit to have come upon such an assembly of fiends in such a dreadful wilderness and without preparation. I would have given everything I had in the world to have been back at my master's station; but that was not to be thought of: my head was failing, and I felt sure that I could never get back alive.

Then came a gust of howling wind, accompanied with a moan from one of the statues above me. I clasped my hands in fear. I felt like a rat caught in a trap, as though I would have turned and bitten at whatever thing was nearest me. The wildness of the wind increased, the moans grew shriller, coming from several statues, and swelling into a chorus. I almost immediately knew what it was, but the sound was so unearthly that this was but little consolation. The inhuman beings into whose hearts the Evil One had put it to conceive these statues, had made their heads into a sort of organ-pipe, so that their mouths should catch the wind and sound with its blowing. It was horrible. However brave a man might be, he could never stand such a concert, from such lips, and in such a place. I heaped every invective upon them that my tongue could utter as I rushed away from them into the mist, and even after I had lost sight of them, and turning my head round could see nothing but the storm-wraiths driving behind me, I heard their ghostly chanting, and felt as though one of them would rush after me and grip me in his hand and throttle me.

I may say here that, since my return to England, I heard a friend playing some chords upon the organ which put me very forcibly in mind of the Erewhonian statues (for Erewhon is the name of the country upon which I was now entering). They rose most vividly to my recollection the moment my friend began. They are as follows, and are by the greatest of all musicians:[1]

Prelude: arpeggio.

[1] See Handel's compositions for the harpsichord, published by Litolf, p. 78.

41

Chapter 6

Into Erewhon

AND NOW I found myself on a narrow path which followed a small watercourse. I was too glad to have an easy track for my flight, to lay hold of the full significance of its existence. The thought, however, soon presented itself to me that I must be in an inhabited country, but one which was yet unknown. What, then, was to be my fate at the hands of its inhabitants? Should I be taken and offered up as a burnt-offering to those hideous guardians of the pass? It might be so. I shuddered at the thought, yet the horrors of solitude had now fairly possessed me; and so dazed was I, and chilled, and woebegone, that I could lay hold of no idea firmly amid the crowd of fancies that kept wandering in upon my brain.

I hurried onward—down, down, down. More streams came in; then there was a bridge, a few pine logs thrown over the water; but they gave me comfort, for savages do not make bridges. Then I had a treat such as I can never convey on paper —a moment, perhaps, the most striking and unexpected of my whole life—the one I think that, with some three or four exceptions, I would most gladly have again, were I able to recall it. I got below the level of the clouds, into a burst of brilliant evening sunshine. I was facing the north-west, and the sun was full upon me. Oh, how its light cheered me! But what I saw! It was such an expanse as was revealed to Moses when he stood upon the summit of Mount Sinai, and beheld that promised land which it was not to be his to enter. The beautiful sunset sky was crimson and gold; blue, silver, and purple; exquisite and tranquillizing; fading away therein were plains, on which I could see many a town and city, with buildings that had lofty steeples and rounded domes. Nearer beneath me lay ridge behind ridge, outline behind outline, sunlight behind shadow, and shadow behind sunlight, gully and serrated ravine. I saw large pine forests, and the glitter of a noble river winding its way upon the plains; also many villages and hamlets, some of them quite near at hand; and it was on these that I pondered most. I sank upon the ground at the foot of a large tree and thought what I had best do; but I could not collect myself. I was quite tired out; and presently, feeling warmed by the sun, and quieted, I fell off into a profound sleep.

I was awoke by the sound of tinkling bells, and looking up, I saw four or five goats feeding near me. As soon as I moved, the creatures turned their heads towards me with an expression of infinite wonder. They did not run away, but stood stock still, and looked at me from every side, as I at them. Then came the sound of chattering and laughter, and there approached two lovely girls, of about seventeen or eighteen years old, dressed each in a sort of linen gaberdine, with a girdle round the waist. They saw me. I sat quite still and looked at them, dazzled with their extreme beauty. For a moment they looked at me and at each other in great amazement; then they gave a little frightened cry and ran off as hard as they could.

"So that's that," said I to myself, as I watched them scampering. I knew that I had better stay where I was and meet my fate, whatever it was to be, and even if there were a better course, I had no strength left to take it. I must come into contact with the inhabitants sooner or later, and it might as well be sooner. Better not to seem afraid of them, as I should do by running away and being caught with a hue and cry tomorrow or next day. So I remained quite still and waited. In about an hour I heard distant voices talking excitedly, and in a few minutes I saw the two girls bringing up a party of six or seven men, well armed with bows and arrows and pikes. There was nothing for it, so I remained sitting quite still, even after they had seen me, until they came close up. Then we all had a good look at one another.

Both the girls and the men were very dark in color, but not more so than the South Italians or Spaniards. The men wore no trousers, but were dressed nearly the same as the Arabs whom I have seen in Algeria. They were of the most magnificent presence, being no less strong and handsome than the women were beautiful; and not only this, but their expression was courteous and benign. I think they would have killed me at once if I had made the slightest show of violence; but they gave me no impression of their being likely to hurt me so long as I was quiet. I am not much given to liking anybody at first sight, but these people impressed me much more favourably than I should have thought possible, so that I could not fear them as I scanned their faces one after another. They were all powerful men. I might have been a match for any one of them singly, for I have been told that I have more to glory in the flesh than in any other respect, being over six feet and proportionately strong; but any two could have soon mastered me, even were I not so bereft of energy by my recent adventures.

43

My colour seemed to surprise them most, for I have light hair, blue eyes, and a fresh complexion. They could not understand how these things could be; my clothes also seemed quite beyond them. Their eyes kept wandering all over me, and the more they looked the less they seemed able to make me out.

At last I raised myself upon my feet, and leaning upon my stick, I spoke whatever came into my head to the man who seemed foremost among them. I spoke in English, though I was very sure that he would not understand. I said that I had no idea what country I was in; that I had stumbled upon it almost by accident, after a series of hairbreadth escapes; and that I trusted they would not allow any evil to overtake me now that I was completely at their mercy. All this I said quietly and firmly, with hardly any change of expression. They could not understand me, but they looked approvingly to one another, and seemed pleased (so I thought) that I showed no fear nor acknowledgment of inferiority—the fact being that I was exhausted beyond the sense of fear. Then one of them pointed to the mountain, in the direction of the statues, and made a grimace in imitation of one of them. I laughed and shuddered expressively, whereon they all burst out laughing too, and chattered hard to one another. I could make out nothing of what they said, but I think they thought it rather a good joke that I had come past the statues. Then one among them came forward and motioned me to follow, which I did without hesitation, for I dared not thwart them; moreover, I liked them well enough, and felt tolerably sure that they had no intention of hurting me.

In about a quarter of an hour we got to a small hamlet built on the side of a hill, with a narrow street and houses huddled up together. The roofs were large and overhanging. Some few windows were glazed, but not many. Altogether the village was exceedingly like one of those that one comes upon in descending the less known passes over the Alps on to Lombardy. I will pass over the excitement which my arrival caused. Suffice it, that though there was abundance of curiosity, there was no rudeness. I was taken to the principal house, which seemed to belong to the people who had captured me. There I was hospitably entertained, and a supper of milk and goat's flesh with a kind of oatcake was set before me, of which I ate heartily. But all the time I was eating I could not help turning my eyes upon the two beautiful girls whom I had first seen, and who seemed to consider me as their lawful prize—which indeed I was, for I would have gone through fire and water for either of them.

Then came the inevitable surprise at seeing me smoke, which

I will spare the reader; but I noticed that when they saw me strike a match, there was a hubbub of excitement which, it struck me, was not altogether unmixed with disapproval: why, I could not guess. Then the women retired, and I was left alone with the men, who tried to talk to me in every conceivable way; but we could come to no understanding, except that I was quite alone, and had come from a long way over the mountains. In the course of time they grew tired, and I very sleepy. I made signs as though I would sleep on the floor in my blankets, but they gave me one of their bunks with plenty of dried fern and grass, on to which I had no sooner laid myself than I fell fast asleep; nor did I awake till well into the following day, when I found myself in the hut with two men keeping guard over me and an old woman cooking. When I woke the men seemed pleased, and spoke to me as though bidding me good morning in a pleasant tone.

I went out of doors to wash in a creek which ran a few yards from the house. My hosts were as engrossed with me as ever; they never took their eyes off me, following every action that I did, no matter how trifling, and each looking towards the other for his opinion at every touch and turn. They took great interest in my ablutions, for they seemed to have doubted whether I was in all respects human like themselves. They even laid hold of my arms and overhauled them, and expressed approval when they saw that they were strong and muscular. They now examined my legs, and especially my feet. When they desisted they nodded approvingly to each other; and when I had combed and brushed my hair, and generally made myself as neat and well arranged as circumstances would allow, I could see that their respect for me increased greatly, and that they were by no means sure that they had treated me with sufficient deference—a matter on which I am not competent to decide. All I know is that they were very good to me, for which I thanked them heartily, as it might well have been otherwise.

For my own part, I liked them and admired them, for their quiet self-possession and dignified ease impressed me pleasurably at once. Neither did their manner make me feel as though I were personally distasteful to them—only that I was a thing utterly new and unlooked for, which they could not comprehend. Their type was more that of the most robust Italians than any other; their manners also were eminently Italian, in their entire unconsciousness of self. Having travelled a good deal in Italy, I was struck with little gestures of the hand and shoulders, which constantly reminded me of that country. My feeling was that my wisest plan would be to go on as I had begun, and be simply myself for better or worse, such as I was, and take my chance accordingly.

I thought of these things while they were waiting for me to have done washing, and on my way back. Then they gave me breakfast—hot bread and milk, and fried flesh of something between mutton and venison. Their ways of cooking and eating were European, though they had only a skewer for a fork, and a sort of butcher's knife to cut with. The more I looked at everything in the house, the more I was struck with its quasi-European character; and had the walls only been pasted over with extracts from *The Illustrated London News* and *Punch,* I could have almost fancied myself in a shepherd's hut upon my master's sheep-run. And yet everything was slightly different. It was much the same with the birds and flowers on the other side, as compared with the English ones. On my arrival I had been pleased at noticing that nearly all the plants and birds were very like common English ones: thus, there was a robin, and a lark, and a wren, and daisies, and dandelions; not quite the same as the English, but still very like them— quite like enough to be called by the same name; so now, here, the ways of these two men, and the things they had in the house, were all very nearly the same as in Europe. It was not at all like going to China or Japan, where everything that one sees is strange. I was, indeed, at once struck with the primitive character of their appliances, for they seemed to be some five or six hundred years behind Europe in their inventions; but this is the case in many an Italian village.

All the time that I was eating my breakfast I kept speculating as to what family of mankind they could belong to; and shortly there came an idea into my head, which brought the blood into my cheeks with excitement as I thought of it. Was it possible that they might be the lost ten tribes of Israel, of whom I had heard both my grandfather and my father make mention as existing in an unknown country, and awaiting a final return to Palestine? Was it possible that *I* might have been designed by Providence as the instrument of their conversion? Oh, what a thought was this! I laid down my skewer and gave them a hasty survey. There was nothing of a Jewish type about them: their noses were distinctly Grecian, and their lips, though full, were not Jewish.

How could I settle this question? I knew neither Greek nor Hebrew, and even if I should get to understand the language here spoken, I should be unable to detect the roots of either of these tongues. I had not been long enough among them to ascertain their habits, but they did not give me the impression of being a religious people. This too was natural: the ten tribes had been always lamentably irreligious. But could I not make them change? To restore the lost ten tribes of Israel to a knowledge of the only truth: here would be indeed an immortal crown of glory! My heart beat fast and furious as I entertained the thought. What a position would it not ensure me in the next world; or perhaps even in this! What folly it would be to throw such a chance away! I should rank next to the Apostles, if not as high as they—certainly above the minor prophets, and possibly above any Old Testament writer except Moses and Isaiah. For such a future as this I would sacrifice all that I have without a moment's hesitation, could I be reasonably assured of it. I had always cordially approved of missionary efforts, and had at times contributed my mite towards their support and extension; but I had never hitherto felt drawn towards becoming a missionary myself; and indeed had always admired, and envied, and respected them, more than I had exactly liked them. But if these people were the lost ten tribes of Israel, the case would be widely different: the opening was too excellent to be lost, and I resolved that should I see indications which appeared to confirm my impression that I had indeed come upon the missing tribes, I would certainly convert them.

I may here mention that this discovery is the one to which I alluded in the opening pages of my story. Time strengthened the impression made upon me at first; and, though I remained in doubt for several months, I feel now no longer uncertain.

When I had done eating, my hosts approached, and pointed down the valley leading to their own country, as though wanting to show that I must go with them; at the same time they laid hold of my arms, and made as though they would take me, but used no violence. I laughed, and motioned my hand across my throat, pointing down the valley as though I was afraid lest I should be killed when I got there. But they divined me at once, and shook their heads with much decision, to show that I was in no danger. Their manner quite reassured me; and in half an hour or so I had packed up my swag, and was eager for the forward journey, feeling wonderfully strengthened and refreshed by good food and sleep, while my hope and curiosity were aroused to their very utmost by the extraordinary position in which I found myself.

But already my excitement had begun to cool; and I reflected that these people might not be the ten tribes after all; in which case I could not but regret that my hopes of making

47

money, which had led me into so much trouble and danger, were almost annihilated by the fact that the country was full to overflowing, with a people who had probably already developed its more available resources. Moreover, how was I to get back? For there was something about my hosts which told me that they had got me, and meant to keep me, in spite of all their goodness.

Chapter 7

First Impressions

WE FOLLOWED an alpine path for some four miles, now hundreds of feet above a brawling stream which descended from the glaciers, and now nearly alongside it. The morning was cold and somewhat foggy, for the autumn had made great strides latterly. Sometimes we went through forests of pine, or rather yew trees, though they looked like pine; and I remember that now and again we passed a little wayside shrine, wherein there would be a statue of great beauty, representing some figure, male or female, in the very heyday of youth, strength, and beauty, or of the most dignified maturity and old age. My hosts always bowed their heads as they passed one of these shrines, and it shocked me to see statues that had no apparent object, beyond the chronicling of some unusual individual excellence or beauty, receive so serious a homage. However, I showed no sign of wonder or disapproval; for I remembered that to be all things to all men was one of the injunctions of the Gentile Apostle, which for the present I should do well to heed. Shortly after passing one of these chapels we came suddenly upon a village which started up out of the mist; and I was alarmed lest I should be made an object of curiosity or dislike. But it was not so. My guides spoke to many in passing, and those spoken to showed much amazement. My guides, however, were well known, and the natural politeness of the people prevented them from putting me to any inconvenience; but they could not help eyeing me, nor I them. I may as well say at once what my after-experience taught me—namely, that with all their faults and extraordinary obliquity of mental vision upon many subjects, they are the very best-bred people that I ever fell in with.

The village was just like the one we had left, only rather

larger. The streets were narrow and unpaved, but very fairly clean. The vine grew outside many of the houses; and there were some with signboards, on which was painted a bottle and a glass, that made me feel much at home. Even on this ledge of human society there was a stunted growth of shoplets, which had taken root and vegetated somehow, though as in an air mercantile of the bleakest. It was here as hitherto: all things were generically the same as in Europe, the differences being of species only; and I was amused at seeing in a window some bottles with barley-sugar and sweetmeats for children, as at home; but the barley-sugar was in plates, not in twisted sticks, and was coloured blue. Glass was plentiful in the better houses.

Lastly, I should say that the people were of a physical beauty which was simply amazing. I never saw anything in the least comparable to them. The women were vigorous, and had a most majestic gait, their heads being set upon their shoulders with a grace beyond all power of expression. Each feature was finished, eyelids, eyelashes, and ears being almost invariably perfect. Their colour was equal to that of the finest Italian paintings; being of the clearest olive, and yet ruddy with a glow of perfect health. Their expression was divine; and as they glanced at me timidly but with parted lips in great bewilderment, I forgot all thoughts of their conversion in feelings that were far more earthly. I was dazzled as I saw one after the other, of whom I could only feel that each was the loveliest I had ever seen. Even in middle age they were still comely, and the old grey-haired women at their cottage doors had a dignity, not to say majesty, of their own.

The men were as handsome as the women beautiful. I have always delighted in and reverenced beauty; but I felt simply abashed in the presence of such a splendid type—a compound of all that is best in Egyptian, Greek and Italian. The children were infinite in number, and exceedingly merry; I need hardly say that they came in for their full share of the prevailing beauty. I expressed by signs my admiration and pleasure to my guides, and they were greatly pleased. I should add that all seemed to take a pride in their personal appearance, and that even the poorest (and none seemed rich) were well-kept and tidy. I could fill many pages with a description of their dress and the ornaments which they wore, and a hundred details which struck me with all the force of novelty; but I must not stay to do so.

When we had got past the village the fog rose, and revealed magnificent views of the snowy mountains and their nearer abutment, while in front I could now and again catch glimpses of the great plains which I had surveyed on the preceding evening. The country was highly cultivated, every ledge being planted with chestnuts, walnuts, and apple-trees from which the apples were now gathering. Goats were abundant; also a kind of small black cattle, in the marshes near the river, which was now fast widening, and running between larger flats from which the hills receded more and more. I saw a few sheep with rounded noses and enormous tails. Dogs were there in plenty, and very English; but I saw no cats, nor indeed are these creatures known, their place being supplied by a sort of small terrier.

In about four hours of walking from the time we started, and after passing two or three more villages, we came upon a considerable town, and my guides made many attempts to make me understand something, but I gathered no inkling of their meaning, except that I need be under no apprehension of danger. I will spare the reader my description of the town, and would only bid him think of Domodossola or Faido. Suffice it that I found myself taken before the chief magistrate, and by his orders was placed in an apartment with two other people, who were the first I had seen looking anything but well and handsome. In fact, one of them was plainly very much out of health, and coughed violently from time to time in spite of manifest efforts to suppress it. The other looked pale and ill but he was marvellously self-contained, and it was impossible to say what was the matter with him. Both of them appeared astonished at seeing one who was evidently a stranger, but they were too ill to come up to me, and form conclusions concerning me. These two were first called out; and in about a quarter of an hour I was made to follow them, which I did in some fear, and with much curiosity.

The chief magistrate was a venerable-looking man, with white hair and beard and a face of great sagacity. He looked me all over for about five minutes, letting his eyes wander from the crown of my head to the soles of my feet, up and down, and down and up; neither did his mind seem in the least clearer when he had done looking than when he began. He at length asked me a single short question, which I supposed meant "Who are you?" I answered in English quite composedly as though he would understand me, and endeavoured to be my very most natural self as well as I could. He appeared more and more puzzled, and then retired, returning with two others much like himself. Then they took me into an inner room, and the two fresh arrivals stripped me, while the chief looked on. They felt my pulse, they looked at my tongue, they listened at my chest, they felt all my muscles; and at the end of each operation they looked at the chief and nodded, and said something in a tone quite pleasant, as though I were all right. They even pulled down my eyelids, and looked, I suppose, to see if they were bloodshot; but it was not so. At length they gave up; and I think that all were satisfied of my being in the most perfect health, and very robust to boot. At last the old magistrate made me a speech of about five minutes long, which the other two appeared to think greatly to the point, but from which I gathered nothing. As soon as it was ended, they proceeded to overhaul my swag and the contents of my pockets. This gave me little uneasiness, for I had no money with me, nor anything which they were at all likely to want, or which I cared about losing. At least I fancied so, but I soon found my mistake.

They got on comfortably at first, though they were much puzzled with my tobacco-pipe and insisted on seeing me use it. When I had shown them what I did with it, they were astonished but not displeased, and seemed to like the smell. But by and by they came to my watch, which I had hidden away in the inmost pocket that I had, and had forgotten when they began their search. They seemed concerned and uneasy as soon as they got hold of it. They then made me open it and show the works; and when I had done so they gave signs of very grave displeasure, which disturbed me all the more because I could not conceive wherein it could have offended them.

I remember that when they first found it I had thought of Paley, and how he tells us that a savage on seeing a watch would at once conclude that it was designed. True, these people were not savages, but I none the less felt that this was the conclusion they would arrive at; and I was thinking what a wonderfully wise man Archbishop Paley must have been, when I was aroused by a look of horror and dismay upon the face of the magistrate, a look which conveyed to me the impression that he regarded my watch not as having been designed, but rather as the designer of himself and of the universe; or as at any rate one of the great first causes of all things.

Then it struck me that this view was quite as likely to be taken as the other by a people who had no experience of European civilization, and I was a little piqued with Paley for having led me so much astray; but I soon discovered that I had misinterpreted the expression on the magistrate's face, and that it was one not of fear, but hatred. He spoke to me solemnly and sternly for two or three minutes. Then, reflecting that this was of no use, he caused me to be conducted through several passages into a large room, which I afterwards found was the museum of the town, and wherein I beheld a sight which astonished me more than anything that I had yet seen.

It was filled with cases containing all manner of curiosities —such as skeletons, stuffed birds and animals, carvings in stone (whereof I saw several that were like those on the saddle, only smaller), but the greater part of the room was occupied by broken machinery of all descriptions. The larger specimens had a case to themselves, and tickets with writing on them in a character which I could not understand. There were fragments of steam engines, all broken and rusted; among them I saw a cylinder and piston, a broken fly-wheel, and part of a crank, which was laid on the ground by their side. Again, there was a very old carriage whose wheels in spite of rust and decay, I could see, had been designed originally for iron rails. Indeed, there were fragments of a great many of our own most advanced inventions; but they seemed all to be several hundred years old, and to be placed where they were, not for instruction, but curiosity. As I said before, all were marred and broken.

We passed many cases, and at last came to one in which there were several clocks and two or three old watches. Here the magistrate stopped, and opening the case began comparing my watch with the others. The design was different, but the thing was clearly the same. On this he turned to me and made me a speech in a severe and injured tone of voice, pointing repeatedly to the watches in the case, and to my own; neither did he seem in the least appeased until I made signs to him that he had better take my watch and put it with the others. This had some effect in calming him. I said in English (trusting to tone and manner to convey my meaning) that I was exceedingly sorry if I had been found to have anything contraband in my possession; that I had had no intention of evading the ordinary tolls, and that I would gladly forfeit the watch if my doing so would atone for an unintentional violation of the law. He began presently to relent, and spoke to me in a kinder manner. I think he saw that I had offended without knowledge; but I believe the chief thing that brought him round was my not seeming to be afraid of him, although I was quite respectful; this, and my having light hair and complexion, on which he had remarked previously by signs, as every one else had done.

I afterwards found that it was reckoned a very great merit to have fair hair, this being a thing of the rarest possible occurrence, and greatly admired and envied in all who were possessed of it. However that might be, my watch was taken from me; but our peace was made, and I was conducted back to the room where I had been examined. The magistrate then made me another speech, whereon I was taken to a building hard by, which I soon discovered to be the common prison of the town, but in which an apartment was assigned me separate from the other prisoners. The room contained a bed, table, and chairs, also a fireplace and a washing-stand. There was another door, which opened on to a balcony, with a flight of steps descending into a walled garden of some size. The man who conducted me into this room made signs to me that I might go down and walk in the garden whenever I pleased, and intimated that I should shortly have something brought me to eat. I was allowed to retain my blankets, and the few things which I had wrapped inside them, but it was plain that I was to consider myself a prisoner—for how long a period I could not by any means determine. He then left me alone.

Chapter 8

In Prison

AND NOW for the first time my courage completely failed me. It is enough to say that I was penniless, and a prisoner in a foreign country, where I had no friend, nor any knowledge of the customs or language of the people. I was at the mercy of men with whom I had little in common. And yet, engrossed as I was with my extremely difficult and doubtful position, I could not help feeling deeply interested in the people among whom I had fallen. What was the meaning of that room full of old machinery which I had just seen, and of the displeasure with which the magistrate had regarded my watch? The people had very little machinery now. I had been struck with this over and over again, though I had not been more than four-and-twenty hours in the country. They were about as far advanced as Europeans of the twelfth or thirteenth century; certainly not more so. And yet they must have had at one time the fullest knowledge of our own most recent inventions. How could it have happened that having been once so far in advance they were now as much behind us? It was evident that it was not from ignorance. They knew my watch as a watch when they saw it; and the care with which the broken machines were preserved and ticketed, proved that they had not lost the recollection of their former civilization. The more I thought, the less I could understand it; but at last I concluded that they must have worked out their mines of coal and iron, till either none were left, or so few, that the use of these metals was restricted to the very highest nobility. This was the only solution I could think of; and, though I afterwards found how entirely mistaken it was, I felt quite sure then that it must be the right one.

I had hardly arrived at this opinion for above four or five minutes, when the door opened, and a young woman made her appearance with a tray, and a very appetizing smell of dinner. I gazed upon her with admiration as she laid a cloth and set a savoury-looking dish upon the table. As I beheld her I felt as though my position was already much ameliorated, for the very sight of her carried great comfort. She was not more than twenty, rather above the middle height, active and strong, but yet most delicately featured; her lips were full and sweet; her eyes were of a deep hazel, and fringed with long and springing eyelashes; her hair was neatly braided from off her forehead; her complexion was simply exquisite; her figure as robust as was consistent with the most perfect female beauty, yet not more so; her hands and feet might have served as models to a sculptor. Having set the stew upon the table, she retired with a glance of pity, whereon (remembering pity's kinsman) I decided that she should pity me a little more. She returned with a bottle and a glass, and found me sitting on the bed with my hands over my face, looking the very picture of abject misery, and, like all pictures, rather untruthful. As I watched her, through my fingers, out of the room again, I felt sure that she was exceedingly sorry for me. Her back being turned, I set to work and ate my dinner, which was excellent.

She returned in about an hour to take away; and there came with her a man who had a great bunch of keys at his waist, and whose manner convinced me that he was the jailor. I afterwards found that he was father to the beautiful creature who had brought me my dinner. I am not a much greater hypocrite than other people, and do what I would, I could not look so very miserable. I had already recovered from my dejection, and felt in a most genial humour both with my jailor and his daughter. I thanked them for their attention towards me; and, though they could not understand, they looked at one another and laughed and chattered till the old man said something or other which I suppose was a joke; for the girl laughed merrily and ran away, leaving her father to take away the dinner things. Then I had another visitor, who was not so prepossessing, and who seemed to have a great idea of himself and a small one of me. He brought a book with him, and pens and paper—all very English; and yet, neither paper, nor printing, nor binding, nor pen, nor ink, were quite the same as ours.

He gave me to understand that he was to teach me the language and that we were to begin at once. This delighted me, both because I should be more comfortable when I could understand and make myself understood, and because I supposed that the authorities would hardly teach me the language if they intended any cruel usage towards me afterwards. We began at once, and I learnt the names of everything in the room, and also the numerals and personal pronouns. I found to my sorrow that the resemblance to European things, which I had so frequently observed hitherto, did not hold good in the matter of language; for I could detect no analogy whatever between this and any tongue of which I have the slightest knowledge— a thing which made me think it possible that I might be learning Hebrew.

I must detail no longer; from this time my days were spent with a monotony which would have been tedious but for the society of Yram, the jailor's daughter, who had taken a great fancy for me and treated me with the utmost kindness. The man came every day to teach me the language, but my real dictionary and grammar were Yram; and I consulted them to such purpose that I made the most extraordinary progress, being able at the end of a month to understand a great deal of the conversation which I overheard between Yram and her father. My teacher professed himself well satisfied, and said he should make a favourable report of me to the authorities. I then questioned him as to what would probably be done with me. He told me that my arrival had caused great excitement throughout the country, and that I was to be detained a close prisoner until the receipt of advices from the Government. My having had a watch, he said, was the only damaging feature in the case. And then, in answer to my asking why this should be so, he gave me a long story of which with my imperfect knowledge of the language I could make nothing whatever, except that it was a very heinous offence, almost as bad (at least, so I thought I understood him) as having typhus fever. But he said he thought my light hair would save me.

I was allowed to walk in the garden; there was a high wall so that I managed to play a sort of hand fives, which prevented my feeling the bad effects of my confinement, though it was stupid work playing alone. In the course of time people from the town and neighbourhood began to pester the jailor to be allowed to see me, and on receiving handsome fees he let them do so. The people were good to me; almost too good, for they were inclined to make a lion of me, which I hated—at least the women were; only they had to beware of Yram, who was a young lady of a jealous temperament, and kept a sharp eye both on me and on my lady visitors. However, I felt so kindly towards her, and was so entirely dependent upon her for almost all that made my life a blessing and a comfort to me, that I took good care not to vex her, and we remained excellent friends. The men were far less inquisitive, and would not, I believe, have come near me of their own accord; but the women made them come as escorts. I was delighted with their handsome mien, and pleasant genial manners.

My food was plain, but always varied and wholesome, and the good red wine was admirable. I had found a sort of wort in the garden, which I sweated in heaps and then dried, obtaining thus a substitute for tobacco; so that what with Yram, the language, visitors, fives in the garden, smoking, and bed, my time slipped by more rapidly and pleasantly than might have been expected. I also made myself a small flute; and being a tolerable player, amused myself at times with playing snatches from operas, and airs such as "O where and oh where," and "Home, sweet home." This was of great advantage to me, for the people of the country were ignorant of the diatonic scale and could hardly believe their ears on hearing some of our most common melodies. Often, too, they would make me sing; and I could at any time make Yram's eyes swim with tears by singing "Villikins and his Dinah," "Billy Taylor," "The Rat-catcher's Daughter," or as much of them as I could remember.

I had one or two discussions with them because I never would sing on Sunday (of which I kept count in my pocket-book), except chants and hymn tunes; of these I regret to say that I had forgotten the words, so that I could only sing the tune. They appeared to have little or no religious feeling, and to have never so much as heard of the divine institution of the Sabbath, so they ascribed my observance of it to a fit of sulki-ness, which they remarked as coming over me upon every seventh day. But they were very tolerant, and one of them said to me quite kindly that she knew how impossible it was to help being sulky at times, only she thought I ought to see some one if it became more serious—a piece of advice which I then failed to understand, though I pretended to take it quite as a matter of course.

Once only did Yram treat me in a way that was unkind and unreasonable—at least so I thought it at the time. It happened thus. I had been playing fives in the garden and got much heated. Although the day was cold, for autumn was now advancing, and Cold Harbour (as the name of the town in which my prison was should be translated) stood fully 3,000 feet above the sea, I had played without my coat and waistcoat, and took a sharp chill on resting myself too long in the open air without protection. The next day I had a severe cold and felt really poorly. Being little used even to the lightest ailments, and thinking that it would be rather nice to be petted and cosseted by Yram, I certainly did not make myself out to be any better than I was; in fact, I remember that I made the worst of things, and took it into my head to consider myself upon the sick list. When Yram brought me my breakfast I complained somewhat dolefully of my indisposition, expecting the sympathy and humouring which I should have received from my mother and sisters at home. Not a bit of it. She fired up in an instant, and asked me what I meant by it, and how I dared to presume to mention such a thing, especially when I considered in what place I was. She had the best mind to tell her father, only that she was afraid the consequences would be so very serious for me. Her manner was so injured and decided, and her anger so evidently unfeigned, that I forgot my cold upon the spot, begging her by all means to tell her father if she wished to do so, and telling her that I had no idea of being shielded by her from anything whatever; presently mollifying, after having said as many biting things as I could, I asked her what it was that I had done amiss, and promised amendment as soon as ever I became aware of it. She saw that I was really ignorant, and had had no intention of being rude to her; whereon it came out that illness of any sort was considered in Erewhon to be highly criminal and immoral; and that I was liable, even for catching cold, to be had up before the magistrates and imprisoned for a considerable period—an announcement which struck me dumb with astonishment.

I followed up the conversation as well as my imperfect knowledge of the language would allow, and caught a glimmering of her position with regard to ill-health; but I did not even then fully comprehend it, nor had I as yet any idea of the other extraordinary perversions of thought which existed among the Erewhonians, but with which I was soon to become familiar. I propose, therefore, to make no mention of what passed between us on this occasion, save that we were reconciled, and that she brought me surreptitiously a glass of hot spirits and water before I went to bed, as also a pile of extra blankets, and that next morning I was quite well. I never remember to have lost a cold so rapidly.

This little affair explained much which had hitherto puzzled me. It seemed that the two men who were examined before the magistrates on the day of my arrival in the country, had been given in charge on account of ill-health, and were both condemned to a long term of imprisonment with hard labour; they were now expiating their offence in this very prison, and their exercise ground was a yard separated by my fives wall from the garden in which I walked. This accounted for the sounds of coughing and groaning which I had often noticed as coming from the other side of the wall: it was high, and I had not dared to climb it for fear the jailor should see me and think that I was trying to escape; but I had often wondered what sort of people they could be on the other side, and had resolved on asking the jailor; but I seldom saw him, and Yram and I generally found other things to talk about.

Another month flew by, during which I made such progress in the language that I could understand all that was said to me, and express myself with tolerable fluency. My instructor professed to be astonished with the progress I had made; I was careful to attribute it to the pains he had taken with me and to his admirable method of explaining my difficulties, so we became excellent friends.

My visitors became more and more frequent. Among them there were some, both men and women, who delighted me entirely by their simplicity, unconsciousness of self, kindly genial manners, and last, but not least, by their exquisite beauty; there came others less well-bred, but still comely and agreeable people, while some were snobs pure and simple.

At the end of the third month the jailor and my instructor came together to visit me and told me that communications had been received from the Government to the effect that if I had behaved well and seemed generally reasonable, and if there could be no suspicion at all about my bodily health and vigour, and if my hair was really light, and my eyes blue and complexion fresh, I was to be sent up at once to the metropolis in order that the King and Queen might see me and converse with me; but that when I arrived there I should be set at liberty, and a suitable allowance would be made me. My teacher also told me that one of the leading merchants had sent me an invitation to repair to his house and to consider myself his guest for as long a time as I chose. "He is a delightful man," continued the interpreter, "but has suffered terribly from" (here there came a long word which I could not quite catch, only it was much longer than kleptomania), "and has but lately recovered from embezzling a large sum of money under singularly distressing circumstances; but he has quite got over it, and the straighteners say that he has made a really wonderful recovery; you are sure to like him."

Chapter 9

To the Metropolis

WITH THE above words the good man left the room before I had time to express my astonishment at hearing such extraordinary language from the lips of one who seemed to be a reputable member of society. "Embezzle a large sum of money under singularly distressing circumstances!" I exclaimed to myself, "and ask *me* to go and stay with him! I shall do nothing of the sort—compromise myself at the very outset in the eyes of all decent people, and give the death-blow to my chances of either converting them if they are the lost tribes of Israel, or making money out of them if they are not! No. I will do anything rather than that." And when I next saw my teacher I told him that I did not at all like the sound of what had been proposed for me, and that I would have nothing to do with it. For by my education and the example of my own parents, and I trust also in some degree from inborn instinct, I have a very genuine dislike for all unhandsome dealings in money matters, though none can have a greater regard for money than I have, if it be got fairly.

The interpreter was much surprised by my answer, and said that I should be very foolish if I persisted in my refusal.

"Mr. Nosnibor," he continued, "is a man of at least 500,000 horse-power" (for their way of reckoning and classifying men is by the number of foot pounds which they have money enough to raise, or more roughly by their horse-power), "and keeps a capital table; besides, his two daughters are among the most beautiful women in Erewhon."

When I heard all this, I confess that I was much shaken, and inquired whether he was favourably considered in the best society.

"Certainly," was the answer; "no man in the country stands higher."

He then went on to say that one would have thought from my manner that my proposed host had had jaundice or pleurisy or been generally unfortunate, and that I was in fear of infection.

"I am not much afraid of infection," said I, impatiently "but I have some regard for my character; and if I know a man to be an embezzler of other people's money, be sure of it, I will give him as wide a berth as I can. If he were ill or poor——"

"Ill or poor!" interrupted the interpreter, with a face of great alarm. "So that's your notion of propriety! You would consort with the basest criminals, and yet deem simple embezzlement a bar to friendly intercourse. I cannot understand you."

"But I am poor myself," cried I.

"You were," said he; "and you were liable to be severely punished for it—indeed, at the council which was held concerning you, this fact was very nearly consigning you to what I should myself consider a well-deserved chastisement" (for he was getting angry, and so was I); "but the Queen was so inquisitive, and wanted so much to see you, that she petitioned the King and made him give you his pardon, and assign you a pension in consideration of your meritorious complexion. It is lucky for you that he has not heard what you have been saying now, or he would be sure to cancel it."

As I heard these words my heart sank within me. I felt the extreme difficulty of my position, and how wicked I should be in running counter to established usage. I remained silent for several minutes, and then said that I should be happy to accept the embezzler's invitation—on which my instructor brightened and said I was a sensible fellow. But I felt very uncomfortable. When he had left the room, I mused over the conversation which had just taken place between us, but I could make nothing out of it, except that it argued an even greater perversity of mental vision than I had been yet prepared for. And this made me wretched; for I cannot bear having much to do with people who think differently from myself. All sorts of wandering thoughts kept coming into my head. I thought of my master's hut, and my seat upon the mountain side, where I had first conceived the insane idea of exploring. What years and years seemed to have passed since I had begun my journey!

I thought of my adventures in the gorge, and on the journey hither, and of Chowbok. I wondered what Chowbok told them about me when he got back—he had done well in going back

Chowbok had. He was not handsome—nay, he was hideous; and it would have gone hardly with him. Twilight drew on, and rain pattered against the windows. Never yet had I felt so unhappy, except during three days of sea-sickness at the beginning of my voyage from England. I sat musing and in great melancholy, until Yram made her appearance with light and supper. She too, poor girl, was miserable; for she had heard that I was to leave them. She had made up her mind that I was to remain always in the town, even after my imprisonment was over; and I fancy had resolved to marry me though I had never so much as hinted at her doing so. So what with the distressingly strange conversation with my teacher, my own friendless condition, and Yram's melancholy, I felt more unhappy than I can describe, and remained so till I got to bed, and sleep sealed my eyelids.

On awaking next morning I was much better. It was settled that I was to make my start in a conveyance which was to be in waiting for me at about eleven o'clock; and the anticipation of change put me in good spirits, which even the tearful face of Yram could hardly altogether derange. I kissed her again and again, assured her that we should meet hereafter, and that in the meanwhile I should be ever mindful of her kindness. I gave her two of the buttons off my coat and a lock of my hair as a keepsake, taking a goodly curl from her own beautiful head in return: and so, having said good-bye a hundred times, till I was fairly overcome with her great sweetness and her sorrow, I tore myself away from her and got downstairs to the *calèche* which was in waiting. How thankful I was when it was all over, and I was driven away and out of sight. Would that I could have felt that it was out of mind also! Pray heaven that it is so now, and that she is married happily among her own people, and has forgotten me!

And now began a long and tedious journey with which I should hardly trouble the reader if I could. He is safe, however, for the simple reason that I was blindfolded during the greater part of the time. A bandage was put upon my eyes every morning, and was only removed at night when I reached the inn at which we were to pass the night. We travelled slowly, although the roads were good. We drove but one horse, which took us our day's journey from morning till evening, about six hours, exclusive of two hours' rest in the middle of the day. I do not suppose we made above thirty or thirty-five miles on an average. Each day we had a fresh horse. As I have said already, I could see nothing of the country. I only know that it was level, and that several times we had to cross large rivers in ferry-boats. The inns were clean and comfortable. In one or two of the larger towns they were quite sumptuous, and the food was good and well cooked. The same wonderful health and grace and beauty prevailed everywhere.

I found myself an object of great interest; so much so, that the driver told me he had to keep our route secret, and at times to go to places that were not directly on our road, in order to avoid the press that would otherwise have awaited us. Every evening I had a reception, and grew heartily tired of having to say the same things over and over again in answer to the same questions, but it was impossible to be angry with people whose manners were so delightful. They never once asked after my health, or even whether I was fatigued with my journey; but their first question was almost invariably an inquiry after my temper, the *naïveté* of which astonished me till I became used to it. One day, being tired and cold, and weary of saying the same thing over and over again, I turned a little brusquely on my questioner and said that I was exceedingly cross, and that I could hardly feel in a worse humour with myself and every one else than at that moment. To my surprise, I was met with the kindest expressions of condolence, and heard it buzzed about the room that I was in an ill temper; whereon people began to give me nice things to smell and to eat, which really did seem to have some temper-mending quality about them, for I soon felt pleased and was at once congratulated upon being better. The next morning two or three people sent their servants to the hotel with sweetmeats, and inquiries whether I had quite recovered from my ill humour. On receiving the good things I felt in half a mind to be ill-tempered every evening; but I disliked the condolences and the inquiries, and found it most comfortable to keep my natural temper, which is smooth enough generally.

Among those who came to visit me were some who had received a liberal education at the Colleges of Unreason, and taken the highest degrees in hypothetics, which are their principal study. These gentlemen had now settled down to various employments in the country, as straighteners, managers and cashiers of the Musical Banks, priests of religion, or what not, and carrying their education with them they diffused a leaven of culture throughout the country. I naturally questioned them about many of the things which had puzzled me since my arrival. I inquired what was the object of meaning of the statues which I had seen upon the plateau of the pass. I was told that they dated from a very remote period, and that there were several other such groups in the country, but none so remarkable as the one which I had seen. They had a religious origin, having been designed to propitiate the gods of deformity and disease. In former times it had been the custom to make expeditions over the ranges, and capture the ugliest of Chowbok's ancestors whom they could find, in order to sacrifice them in the presence of these deities, and thus avert ugliness and disease from the Erewhonians themselves. It had been whispered (but my informant assured me untruly) that centuries ago they had even offered up some of their own people who were ugly or out of health, in order to make examples of them; these detestable customs, however, had been long discontinued; neither was there any present observance of the statues.

I had the curiosity to inquire what would be done to any of Chowbok's tribe if they crossed over into Erewhon. I was told that nobody knew, inasmuch as such a thing had not happened for ages. They would be too ugly to be allowed to go at large, but not so much so as to be criminally liable. Their offence in having come would be a moral one; but they would be beyond the straightener's art. Possibly they would be consigned to the Hospital for Incurable Bores, and made to work at being bored for so many hours a day by the Erewhonian inhabitants of the hospital, who are extremely impatient of one another's boredom, but would soon die if they had no one whom they might bore—in fact, that they would be kept as professional borees. When I heard this, it occurred to me that some rumours of its substance might perhaps have become current among Chowbok's people; for the agony of his fear had been too great to have been inspired by the mere dread of being burnt alive before the statues.

I also questioned them about the museum of old machines, and the cause of the apparent retrogression in all arts, sciences, and inventions. I learnt that about four hundred years previously, the state of mechanical knowledge was far beyond our own, and was advancing with prodigious rapidity, until one of the most learned professors of hypothetics wrote an extraordinary book (from which I propose to give extracts later on), proving that the machines were ultimately destined to supplant the race of man, and to become instinct with a vitality as different from, and superior to, that of animals, as animal to vegetable life. So convincing was his reasoning, or unreasoning, to this effect, that he carried the country with him; and they made a clean sweep of all machinery that had not been in use for more than two hundred and seventy-one years (which period was arrived at after a series of compromises), and strictly forbade all further improvements and inventions under pain of being considered in the eye of the law to be labouring under typhus fever, which they regard as one of the worst of all crimes.

This is the only case in which they have confounded mental and physical diseases, and they do it even here as by an avowed legal fiction. I became uneasy when I remembered about my watch; but they comforted me with the assurance that transgression in this matter was now so unheard of, that the law could afford to be lenient towards an utter stranger, especially towards one who had such a good character (they meant physique), and such beautiful light hair. Moreover the watch was a real curiosity, and would be a welcome addition to the metropolitan collection; so they did not think I need let it trouble me seriously.

I will write, however, more fully upon this subject when I deal with the Colleges of Unreason, and the Book of the Machines.

In about a month from the time of our starting I was told that our journey was nearly over. The bandage was now dispensed with, for it seemed impossible that I should ever be able to find my way back without being captured. Then we rolled merrily along through the streets of a handsome town, and got on to a long, broad, and level road, with poplar trees on either side. The road was raised slightly above the surrounding country, and had formerly been a railway; the fields on either side were in the highest conceivable cultivation, but the harvest and also the vintage had been already gathered. The weather had got cooler more rapidly than could be quite accounted for by the progress of the season; so I rather thought that we must have been making away from the sun, and were some degrees farther from the equator than when we started. Even here the vegetation showed that the climate was a hot one, yet there was no lack of vigour among the people; on the contrary, they were a very hardy race, and capable of great endurance. For the hundredth time I thought that, take them all round, I had never seen their equals in respect of physique, and they looked as good-natured as they were robust. The flowers were for the most part over, but their absence was in some measure compensated for by a profusion of delicious fruit, closely resembling the figs, peaches, and pears of Italy and France. I saw no wild animals, but birds were plentiful and much as in Europe, but not tame as they had been on the other side the ranges. They were shot at with the cross-bow and with arrows, gunpowder being unknown, or at any rate not in use.

We were now nearing the metropolis and I could see great towers and fortifications, and lofty buildings that looked like palaces. I began to be nervous as to my reception; but I had got on very well so far, and resolved to continue upon the same plan as hitherto—namely, to behave just as though I were in England until I saw that I was making a blunder, and then to say nothing till I could gather how the land lay. We drew nearer and nearer. The news of my approach had got abroad, and there was a great crowd collected on either side the road, who greeted me with marks of most respectful curiosity, keeping me bowing constantly in acknowledgment from side to side.

When we were about a mile off, we were met by the Mayor and several Councillors, among whom was a venerable old man, who was introduced to me by the Mayor (for so I suppose I should call him) as the gentleman who had invited me to his house. I bowed deeply and told him how grateful I felt to him, and how gladly I would accept his hospitality. He forbade me to say more, and pointing to his carriage, which was close at hand, he motioned me to a seat therein. I again bowed profoundly to the Mayor and Councillors, and drove off with my entertainer, whose name was Senoj Nosnibor. After about half a mile the carriage turned off the main road, and we drove under the walls of the town till we reached a *palazzo* on a slight eminence, and just on the outskirts of the city. This was Senoj Nosnibor's house, and nothing can be imagined finer. It was situated near the magnificent and venerable ruins of the old railway station, which formed an imposing feature from the gardens of the house. The grounds, some ten or a dozen acres in extent, were laid out in terraced gardens, one above the other, with flights of broad steps ascending and descending the declivity of the garden. On these steps there were statues of most exquisite workmanship. Besides the statues there were vases filled with various shrubs that were new to me; and on either side the flights of steps there were rows of old cypresses and cedars, with grassy alleys between them. Then came choice vineyards and orchards of fruit-trees in full bearing.

The house itself was approached by a court-yard, and round it was a corridor on to which rooms opened, as at Pompeii. In the middle of the court there was a bath and a fountain. Having passed the court we came to the main body of the house, which was two stories in height. The rooms were large and lofty; perhaps at first they looked rather bare of furniture, but in hot climates people generally keep their rooms more bare than they do in colder ones. I missed also the sight of a grand piano or some similar instrument, there being no means of producing music in any of the rooms save the larger drawing-room, where there were half a dozen large bronze gongs, which the ladies used occasionally to beat about at random. It was not pleasant to hear them, but I have heard quite as unpleasant music both before and since.

Mr. Nosnibor took me through several spacious rooms till we reached a boudoir where were his wife and daughters, of whom I had heard from the interpreter. Mrs. Nosnibor was about forty years old, and still handsome, but she had grown very stout: her daughters were in the prime of youth and ex-quisitely beautiful. I gave the preference almost at once to the younger, whose name was Arowhena; for the elder sister was haughty, while the younger had a very winning manner. Mrs. Nosnibor received me with the perfection of courtesy, so that I must have indeed been shy and nervous if I had not at once felt welcome. Scarcely was the ceremony of my introduction well completed before a servant announced that dinner was ready in the next room. I was exceedingly hungry, and the dinner was beyond all praise. Can the reader wonder that I began to consider myself in excellent quarters? "That man em-bezzle money?" thought I to myself; "impossible."

But I noticed that my host was uneasy during the whole meal, and that he ate nothing but a little bread and milk; towards the end of dinner there came a tall lean man with a black beard, to whom Mr. Nosnibor and the whole family paid great attention: he was the family straightener. With this gentleman Mr. Nosnibor retired into another room, from which there presently proceeded a sound of weeping and wailing. I could hardly believe my ears, but in a few minutes I got to know for a certainty that they came from Mr. Nosnibor him-self.

"Poor papa," said Arowhena, as she helped herself com-posedly to the salt, "how terrible he has suffered."

"Yes," answered her mother; "but I think he is quite out of danger now."

Then they went on to explain to me the circumstances of the case, and the treatment which the straightener had pre-scribed, and how successful he had been—all which I will reserve for another chapter, and put rather in the form of a general summary of the opinions current upon these subjects than in the exact words in which the facts were delivered to me; the reader, however, is earnestly requested to believe that both in this next chapter and in those that follow it I have endeavoured to adhere most conscientiously to the strictest accuracy, and that I have never willingly misrepresented, though I may have sometimes failed to understand all the bearings of an opinion or custom.

Chapter 10

Current Opinions

THIS IS what I gathered. That in that country if a man falls into ill health, or catches any disorder, or fails bodily in any way before he is seventy years old, he is tried before a jury of his countrymen, and if convicted is held up to public scorn and sentenced more or less severely as the case may be. There are subdivisions of illness into crimes and misdemeanours as with offences amongst ourselves—a man being punished very heavily for serious illness, while failure of eyes or hearing in one over sixty-five, who has had good health hitherto, is dealt with by fine only, or imprisonment in default of payment. But if a man forges a cheque, or sets his house on fire, or robs with violence from the person, or does any other such things as are criminal in our own country, he is either taken to a hospital and most carefully tended at the public expense, or if he is in good circumstances, he lets it be known to all his friends that he is suffering from a severe fit of immorality, just as we do when we are ill, and they come and visit him with great solicitude, and inquire with interest how it all came about, what symptoms first showed themselves, and so forth—questions which he will answer with perfect unreserve; for bad conduct, though considered no less deplorable than illness with ourselves, and as unquestionably indicating something seriously wrong with the individual who misbehaves, is nevertheless held to be the result of either pre-natal or post-natal misfortune.

The strange part of the story, however, is that though they ascribe moral defects to the effect of misfortune either in character or surroundings, they will not listen to the plea of misfortune in cases that in England meet with sympathy and commiseration only. Ill luck of any kind, or even ill treatment at the hands of others, is considered an offence against society, inasmuch as it makes people uncomfortable to hear of it. Loss of fortune, therefore, or loss of some dear friend on whom another was much dependent, is punished hardly less severely than physical delinquency.

Foreign, indeed, as such ideas are to our own, traces of somewhat similar opinions can be found even in nineteenth-century England. If a person has an abscess, the medical man will say that it contains "peccant" matter, and people say that they have a "bad" arm or finger, or that they are very "bad" all over, when they only mean "diseased." Among foreign nations Erewhonian opinion may be still more clearly noted. The Mohammedans, for example, to this day, send their female prisoners to hospitals, and the New Zealand Maoris visit any misfortune with forcible entry into the house of the offender, and the breaking up and burning of all his goods. The Italians, again, use the same word for "disgrace" and "misfortune." I once heard an Italian lady speak of a young friend whom she described as endowed with every virtue under heaven, "ma," she exclaimed, "povero disgraziato, ha ammazzato suo zio." ("Poor unfortunate fellow, he has murdered his uncle.")

On mentioning this, which I heard when taken to Italy as a boy by my father, the person to whom I told it showed no surprise. He said that he had been driven for two or three years in a certain city by a young Sicilian cabdriver of prepossessing manners and appearance, but then lost sight of him. On asking what had become of him, he was told that he was in prison for having shot at his father with intent to kill him—happily without serious result. Some years later my informant again found himself warmly accosted by the prepossessing young cabdriver. "Ah, caro signore," he exclaimed, "sono cinque anni che non lo vedo—tre anni di militare, e due anni di disgrazia," etc. ("My dear sir, it is five years since I saw you—three years of military service, and two of misfortune") —during which last the poor fellow had been in prison. Of moral sense he showed not so much as a trace. He and his father were now on excellent terms, and were likely to remain so unless either of them should again have the misfortune mortally to offend the other.

In the following chapter I will give a few examples of the way in which what we should call misfortune, hardship, or disease are dealt with by the Erewhonians, but for the moment will return to their treatment of cases that with us are criminal. As I have already said, these, though not judicially punishable, are recognized as requiring correction. Accordingly, there exists a class of men trained in soul-craft, whom they call straighteners, as nearly as I can translate a word which literally means "one who bends back the crooked." These men practise much as medical men in England, and receive a quasi-surreptitious fee on every visit. They are treated with the same unreserve, and obeyed as readily, as our own doctors—that is to say, on the whole sufficiently—because people know that it is their interest to get well as soon as they can, and that they will not be scouted as they would be if their bodies were out of order, even though they may have to undergo a very painful course of treatment.

When I say that they will not be scouted, I do not mean that an Erewhonian will suffer no special inconvenience in consequence, we will say, of having committed fraud. Friends will fall away from him because of his being less pleasant company, just as we ourselves are disinclined to make companions of those who are either poor or poorly. No one with any sense of self-respect will place himself on an equality in the matter of affection with those who are less lucky than himself in birth, health, money, good looks, capacity, or anything else. Indeed, that dislike and even disgust should be felt by the fortunate for the unfortunate, or at any rate for those who have been discovered to have met with any of the more serious and less familiar misfortunes, is not only natural, but desirable for any society, whether of man or brute.

The fact, therefore, that the Erewhonians attach none of that guilt to crime which they do to physical ailments, does not prevent the more selfish among them from neglecting a friend who has robbed a bank, for instance, till he has fully recovered; but it does prevent them from even thinking of treating criminals with that contemptuous tone which would seem to say, "I, if I were you, should be a better man than you are," a tone which is held quite reasonable in regard to physical ailment. Hence, though they conceal ill health by every cunning and hypocrisy and artifice which they can devise, they are quite open about the most flagrant mental diseases, should they happen to exist, which to do the people justice is not often. Indeed, there are some who are, so to speak, spiritual valetudinarians, and who make themselves exceedingly ridiculous by their nervous supposition that they are wicked, while they are very tolerable people all the time. This however is exceptional; and on the whole they use much the same reserve or unreserve about the state of their moral welfare as we do about our health.

Hence all the ordinary greetings among ourselves, such as,

How do you do? and the like, are considered signs of gross ill-breeding; nor do the politer classes tolerate even such a common complimentary remark as telling a man that he is looking well. They salute each other with "I hope you are good this morning"; or "I hope you have recovered from the snappishness from which you were suffering when I last saw you"; and if the person saluted has not been good, or is still snappish, he says so at once and is condoled with accordingly. Indeed, the straighteners have gone so far as to give names from the hypothetical language (as taught at the Colleges of Unreason) to all known forms of mental indisposition, and to classify them according to a system of their own, which, though I could not understand it, seemed to work well in practise; for they are always able to tell a man what is the matter with him as soon as they have heard his story, and their familiarity with the long names assures him that they thoroughly understand his case.

The reader will have no difficulty in believing that the laws regarding ill health were frequently evaded by the help of recognized fictions, which every one understood, but which it would be considered gross ill-breeding to even seem to understand. Thus, a day or two after my arrival at the Nosnibors', one of the many ladies who called on me made excuses for her husband's only sending his card, on the ground that when going through the public market-place that morning he had stolen a pair of socks. I had already been warned that I should never show surprise, so I merely expressed my sympathy, and said that though I had only been in the capital so short a time, I had already had a very narrow escape from stealing a clothes-brush, and that though I had resisted temptation so far, I was sadly afraid that if I saw any object of special interest that was neither too hot nor too heavy, I should have to put myself in the straightener's hands.

Mrs. Nosnibor, who had been keeping an ear on all that I had been saying, praised me when the lady had gone. Nothing, she said, could have been more polite according to Erewhonian etiquette. She then explained that to have stolen a pair of socks, or "to have the socks" (in more colloquial language), was a recognized way of saying that the person in question was slightly indisposed.

In spite of all this they have a keen sense of the enjoyment consequent upon what they call being "well." They admire mental health and love it in other people, and take all the pains they can (consistently with their other duties) to secure it for themselves. They have an extreme dislike to marrying into

70

what they consider unhealthy families. They send for the straightener at once whenever they have been guilty of anything seriously flagitious—often even if they think that they are on the point of committing it; and though his remedies are sometimes exceedingly painful, involving close confinement for weeks, and in some cases the most cruel physical tortures, I never heard of a reasonable Erewhonian refusing to do what his straightener told him, any more than of a reasonable Englishman refusing to undergo even the most frightful operation, if his doctors told him it was necessary.

We in England never shrink from telling our doctor what is the matter with us merely through the fear that he will hurt us. We let him do his worst upon us, and stand it without a murmur, because we are not scouted for being ill, and because we know that the doctor is doing his best to cure us, and that he can judge of our case better than we can; but we should conceal all illness if we were treated as the Erewhonians are when they have anything the matter with them; we should do the same as with moral and intellectual diseases—we should feign health with the most consummate art, till we were found out, and should hate a single flogging given in the way of mere punishment more than the amputation of a limb, if it were kindly and courteously performed from a wish to help us out of our difficulty, and with the full consciousness on the part of the doctor that it was only by an accident of constitution that he was not in the like plight himself. So the Erewhonians take a flogging once a week, and a diet of bread and water for two or three months together, whenever their straightener recommends it.

I do not suppose that even my host, on having swindled a confiding widow out of the whole of her property, was put to more actual suffering than a man will readily undergo at the hands of an English doctor. And yet he must have had a very bad time of it. The sounds I heard were sufficient to show that his pain was exquisite, but he never shrank from undergoing it. He was quite sure that it did him good; and I think he was right. I cannot believe that that man will ever embezzle money again. He may—but it will be a long time before he does so.

During my confinement in prison, and on my journey, I had already discovered a great deal of the above; but it still seemed surpassingly strange, and I was in constant fear of committing some piece of rudeness, through my inability to look at things from the same stand-point as my neighbours; but after a few weeks' stay with the Nosnibors, I got to under-

71

stand things better, especially on having heard all about my host's illness, of which he told me fully and repeatedly.

It seemed that he had been on the Stock Exchange of the city for many years and had amassed enormous wealth, without exceeding the limits of what was generally considered justifiable, or at any rate, permissible dealing; but at length on several occasions he had become aware of a desire to make money by fraudulent representations, and had actually dealt with two or three sums in a way which had made him rather uncomfortable. He had unfortunately made light of it and pooh-poohed the ailment, until circumstances eventually presented themselves which enabled him to cheat upon a very considerable scale—he told me what they were, and they were about as bad as anything could be, but I need not detail them—he seized the opportunity, and became aware, when it was too late, that he must be seriously out of order. He had neglected himself too long.

He drove home at once, broke the news to his wife and daughters as gently as he could, and sent off for one of the most celebrated straighteners of the kingdom to a consultation with the family practitioner, for the case was plainly serious. On the arrival of the straightener he told his story, and expressed his fear that his morals must be permanently impaired.

The eminent man reassured him with a few cheering words, and then proceeded to make a more careful diagnosis of the case. He inquired concerning Mr. Nosnibor's parents—had their moral health been good? He was answered that there had not been anything seriously amiss with them, but that his maternal grandfather, whom he was supposed to resemble somewhat in person, had been a consummate scoundrel and had ended his days in a hospital—while a brother of his father's, after having led a most flagitious life for many years, had been at last cured by a philosopher of a new school, which as far as I could understand it bore much the same relation to the old as homoeopathy to allopathy. The straightener shook his head at this, and laughingly replied that the cure must have been due to nature. After a few more questions he wrote a prescription and departed.

I saw the prescription. It ordered a fine to the State of double the money embezzled; no food but bread and milk for six months, and a severe flogging once a month for twelve. I was surprised to see that no part of the fine was to be paid to the poor woman whose money had been embezzled, but on inquiry I learned that she would have been prosecuted in

72

the Misplaced Confidence Court, if she had not escaped its clutches by dying shortly after she had discovered her loss.

As for Mr. Nosnibor, he had received his eleventh flogging on the day of my arrival. I saw him later on the same afternoon, and he was still twinged; but there had been no escape from following out the straightener's prescription, for the so-called sanitary laws of Erewhon are very rigorous, and unless the straightener was satisfied that his orders had been obeyed, the patient would have been taken to a hospital (as the poor are), and would have been much worse off. Such at least is the law, but it is never necessary to enforce it.

On a subsequent occasion I was present at an interview between Mr. Nosnibor and the family straightener, who was considered competent to watch the completion of the cure. I was struck with the delicacy with which he avoided even the remotest semblance of inquiry after the physical well-being of his patient, though there was a certain yellowness about my host's eyes which argued a bilious habit of body. To have taken notice of this would have been a gross breach of professional etiquette. I was told, however, that a straightener sometimes thinks it right to glance at the possibility of some slight physical disorder if he finds it important in order to assist him in his diagnosis; but the answers which he gets are generally untrue or evasive, and he forms his own conclusions upon the matter as well as he can. Sensible men have been known to say that the straightener should in strict confidence be told of every physical ailment that is likely to bear upon the case; but people are naturally shy of doing this, for they do not like lowering themselves in the opinion of the straightener, and his ignorance of medical science is supreme. I heard of one lady, indeed, who had the hardihood to confess that a furious outbreak of ill-humour and extravagant fancies for which she was seeking advice was possibly the result of indisposition. "You should resist that," said the straightener, in a kind, but grave voice; "we can do nothing for the bodies of our patients; such matters are beyond our province, and I desire that I may hear no further particulars." The lady burst into tears, and promised faithfully that she would never be unwell again.

But to return to Mr. Nosnibor. As the afternoon wore on many carriages drove up with callers to inquire how he had stood his flogging. It had been very severe, but the kind inquiries upon every side gave him great pleasure, and he assured me that he felt almost tempted to do wrong again by the solicitude with which his friends had treated him during his recovery; in this I need hardly say that he was not serious.

During the remainder of my stay in the country Mr. Nosnibor was constantly attentive to his business, and largely increased his already great possessions; but I never heard a whisper to the effect of his having been indisposed a second time, or made money by other than the most strictly honourable means. I did hear afterwards in confidence that there had been reason to believe that his health had been not a little affected by the straightener's treatment, but his friends did not choose to be over-curious upon the subject, and on his return to his affairs it was by common consent passed over as hardly criminal in one who was otherwise so much afflicted. For they regard bodily ailments as the more venial in proportion as they have been produced by causes independent of the constitution. Thus if a person ruin his health by excessive indulgence at the table or by drinking, they count it to be almost a part of the mental disease which brought it about, and so it goes for little, but they have no mercy on such illnesses as fevers or catarrhs or lung diseases, which to us appear to be beyond the control of the individual. They are only more lenient towards the diseases of the young—such as measles, which they think to be like sowing one's wild oats—and look over them as pardonable indiscretions if they have not been too serious, and if they are atoned for by complete subsequent recovery.

It is hardly necessary to say that the office of straightener is one which requires long and special training. It stands to reason that he who would cure a moral ailment must be practically acquainted with it in all its bearings. The student for the profession of straightener is required to set apart certain seasons for the practise of each vice in turn, as a religious duty. These seasons are called "fasts," and are continued by the student until he finds that he really can subdue all the more usual vices in his own person, and hence can advise his patients from the results of his own experience.

Those who intend to be specialists, rather than general practitioners, devote themselves more particularly to the branch in which their practise will mainly lie. Some students have been obliged to continue their exercises during their whole lives, and some devoted men have actually died as martyrs to the drink, or gluttony, or whatever branch of vice they may have chosen for their especial study. The greater number, however, take no harm by the excursions into the various departments of vice which it is incumbent upon them to study.

For the Erewhonians hold that unalloyed virtue is not a thing to be immoderately indulged in. I was shown more than one case in which the real or supposed virtues of parents were visited upon the children to the third and fourth generation. The straighteners say that the most that can be truly said for virtue is that there is a considerable balance in its favour, and that it is on the whole a good deal better to be on its side than against it; but they urge that there is much pseudo-virtue going about, which is apt to let people in very badly before they find it out. Those men, they say, are best who are not remarkable either for vice or virtue. I told them about Hogarth's idle and industrious apprentices, but they did not seem to think that the industrious apprentice was a very nice person.

Chapter 11

Some Erewhonian Trials

IN EREWHON as in other countries there are some courts of justice that deal with special subjects. Misfortune generally, as I have above explained, is considered more or less criminal, but it admits of classification, and a court is assigned to each of the main heads under which it can be supposed to fall. Not very long after I had reached the capital I strolled into the Personal Bereavement Court, and was much both interested and pained by listening to the trial of a man who was accused of having just lost a wife to whom he had been tenderly attached, and who had left him with three little children, of whom the eldest was only three years old.

The defence which the prisoner's counsel endeavoured to establish was, that the prisoner had never really loved his wife; but it broke down completely, for the public prosecutor called witness after witness who deposed to the fact that the couple had been devoted to one another, and the prisoner repeatedly wept as incidents were put in evidence that reminded him of the irreparable nature of the loss he had sustained. The jury returned a verdict of guilty after very little deliberation, but recommended the prisoner to mercy on the ground that he had but recently insured his wife's life for a considerable sum, and might be deemed lucky inasmuch as he had received the money without demur from the insurance company, though he had only paid two premiums.

I have just said that the jury found the prisoner guilty. When the judge passed sentence, I was struck with the way in which the prisoner's counsel was rebuked for having referred to a work in which the guilt of such misfortunes as the prisoner's was extenuated to a degree that roused the indignation of the court.

"We shall have," said the judge, "these crude and subversionary books from time to time until it is recognized as an axiom of morality that luck is the only fit object of human veneration. How far a man has any right to be more lucky and hence more venerable than his neighbours, is a point that always has been, and always will be, settled proximately by a kind of higgling and haggling of the market, and ultimately by brute force; but however this may be, it stands to reason that no man should be allowed to be unlucky to more than a very moderate extent."

Then, turning to the prisoner, the judge continued: "You have suffered a great loss. Nature attaches a severe penalty to such offences, and human law must emphasize the decrees of nature. But for the recommendation of the jury I should have given you six months' hard labour. I will, however, commute your sentence to one of three months, with the option of a fine of twenty-five per cent of the money you have received from the insurance company."

The prisoner thanked the judge, and said that as he had no one to look after his children if he was sent to prison, he would embrace the option mercifully permitted him by his lordship, and pay the sum he had named. He was then removed from the dock.

The next case was that of a youth barely arrived at man's estate, who was charged with having been swindled out of large property during his minority by his guardian, who was also one of his nearest relations. His father had been long dead, and it was for this reason that his offence came on for trial in the Personal Bereavement Court. The lad, who was undefended, pleaded that he was young, inexperienced, greatly in awe of his guardian, and without independent professional advice. "Young man," said the judge sternly, "do not talk nonsense. People have no right to be young, inexperienced, greatly in awe of their guardians, and without independent professional advice. If by such indiscretions they outrage the moral sense of their friends, they must expect to suffer accordingly." He then ordered the prisoner to apologize to his guardian, and to receive twelve strokes with a cat-of-nine-tails.

But I shall perhaps best convey to the reader an idea of the entire perversion of thought which exists among this extraordinary people, by describing the public trial of a man who was accused of pulmonary consumption—an offence which was punished with death until quite recently. It did not occur till I had been some months in the country, and I am deviating from chronological order in giving it here; but I had perhaps better do so in order that I may exhaust this subject before proceeding to others. Moreover, I should never come to an end were I to keep to a strictly narrative form, and detail the infinite absurdities with which I daily came in contact.

The prisoner was placed in the dock, and the jury were sworn much as in Europe; almost all our own modes of procedure were reproduced, even to the requiring the prisoner to plead guilty or not guilty. He pleaded not guilty, and the case proceeded. The evidence for the prosecution was very strong; but I must do the court the justice to observe that the trial was absolutely impartial. Counsel for the prisoner was allowed to urge everything that could be said in his defence: the line taken was that the prisoner was simulating consumption in order to defraud an insurance company, from which he was about to buy an annuity, and that he hoped thus to obtain it on more advantageous terms. If this could have been shown to be the case he would have escaped a criminal prosecution, and been sent to a hospital as for a moral ailment. The view, however, was one which could not be reasonably sustained, in spite of all the ingenuity and eloquence of one of the most celebrated advocates of the country. The case was only too clear, for the prisoner was almost at the point of death, and it was astonishing that he had not been tried and convicted long previously. His coughing was incessant during the whole trial, and it was all that the two jailors in charge of him could do to keep him on his legs until it was over.

The summing up of the judge was admirable. He dwelt upon every point that could be construed in favour of the prisoner, but as he proceeded it became clear that the evidence was too convincing to admit of doubt, and there was but one opinion in the court as to the impending verdict when the jury retired from the box. They were absent for about ten minutes, and on their return the foreman pronounced the prisoner guilty. There was a faint murmur of applause, but it was instantly repressed. The judge then proceeded to pronounce sentence in words which I can never forget, and which I copied out into a note-book next day from the report that was published in the leading newspaper. I must condense it somewhat, and nothing which I could say would give more than a faint idea of the solemn, not to say majestic, severity with which it was delivered. The sentence was as follows:

"Prisoner at the bar, you have been accused of the great crime of labouring under pulmonary consumption, and after an impartial trial before a jury of your countrymen, you have been found guilty. Against the justice of the verdict I can say nothing: the evidence against you was conclusive, and it only remains for me to pass such a sentence upon you, as shall satisfy the ends of the law. That sentence must be a very severe one. It pains me much to see one who is yet so young, and whose prospects in life were otherwise so excellent, brought to this distressing condition by a constitution which I can only regard as radically vicious; but yours is no case for compassion: this is not your first offence: you have led a career of crime, and have only profited by the leniency shown you upon past occasions to offend yet more seriously against the laws and institutions of your country. You were convicted of aggravated bronchitis last year: and I find that though you are now only twenty-three years old, you have been imprisoned on no less than fourteen occasions for illnesses of a more or less hateful character; in fact, it is not too much to say that you have spent the greater part of your life in a jail.

"It is all very well for you to say that you came of unhealthy parents, and had a severe accident in your childhood which permanently undermined your constitution; excuses such as these are the ordinary refuge of the criminal; but they cannot for one moment be listened to by the ear of justice. I am not here to enter upon curious metaphysical questions as to the origin of this or that—questions to which there would be no end were their introduction once tolerated, and which would result in throwing the only guilt on the tissues of the primordial cell, or on the elementary gases. There is no question of how you came to be wicked, but only this—namely, are you wicked or not? This has been decided in the affirmative, neither can I hesitate for a single moment to say that it has been decided justly. You are a bad and dangerous person, and stand branded in the eyes of your fellow-countrymen with one of the most heinous known offences.

"It is not my business to justify the law: the law may in some cases have its inevitable hardships, and I may feel regret at times that I have not the option of passing a less severe sentence than I am compelled to do. But yours is no such case; on the contrary, had not the capital punishment for consumption been abolished, I should certainly inflict it now.

"It is intolerable that an example of such terrible enormity should be allowed to go at large unpunished. Your presence in the society of respectable people would lead the less able-bodied to think more lightly of all forms of illness; neither can it be permitted that you should have the chance of corrupting unborn beings who might hereafter pester you. The unborn must not be allowed to come near you: and this not so much for their protection (for they are our natural enemies), as for our own; for since they will not be utterly gainsaid, it must be seen to that they shall be quartered upon those who are least likely to corrupt them.

"But independently of this consideration, and independently of the physical guilt which attaches itself to a crime so great as yours, there is yet another reason why we should be unable to show you mercy, even if we were inclined to do so. I refer to the existence of a class of men who lie hidden among us, and who are called physicians. Were the severity of the law or the current feeling of the country to be relaxed never so slightly, these abandoned persons, who are now compelled to practise secretly and who can be consulted only at the greatest risk, would become frequent visitors in every household; their organization and their intimate acquaintance with all family secrets would give them a power, both social and political, which nothing could resist. The head of the household would become subordinate to the family doctor, who would interfere between man and wife, between master and servant, until the doctors should be the only depositaries of power in the nation, and have all that we hold precious at their mercy. A time of universal dephysicalization would ensue; medicine-vendors of all kinds would abound in our streets and advertise in all our newspapers. There is one remedy for this, and one only. It is that which the laws of this country have long received and acted upon, and consists in the sternest repression of all diseases whatsoever, as soon as their existence is made manifest to the eye of the law. Would that that eye were far more piercing than it is.

"But I will enlarge no further upon things that are themselves so obvious. You may say that it is not your fault. The answer is ready enough at hand, and it amounts to this—that if you had been born of healthy and well-to-do parents, and been well taken care of when you were a child, you would never have offended against the laws of your country, nor found yourself in your present disgraceful position. If you tell me that you had no hand in your parentage and education, and that it is therefore unjust to lay these things to your charge, I answer that whether your being in a consumption is your fault or no, it is a fault in you, and it is my duty to see that against such faults as this the commonwealth shall be protected. You may say that it is your misfortune to be criminal; I answer that it is your crime to be unfortunate.

"Lastly, I should point out that even though the jury had acquitted you—a supposition that I cannot seriously entertain —I should have felt it my duty to inflict a sentence hardly less severe than that which I must pass at present; for the more you had been found guiltless of the crime imputed to you, the more you would have been found guilty of one hardly less heinous— I mean the crime of having been maligned unjustly.

"I do not hesitate therefore to sentence you to imprisonment, with hard labour, for the rest of your miserable existence. During that period I would earnestly entreat you to repent of the wrongs you have done already, and to entirely reform the constitution of your whole body. I entertain but little hope that you will pay attention to my advice; you are already far too abandoned. Did it rest with myself, I should add nothing in mitigation of the sentence which I have passed, but it is the merciful provision of the law that even the most hardened criminal shall be allowed some one of the three official remedies, which is to be prescribed at the time of his conviction. I shall therefore order that you receive two tablespoonfuls of castor oil daily, until the pleasure of the court be further known."

When the sentence was concluded the prisoner acknowledged in a few scarcely audible words that he was justly punished, and that he had had a fair trial. He was then removed to the prison from which he was never to return. There was a second attempt at applause when the judge had finished speaking, but as before it was at once repressed; and though the feeling of the court was strongly against the prisoner, there was no show of any violence against him, if one may except a little hooting from the bystanders when he was being removed in the prisoners' van. Indeed, nothing struck me more during my whole sojourn in the country, than the general respect for law and order.

Chapter 12

Malcontents

I confess that I felt rather unhappy when I got home, and thought more closely over the trial that I had just witnessed. For the time I was carried away by the opinion of those among whom I was. They had no misgivings about what they were doing. There did not seem to be a person in the whole court who had the smallest doubt but that all was exactly as it should be. This universal unsuspecting confidence was imparted by sympathy to myself, in spite of all my training in opinions so widely different. So it is with most of us: that which we observe to be taken as a matter of course by those round us, we take as a matter of course ourselves. And after all, it is our duty to do this, save upon grave occasion.

But when I was alone, and began to think the trial over, it certainly did strike me as betraying a strange and untenable position. Had the judge said that he acknowledged the probable truth, namely, that the prisoner was born of unhealthy parents, or had been starved in infancy, or had met with some accidents which had developed consumption; and had he then gone on to say that though he knew all this, and bitterly regretted that the protection of society obliged him to inflict additional pain on one who had suffered so much already, yet that there was no help for it, I could have understood the position, however mistaken I might have thought it. The judge was fully persuaded that the infliction of pain upon the weak and sickly was the only means of preventing weakness and sickliness from spreading, and that ten times the suffering now inflicted upon the accused was eventually warded off from others by the present apparent severity. I could therefore perfectly understand his inflicting whatever pain he might consider necessary in order to prevent so bad an example from spreading further and lowering the Erewhonian standard; but it seemed almost childish to tell the prisoner that he could have been in good health, if he had been more fortunate in his constitution, and been exposed to less hardships when he was a boy.

I write with great diffidence, but it seems to me that there is no unfairness in punishing people for their misfortunes, or rewarding them for their sheer good luck; it is the normal condition of human life that this should be done, and no right-minded person will complain of being subjected to the common treatment. There is no alternative open to us. It is idle to say that men are not responsible for their misfortunes. What is responsibility? Surely to be responsible means to be liable to have to give an answer should it be demanded, and all things which live are responsible for their lives and actions should society see fit to question them through the mouth of its authorized agent.

What is the offence of a lamb that we should rear it, and tend it, and lull it into security, for the express purpose of killing it? Its offence is the misfortune of being something which society wants to eat, and which cannot defend itself. This is ample. Who shall limit the right of society except society itself? And what consideration for the individual is tolerable unless society be the gainer thereby? Wherefore should a man be so richly rewarded for having been son to a millionaire, were it not clearly provable that the common welfare is thus better furthered? We cannot seriously detract from a man's merit in having been the son of a rich father without imperilling our own tenure of things which we do not wish to jeopardize; if this were otherwise we should not let him keep his money for a single hour; we would have it ourselves at once. For property *is* robbery, but then, we are all robbers or would-be robbers together, and have found it essential to organize our thieving, as we have found it necessary to organize our lust and our revenge. Property, marriage, the law; as the bed to the river, so rule and convention to the instinct; and woe to him who tampers with the banks while the flood is flowing.

But to return. Even in England a man on board a ship with yellow fever is held responsible for his mischance, no matter what his being kept in quarantine may cost him. He may catch the fever and die; we cannot help it; he must take his chance as other people do; but surely it would be desperate unkindness to add contumely to our self-protection, unless, indeed, we believe that contumely is one of our best means of self-protection. Again, take the case of maniacs. We say that they are irresponsible for their actions, but we take good care, or ought to take good care, that they shall answer to us for their insanity, and we imprison them in what we call an asylum (that modern sanctuary!) if we do not like their answers. This is a strange kind of irresponsibility. What we ought to say is that we can afford to be satisfied with a less satisfactory answer from a lunatic than from one who is not mad, because lunacy is less infectious than crime.

We kill a serpent if we go in danger by it, simply for being such and such a serpent in such and such a place; but we never say that the serpent has only itself to blame for not having been a harmless creature. Its crime is that of being the thing which it is: but this is a capital offence, and we are right in killing it out of the way, unless we think it more danger to do so than to let it escape; nevertheless we pity the creature, even though we kill it.

But in the case of him whose trial I have described above, it was impossible that any one in the court should not have known that it was but by an accident of birth and circumstances that he was not himself also in a consumption; and yet none thought that it disgraced them to hear the judge give vent to the most cruel truisms about him. The judge himself was a kind and thoughtful person. He was a man of magnificent and benign presence. He was evidently of an iron constitution, and his face wore an expression of the maturest wisdom and experience; yet for all this, old and learned as he was, he could not see things which one would have thought would have been apparent even to a child. He could not emancipate himself from, nay, it did not even occur to him to feel, the bondage of the ideas in which he had been born and bred.

So was it also with the jury and bystanders; and—most wonderful of all—so was it even with the prisoner. Throughout he seemed fully impressed with the notion that he was being dealt with justly: he saw nothing wanton in his being told by the judge that he was to be punished, not so much as a necessary protection to society (although this was not entirely lost sight of), as because he had not been better born and bred than he was. But this led me to hope that he suffered less than he would have done if he had seen the matter in the same light that I did. And, after all, justice is relative.

I may here mention that only a few years before my arrival in the country, the treatment of all convicted invalids had been much more barbarous than now, for no physical remedy was provided, and prisoners were put to the severest labour in all sorts of weather, so that most of them soon succumbed to the extreme hardships which they suffered; this was supposed to be beneficial in some ways, inasmuch as it put the country to less expense for the maintenance of its criminal class; but the growth of luxury had induced a relaxation of the old severity, and a sensitive age would no longer tolerate what appeared to be an excess of rigour, even towards the most guilty; moreover, it was found that juries were less willing to convict, and justice was often cheated because there was no alternative between virtually condemning a man to death and letting him go free; it was also held that the country paid in recommittals for its over-severity; for those who had been imprisoned even for trifling ailments were often permanently disabled by their imprisonment; and when a man had been once convicted, it was probable that he would seldom afterwards be off the hands of the country.

These evils had long been apparent and recognized; yet people were too indolent, and too indifferent to suffering not their own, to bestir themselves about putting an end to them, until at last a benevolent reformer devoted his whole life to effecting the necessary changes. He divided all illnesses into three classes

—those affecting the head, the trunk, and the lower limbs—and obtained an enactment that all diseases of the head, whether internal or external, should be treated with laudanum, those of the body with castor oil, and those of the lower limbs with an embrocation of strong sulphuric acid and water.

It may be said that the classification was not sufficiently careful, and that the remedies were ill chosen; but it is a hard thing to initiate any reform, and it was necessary to familiarize the public mind with the principle, by inserting the thin end of the wedge first: it is not, therefore, to be wondered at that among so practical a people there should still be some room for improvement. The mass of the nation are well pleased with existing arrangements, and believe that their treatment of criminals leaves little or nothing to be desired; but there is an energetic minority who hold what are considered to be extreme opinions, and who are not at all disposed to rest contented until the principle lately admitted has been carried further.

I was at some pains to discover the opinions of these men, and their reasons for entertaining them. They are held in great odium by the generality of the public, and are considered as subverters of all morality whatever. The malcontents, on the other hand, assert that illness is the inevitable result of certain antecedent causes, which, in the great majority of cases, were beyond the control of the individual, and that therefore a man is only guilty for being in a consumption in the same way as rotten fruit is guilty for having gone rotten. True, the fruit must be thrown on one side as unfit for man's use, and the man in a consumption must be put in prison for the protection of his fellow-citizens; but these radicals would not punish him further than by loss of liberty and a strict surveillance. So long as he was prevented from injuring society, they would allow him to make himself useful by supplying whatever of society's wants he could supply. If he succeeded in thus earning money, they would have him made as comfortable in prison as possible, and would in no way interfere with his liberty more than was necessary to prevent him from escaping, or from becoming more severely indisposed within the prison walls; but they would deduct from his earnings the expenses of his board, lodging, surveillance, and half those of his conviction. If he was too ill to do anything for his support in prison, they would allow him nothing but bread and water, and very little of that.

They say that society is foolish in refusing to allow itself to be benefited by a man merely because he has done it harm hitherto, and that objection to the labour of the diseased classes is only protection in another form. It is an attempt to raise the natural price of a commodity by saying that such and such persons, who are able and willing to produce it, shall not do so, whereby every one has to pay more for it.

Besides, so long as a man has not been actually killed he is our fellow-creature, though perhaps a very unpleasant one. It is in a great degree the doing of others that he is what he is, or in other words, the society which now condemns him is partly answerable concerning him. They say that there is no fear of any increase of disease under these circumstances; for the loss of liberty, the surveillance, the considerable and compulsory deduction from the prisoner's earnings, the very sparing use of stimulants (of which they would allow but little to any, and none to those who did not earn them), the enforced celibacy, and above all, the loss of reputation among friends, are in their opinion as ample safeguards to society against a general neglect of health as those now resorted to. A man, therefore (so they say), should carry his profession or trade into prison with him if possible; if not, he must earn his living by the nearest thing to it that he can; but if he be a gentleman born and bred to no profession, he must pick oakum, or write art criticisms for a newspaper.

These people say further, that the greater part of the illness which exists in their country is brought about by the insane manner in which it is treated.

They believe that illness is in many cases just as curable as the moral diseases which they see daily cured round them, but that a great reform is impossible till men learn to take a juster view of what physical obliquity proceeds from. Men will hide their illnesses as long as they are scouted on its becoming known that they are ill; it is the scouting, not the physic, which produces the concealment; and if a man felt that the news of his being in ill-health would be received by his neighbours as a deplorable fact, but one as much the result of necessary antecedent causes as though he had broken into a jeweller's shop and stolen a valuable diamond necklace—as a fact which might just as easily have happened to themselves, only that they had the luck to be better born or reared; and if they also felt that they would not be made more uncomfortable in the prison than the protection of society against infection and the proper treatment of their own disease actually demanded, men would give themselves up to the police as readily on perceiving that they had taken smallpox, as they go now to the straightener when they feel that they are on the point of forging a will, or running away with somebody else's wife.

But the main argument on which they rely is that of economy: for they know that they will sooner gain their end by appealing to men's pockets, in which they have generally something of their own, than to their heads, which contain for the most part little but borrowed or stolen property; and also, they believe it to be the readiest test and the one which has most to show for itself. If a course of conduct can be shown to cost a country less, and this by no dishonourable saving and with no indirectly increased expenditure in other ways, they hold that it requires a good deal to upset the arguments in favour of its being adopted, and whether rightly or wrongly I cannot pretend to say, they think that the more medicinal and humane treatment of the diseased of which they are the advocates would in the long run be much cheaper to the country: but I did not gather that these reformers were opposed to meeting some of the more violent forms of illness with the cat-of-nine-tails, or with death; for they saw no so effectual way of checking them; they would therefore both flog and hang, but they would do so pitifully.

I have perhaps dwelt too long upon opinions which can have no possible bearing upon our own, but I have not said the tenth part of what these would-be reformers urged upon me. I feel, however, that I have sufficiently trespassed upon the attention of the reader.

Chapter 13

The Views of the Erewhonians
Concerning Death

THE EREWHONIANS regard death with less abhorrence than disease. If it is an offence at all, it is one beyond the reach of the law, which is therefore silent on the subject; but they insist that the greater number of those who are commonly said to die, have never yet been born—not, at least, into that unseen world which is alone worthy of consideration. As regards this unseen world I understand them to say that some miscarry in respect to it before they have even reached the seen, and some after, while few are ever truly born into it at all—the greater part of all the men and women over the whole country miscarrying before they reach it. And they say that this does not matter so much as we think it does.

As for what we call death, they argue that too much has

been made of it. The mere knowledge that we shall one day die does not make us very unhappy; no one thinks that he or she will escape, so that none are disappointed. We do not care greatly even though we know that we have not long to live; the only thing that would seriously affect us would be the knowing —or rather thinking that we know—the precise moment at which the blow will fall. Happily no one can ever certainly know this, though many try to make themselves miserable by endeavouring to find it out. It seems as though there were some power somewhere which mercifully stays us from putting that sting into the tail of death, which we would put there if we could, and which ensures that though death must always be a bugbear, it shall never under any conceivable circumstances be more than a bugbear.

For even though a man is condemned to die in a week's time and is shut up in a prison from which it is certain that he cannot escape, he will always hope that a reprieve may come before the week is over. Besides, the prison may catch fire, and he may be suffocated not with a rope, but with common ordinary smoke; or he may be struck dead by lightning while exercising in the prison yards. When the morning is come on which the poor wretch is to be hanged, he may choke at his breakfast, or die from failure of the heart's action before the drop has fallen; and even though it has fallen, he cannot be quite certain that he is going to die, for he cannot know this till his death has actually taken place, and it will be too late then for him to discover that he was going to die at the appointed hour after all. The Erewhonians, therefore, hold that death, like life, is an affair of being more frightened than hurt.

They burn their dead, and the ashes are presently scattered over any piece of ground which the deceased may himself have chosen. No one is permitted to refuse this hospitality to the dead: people, therefore, generally choose some garden or orchard which they may have known and been fond of when they were young. The superstitious hold that those whose ashes are scattered over any land become its jealous guardians from that time forward; and the living like to think that they shall become identified with this or that locality where they have once been happy.

They do not put up monuments, nor write epitaphs, for their dead, though in former ages their practise was much as ours, but they have a custom which comes to much the same thing, for the instinct of preserving the name alive after the death of the body seems to be common to all mankind. They have statues of themselves made while they are still alive (those, that is,

87

who can afford it), and write inscriptions under them, which are often quite as untruthful as our own epitaphs—only in another way. For they do not hesitate to describe themselves as victims to ill temper, jealousy, covetousness, and the like, but almost always lay claim to personal beauty, whether they have it or not, and, often, to the possession of a large sum in the funded debt of the country. If a person is ugly he does not sit as a model for his own statue, although it bears his name. He gets the handsomest of his friends to sit for him, and one of the ways of paying a compliment to another is to ask him to sit for such a statue. Women generally sit for their own statues, from a natural disinclination to admit the superior beauty of a friend, but they expect to be idealized. I understood that the multitude of these statues was beginning to be felt as an encumbrance in almost every family, and that the custom would probably before long fall into desuetude.

Indeed, this has already come about to the satisfaction of every one, as regards the statues of public men—not more than three of which can be found in the whole capital. I expressed my surprise at this, and was told that some five hundred years before my visit, the city had been so overrun with these pests, that there was no getting about, and people were worried beyond endurance by having their attention called at every touch and turn to something, which, when they had attended to it, they found not to concern them. Most of these statues were mere attempts to do for some man or woman what an animal-stuffer does more successfully for a dog, or bird, or pike. They were generally foisted on the public by some coterie that was trying to exalt itself in exalting some one else, and not unfrequently they had no other inception than desire on the part of some member of the coterie to find a job for a young sculptor to whom his daughter was engaged. Statues so begotten could never be anything but deformities, and this is the way in which they are sure to be begotten, as soon as the art of making them at all has become widely practised.

I know not why, but all the noblest arts hold in perfection but for a very little moment. They soon reach a height from which they begin to decline, and when they have begun to decline it is a pity that they cannot be knocked on the head; for an art is like a living organism—better dead than dying. There is no way of making an aged art young again; it must be born anew and grow up from infancy as a new thing, working out its own salvation from effort to effort in all fear and trembling.

The Erewhonians five hundred years ago understood nothing of all this—I doubt whether they even do so now. They wanted to get the nearest thing they could to a stuffed man whose stuffing should not grow mouldy. They should have had some such an establishment as our Madame Tussaud's, where the figures wear real clothes, and are painted up to nature. Such an institution might have been made self-supporting, for people might have been made to pay before going in. As it was, they had let their poor cold grimy colourless heroes and heroines loaf about in squares and in corners of streets in all weathers, without any attempt at artistic sanitation—for there was no provision for burying their dead works of art out of their sight —no drainage, so to speak, whereby statues that had been sufficiently assimilated, so as to form part of the residuary impression of the country, might be carried away out of the system. Hence they put them up with a light heart on the cackling of their coteries, and they and their children had to live, often enough, with some wordy windbag whose cowardice had cost the country untold loss in blood and money.

At last the evil reached such a pitch that the people rose, and with indiscriminate fury destroyed good and bad alike. Most of what was destroyed was bad, but some few works were good, and the sculptors of to-day wring their hands over some of the fragments that have been preserved in museums up and down the country. For a couple of hundred years or so, not a statue was made from one end of the kingdom to the other, but the instinct for having stuffed men and women was so strong, that people at length again began to try to make them. Not knowing how to make them, and having no academies to mislead them, the earliest sculptors of this period thought things out for themselves, and again produced works that were full of interest, so that in three or four generations they reached a perfection hardly if at all inferior to that of several hundred years earlier.

On this the same evils recurred. Sculptors obtained high prices—the art became a trade—schools arose which professed to sell the holy spirit of art for money; pupils flocked from far and near to buy it, in the hopes of selling it later on, and were struck purblind as a punishment for the sin of those who sent them. Before long a second iconoclastic fury would infallibly have followed, but for the prescience of a statesman who succeeded in passing an Act to the effect that no statue of any public man or woman should be allowed to remain unbroken for more than fifty years, unless at the end of that time a jury of twenty-four men taken at random from the street pronounced in favour of its being allowed a second fifty years of life. Every fifty years this reconsideration was to be repeated, and unless there was a majority of eighteen in favour of the

89

retention of the statue, it was to be destroyed.

Perhaps a simpler plan would have been to forbid the erection of a statue to any public man or woman till he or she had been dead at least one hundred years, and even then to insist on reconsideration of the claims of the deceased and the merit of the statue every fifty years—but the working of the Act brought about results that on the whole were satisfactory. For in the first place, many public statues that would have been voted under the old system, were not ordered, when it was known that they would be almost certainly broken up after fifty years, and in the second, public sculptors knowing their work to be so ephemeral, scamped it to an extent that made it offensive even to the most uncultured eye. Hence before long subscribers took to paying the sculptor for the statue of their dead statesman, on condition that he did not make it. The tribute of respect was thus paid to the deceased, the public sculptors were not mulcted, and the rest of the public suffered no inconvenience.

I was told, however, that an abuse of this custom is growing up, inasmuch as the competition for the commission not to make a statue is so keen, that sculptors have been known to return a considerable part of the purchase money to the subscribers, by an arrangement made with them beforehand. Such transactions, however, are always clandestine. A small inscription is let into the pavement, where the public statue would have stood, which informs the reader that such a statue has been ordered for the person, whoever he or she may be, but that as yet the sculptor has not been able to complete it. There has been no Act to repress statues that are intended for private consumption, but as I have said, the custom is falling into desuetude.

Returning to Erewhonian customs in connection with death, there is one which I can hardly pass over. When any one dies, the friends of the family write no letters of condolence, neither do they attend the scattering, nor wear mourning, but they send little boxes filled with artificial tears, and with the name of the sender painted neatly upon the outside of the lid. The tears vary in number from two to fifteen or sixteen, according to degree of intimacy or relationship; and people sometimes find it a nice point of etiquette to know the exact number which they ought to send. Strange as it may appear, this attention is highly valued, and its omission by those from whom it might be expected is keenly felt. These tears were formerly stuck with adhesive plaster to the cheeks of the bereaved, and were worn in public for a few months after the death of a relative;

they were then banished to the hat or bonnet, and are now no longer worn.

The birth of a child is looked upon as a painful subject on which it is kinder not to touch: the illness of the mother is carefully concealed until the necessity for signing the birth formula (of which hereafter) renders further secrecy impossible, and for some months before the event the family live in retirement, seeing very little company. When the offence is over and done with, it is condoned by the common want of logic; for this merciful provision of nature, this buffer against collisions, this friction which upsets our calculations but without which existence would be intolerable, this crowning glory of human invention whereby we can be blind and see at one and the same moment, this blessed inconsistency, exists here as elsewhere; and though the strictest writers on morality have maintained that it is wicked for a woman to have children at all, inasmuch as it is wrong to be out of health that good may come, yet the necessity of the case has caused a general feeling in favour of passing over such events in silence, and of assuming their non-existence except in such flagrant cases as force themselves on the public notice. Against these the condemnation of society is inexorable, and if it is believed that the illness has been dangerous and protracted, it is almost impossible for a woman to recover her former position in society.

The above conventions struck me as arbitrary and cruel, but they put a stop to many fancied ailments; for the situation, so far from being considered interesting, is looked upon as savouring more or less distinctly of a very reprehensible condition of things, and the ladies take care to conceal it as long as they can even from their own husbands, in anticipation of a severe scolding as soon as the misdemeanour is discovered. Also the baby is kept out of sight, except on the day of signing the birth formula, until it can walk and talk. Should the child unhappily die, a coroner's inquest is inevitable, but in order to avoid disgracing a family which may have been hitherto respected, it is almost invariably found that the child was over seventy-five years old, and died from the decay of nature.

Chapter 14

Mahaina

I CONTINUED my sojourn with the Nosnibors. In a few days Mr. Nosnibor had recovered from his flogging, and was looking forward with glee to the fact that the next would be the last. I did not think that there seemed any occasion even for this; but he said it was better to be on the safe side, and he would make up the dozen. He now went to his business as usual; and I understood that he was never more prosperous, in spite of his heavy fine. He was unable to give me much of his time during the day; for he was one of those valuable men who are paid, not by the year, month, week, or day, but by the minute. His wife and daughters, however, made much of me, and introduced me to their friends, who came in shoals to call upon me.

One of these persons was a lady called Mahaina. Zulora (the elder of my host's daughters) ran up to her and embraced her as soon as she entered the room, at the same time inquiring tenderly after her "poor dipsomania." Mahaina answered that it was just as bad as ever; she was a perfect martyr to it, and her excellent health was the only thing which consoled her under her affliction.

Then the other ladies joined in with condolences and the never-failing suggestions which they had ready for every mental malady. They recommended their own straightener and disparaged Mahaina's. Mrs. Nosnibor had a favourite nostrum, but I could catch little of its nature. I heard the words "full confidence that the desire to drink will cease when the formula has been repeated . . . this confidence is *everything* . . . far from undervaluing a thorough determination never to touch spirits again . . . fail too often . . . formula a *certain cure* (with great emphasis) . . . prescribed form . . . full conviction." This conversation then became more audible, and was carried on at considerable length. I should perplex myself and the reader by endeavouring to follow the ingenious perversity of all they said; enough, that in the course of time the visit came to an end, and Mahaina took her leave receiving affectionate embraces from all the ladies. I had remained in the background after the first ceremony of introduction, for I did not like the looks of Mahaina, and the conversation displeased me. When she left the room I had some consolation in the remarks called forth by her departure.

At first they fell to praising her very demurely. She was all this, that, and the other, till I disliked her more and more at every word, and inquired how it was that the straighteners had not been able to cure her as they had cured Mr. Nosnibor.

There was a shade of significance on Mrs. Nosnibor's face as I said this, which seemed to imply that she did not consider Mahaina's case to be quite one for a straightener. It flashed across me that perhaps the poor woman did not drink at all. I knew that I ought not to have inquired, but I could not help it, and asked point-blank whether she did or not.

"We can none of us judge of the condition of other people," said Mrs. Nosnibor in a gravely charitable tone and with a look towards Zulora.

"Oh, mamma," answered Zulora, pretending to be half angry but rejoiced at being able to say out what she was already longing to insinuate; "I don't believe a word of it. It's all indigestion. I remember staying in the house with her for a whole month last summer, and I am sure she never once touched a drop of wine or spirits. The fact is, Mahaina is a very weakly girl, and she pretends to get tipsy in order to win a forbearance from her friends to which she is not entitled. She is not strong enough for her calisthenic exercises, and she knows she would be made to do them unless her inability was referred to moral causes."

Here the younger sister, who was ever sweet and kind, remarked that she thought Mahaina did tipple occasionally. "I also think," she added, "that she sometimes takes poppy juice."

"Well, then, perhaps she does drink sometimes," said Zulora; "but she would make us all think that she does it much oftener in order to hide her weakness."

And so they went on for half an hour and more, bandying about the question as to how far their late visitor's intemperance was real or no. Every now and then they would join in some charitable commonplace, and would pretend to be all of one mind that Mahaina was a person whose bodily health would be excellent if it were not for her unfortunate inability to refrain from excessive drinking; but as soon as this appeared to be fairly settled they began to be uncomfortable until they had undone their work and left some serious imputation upon her constitution. At last, seeing that the debate had assumed the character of a cyclone or circular storm, going round and round and round till one could never say where it began nor where it ended, I made some apology for an abrupt departure

93

and retired to my own room.

Here at least I was alone, but I was very unhappy. I had fallen upon a set of people who, in spite of their high civilization and many excellences, had been so warped by the mistaken views presented to them during childhood from generation to generation, that it was impossible to see how they could ever clear themselves. Was there nothing which I could say to make them feel that the constitution of a person's body was a thing over which he or she had had at any rate no initial control whatever, while the mind was a perfectly different thing, and capable of being created anew and directed according to the pleasure of its possessor? Could I never bring them to see that while habits of mind and character were entirely independent of initial mental force and early education, the body was so much a creature of parentage and circumstances, that no punishment for ill-health should be ever tolerated save as a protection from contagion, and that even where punishment was inevitable it should be attended with compassion? Surely, if the unfortunate Mahaina were to feel that she could avow her bodily weakness without fear of being despised for her infirmities, and if there were medical men to whom she could fairly state her case, she would not hesitate about doing so through the fear of taking nasty medicine. It was possible that her malady was incurable (for I had heard enough to convince me that her dipsomania was only a pretence and that she was temperate in all her habits); in that case she might perhaps be justly subject to annoyances or even to restraint; but who could say whether she was curable or not, until she was able to make a clean breast of her symptoms instead of concealing them? In their eagerness to stamp out disease, these people overshot their mark; for people had become so clever at dissembling—they painted their faces with such consummate skill—they repaired the decay of time and the effects of mischance with such profound dissimulation—that it was really impossible to say whether any one was well or ill till after an intimate acquaintance of months or years. Even then the shrewdest were constantly mistaken in their judgements, and marriages were often contracted with most deplorable results, owing to the art with which infirmity had been concealed.

It appeared to me that the first step towards the cure of diseases should be the announcement of the fact to a person's near relations and friends. If any one had a headache, he ought to be permitted within reasonable limits to say so at once, and to retire to his own bedroom and take a pill, without every one's looking grave and tears being shed and all the rest of it. As it

94

was, even upon hearing it whispered that somebody else was subject to headaches, a whole company must look as though they had never had a headache in their lives. It is true they were not very prevalent, for the people were the healthiest and most comely imaginable, owing to the severity with which ill-health was treated; still, even the best were liable to be out of sorts sometimes, and there were few families that had not a medicine-chest in a cupboard somewhere.

Chapter 15

The Musical Banks

ON MY return to the drawing-room, I found that the Mahaina current had expended itself. The ladies were just putting away their work and preparing to go out. I asked them where they were going. They answered with a certain air of reserve that they were going to the bank to get some money.

Now I had already collected that the mercantile affairs of the Erewhonians were conducted on a totally different system from our own; I had, however, gathered little hitherto, except that they had two distinct commercial systems, of which the one appealed more strongly to the imagination than anything to which we are accustomed in Europe, inasmuch as the banks that were conducted upon this system were decorated in the most profuse fashion, and all mercantile transactions were accompanied with music, so that they were called Musical Banks, though the music was hideous to a European ear.

As for the system itself I never understood it, neither can I do so now: they have a code in connection with it, which I have not the slightest doubt that they understand, but no foreigner can hope to do so. One rule runs into, and against, another as in a most complicated grammar, or as in Chinese pronunciation, wherein I am told that the slightest change in accentuation or tone of voice alters the meaning of a whole sentence. Whatever is incoherent in my description must be referred to the fact of my never having attained to a full comprehension of the subject.

So far, however, as I could collect anything certain, I gathered that they have two distinct currencies, each under the control of its own banks and mercantile codes. One of these (the one with the Musical Banks) was supposed to be *the* system,

95

and to give out the currency in which all monetary transactions should be carried on; and as far as I could see, all who wished to be considered respectable, kept a larger or smaller balance at these banks. On the other hand, if there is one thing of which I am more sure than another, it is that the amount so kept had no direct commercial value in the outside world; I am sure that the managers and cashiers of the Musical Banks were not paid in their own currency. Mr. Nosnibor used to go to these banks, or rather to the great mother bank of the city, sometimes, but not very often. He was a pillar of one of the other kind of banks, though he appeared to hold some minor office also in the musical ones. The ladies generally went alone; as indeed was the case in most families, except on state occasions.

I had long wanted to know more of this strange system, and had the greatest desire to accompany my hostess and her daughters. I had seen them go out almost every morning since my arrival and had noticed that they carried their purses in their hands, not exactly ostentatiously, yet just so as that those who met them should see whither they were going. I had never, however, yet been asked to go with them myself.

It is not easy to convey a person's manner by words, and I can hardly give any idea of the peculiar feeling that came upon me when I saw the ladies on the point of starting for the bank. There was a something of regret, a something as though they would wish to take me with them, but did not like to ask me, and yet as though I were hardly to ask to be taken. I was determined, however, to bring matters to an issue with my hostess about my going with them, and after a little parleying, and many inquires as to whether I was perfectly sure that I myself wished to go, it was decided that I might do so.

We passed through several streets of more or less considerable houses, and at last turning round a corner we came upon a large piazza, at the end of which was a magnificent building, of a strange but noble architecture and of great antiquity. It did not open directly on to the piazza, there being a screen, through which was an archway, between the piazza and the actual precincts of the bank. On passing under the archway we entered upon a green sward, round which there ran an arcade or cloister, while in front of us uprose the majestic towers of the bank and its venerable front, which was divided into three deep recesses and adorned with all sorts of marbles and many sculptures. On either side there were beautiful old trees wherein the birds were busy by the hundred, and a number of quaint but substantial houses of singularly comfortable appearance; they were situated in the midst of orchards and gardens, and gave me an impression of great peace and plenty.

Indeed, it had been no error to say that this building was one that appealed to the imagination; it did more—it carried both imagination and judgement by storm. It was an epic in stone and marble, and so powerful was the effect it produced on me, that as I beheld it I was charmed and melted. I felt more conscious of the existence of a remote past. One knows of this always, but the knowledge is never so living as in the actual presence of some witness of the life of bygone ages. I felt how short a space of human life was the period of our own existence. I was more impressed with my own littleness, and much more inclinable to believe that the people whose sense of the fitness of things was equal to the upraising of so serene a handiwork, were hardly likely to be wrong in the conclusions they might come to upon any subject. My feeling certainly was that the currency of this bank must be the right one.

We crossed the sward and entered the building. If the outside had been impressive the inside was even more so. It was very lofty and divided into several parts by walls which rested upon massive pillars; the windows were filled with stained glass descriptive of the principal commercial incidents of the bank for many ages. In a remote part of the building there were men and boys singing; this was the only disturbing feature, for as the gamut was still unknown, there was no music in the country which could be agreeable to a European ear. The singers seemed to have derived their inspirations from the songs of birds and the wailing of the wind, which last they tried to imitate in melancholy cadences that at times degenerated into a howl. To my thinking the noise was hideous, but it produced a great effect upon my companions, who professed themselves much moved. As soon as the singing was over, the ladies requested me to stay where I was while they went inside the place from which it had seemed to come.

During their absence certain reflections forced themselves upon me.

In the first place, it struck me as strange that the building should be so nearly empty; I was almost alone, and the few besides myself had been led by curiosity, and had no intention of doing business with the bank. But there might be more inside. I stole up to the curtain and ventured to draw the extreme edge of it on one side. No, there was hardly any one there. I saw a large number of cashiers, all at their desks ready to pay cheques, and one or two who seemed to be the managing partners. I also saw my hostess and her daughters and two or three other ladies; also three or four old women and the boys from one of the neighbouring Colleges of Unreason; but there was no one else. This did not look as though the bank was doing a very large business; and yet I had always been told that every one in the city dealt with this establishment.

I cannot describe all that took place in these inner precincts, for a sinister-looking person in a black gown came and made unpleasant gestures at me for peeking. I happened to have in my pocket one of the Musical Bank pieces, which had been given me by Mrs. Nosnibor, so I tried to tip him with it; but having seen what it was, he became so angry that I had to give him a piece of the other kind of money to pacify him. When I had done this he became civil directly. As soon as he was gone I ventured to take a second look, and saw Zulora in the very act of giving a piece of paper which looked like a cheque to one of the cashiers. He did not examine it, but putting his hand into an antique coffer hard by, he pulled out a quantity of metal pieces apparently at random, and handed them over without counting them; neither did Zulora count them, but put them into her purse and went back to her seat after dropping a few pieces of the other coinage into an alms box that stood by the cashier's side. Mrs. Nosnibor and Arowhena then did likewise, but a little later they gave all (so far as I could see) that they had received from the cashier back to a verger, who I have no doubt put it back into the coffer from which it had been taken. They then began making towards the curtain; whereon I let it drop and retreated to a reasonable distance.

They soon joined me. For some few minutes we all kept silence, but at last I ventured to remark that the bank was not so busy to-day as it probably often was. On this Mrs. Nosnibor said that it was indeed melancholy to see what little heed people paid to the most precious of all institutions. I could say nothing in reply, but I have ever been of opinion that the greater part of mankind do approximately know where they get that which does them good.

Mrs. Nosnibor went on to say that I must not think there was any want of confidence in the bank because I had seen so few people there; the heart of the country was thoroughly devoted to these establishments, and any sign of their being in danger would bring a support from the most unexpected quarters. It was only because people knew them to be so very safe, that in some cases (as she lamented to say in Mr. Nosnibor's) they felt that their support was unnecessary. Moreover, these institutions never departed from the safest and most approved banking principles. Thus they never allowed interest on deposit, a thing now frequently done by certain bubble companies, which by doing an illegitimate trade had drawn many customers away; and even the shareholders were fewer than formerly, owing to the innovations of these unscrupulous persons, for the Musical Banks paid little or no dividend, but divided their profits by way of bonus on the original shares once in every thirty thousand years; and as it was now only two thousand years since there had been one of these distributions, people felt that they could not hope for another in their own time and preferred investments whereby they got some more tangible return; all which, she said, was very melancholy to think of.

Having made these last admissions, she returned to her original statement, namely, that every one in the country really supported these banks. As to the fewness of the people, and the absence of the able-bodied, she pointed out to me with some justice that this was exactly what we ought to expect. The men who were most conversant about the stability of human institutions, such as the lawyers, men of science, doctors, statesmen, painters, and the like, were just those who were most likely to be misled by their own fancied accomplishments, and to be made unduly suspicious by their licentious desire for greater present return, which was at the root of nine-tenths of the opposition; by their vanity, which would prompt them to affect superiority to the prejudices of the vulgar; and by the stings of their own conscience, which was constantly upbraiding them in the most cruel manner on account of their bodies, which were generally diseased.

Let a person's intellect (she continued) be never so sound, unless his body is in absolute health, he can form no judgement worth having on matters of this kind. The body is everything: it need not perhaps be such a strong body (she said this because she saw that I was thinking of the old and infirm-looking folks whom I had seen in the bank), but it must be in perfect health; in this case, the less active strength it had the more free would be the working of the intellect, and therefore the sounder the conclusion. The people, then, whom I had seen at the bank were in reality the very ones whose opinions were most worth having; they declared its advantages to be incalculable, and even professed to consider the immediate return to be far larger than they were entitled to; and so she ran on, nor did she leave off till we had got back to the house.

She might say what she pleased, but her manner carried

no conviction, and later on I saw signs of general indifference to these banks that were not to be mistaken. Their supporters often denied it, but the denial was generally so couched as to add another proof of its existence. In commercial panics, and in times of general distress, the people as a mass did not so much as even think of turning to these banks. A few might do so, some from habit and early training, some from the instinct that prompts us to catch at any straw when we think ourselves drowning, but few from a genuine belief that the Musical Banks could save them from financial ruin, if they were unable to meet their engagements in the other kind of currency.

In conversation with one of the Musical Bank managers I ventured to hint this as plainly as politeness would allow. He said that it had been more or less true till lately; but that now they had put fresh stained glass windows into all the banks in the country, and repaired the buildings, and enlarged the organs; the presidents, moreover, had taken to riding in omnibuses and talking nicely to people in the streets, and to remembering the ages of their children, and giving them things when they were naughty, so that all would henceforth go smoothly.

"But haven't you done anything to the money itself?" said I, timidly.

"It is not necessary," he rejoined; "not in the least necessary, I assure you."

And yet any one could see that the money given out at these banks was not that with which people bought their bread, meat, and clothing. It was like it at a first glance, and was stamped with designs that were often of great beauty; it was not, again, a spurious coinage, made with the intention that it should be mistaken for the money in actual use; it was more like a toy money, or the counters used for certain games at cards; for, notwithstanding the beauty of the designs, the material on which they were stamped was as nearly valueless as possible. Some were covered with tin foil, but the greater part were frankly of a cheap base metal the exact nature of which I was not able to determine. Indeed they were made of a great variety of metals, or, perhaps more accurately, alloys, some of which were hard, while others would bend easily and assume almost any form which their possessor might desire at the moment.

Of course, every one knew that their commercial value was *nil*, but all those who wished to be considered respectable thought it incumbent upon them to retain a few coins in their possession, and to let them be seen from time to time in their hands and purses. Not only this, but they would stick to it that the current coin of the realm was dross in comparison with the Musical Bank coinage. Perhaps, however, the strangest thing of all was that these very people would at times make fun in small ways of the whole system; indeed, there was hardly any insinuation against it which they would not tolerate and even applaud in their daily newspapers if written anonymously, while if the same thing were said without ambiguity to their faces—nominative case, verb, and accusative being all in their right places, and doubt impossible—they would consider themselves very seriously and justly outraged, and accuse the speaker of being unwell.

I never could understand (neither can I quite do so now, though I begin to see better what they mean) why a single currency should not suffice them; it would seem to me as though all their dealings would have been thus greatly simplified; but I was met with a look of horror if ever I dared to hint at it. Even those who to my certain knowledge kept only just enough money at the Musical Banks to swear by, would call the other banks (where their securities really lay) cold, deadening, paralysing, and the like.

I noticed another thing, moreover, which struck me greatly. I was taken to the opening of one of these banks in a neighbouring town, and saw a large assemblage of cashiers and managers. I sat opposite them and scanned their faces attentively. They did not please me; they lacked, with few exceptions, the true Erewhonian frankness; and an equal number from any other class would have looked happier and better men. When I met them in the streets they did not seem like other people, but had, as a general rule, a cramped expression upon their faces which pained and depressed me.

Those who came from the country were better; they seemed to have lived less as a separate class, and to be freer and healthier; but in spite of my seeing not a few whose looks were benign and noble, I could not help asking myself concerning the greater number of those whom I met, whether Erewhon would be a better country if their expression were to be transferred to the people in general. I answered myself emphatically, no. The expression on the faces of the high Ydgrunites was that which one would wish to diffuse, and not that of the cashiers.

A man's expression is his sacrament; it is the outward and visible sign of his inward and spiritual grace, or want of grace; and as I looked at the majority of these men, I could not help feeling that there must be a something in their lives which had stunted their natural development, and that they would have been more healthily minded in any other profession. I was always sorry for them, for in nine cases out of ten they were well-meaning persons; they were in the main very poorly paid; their constitutions were as a rule above suspicion; and there were recorded numberless instances of their self-sacrifice and generosity; but they had had the misfortune to have been betrayed into a false position at an age for the most part when their judgement was not matured, and after having been kept in studied ignorance of the real difficulties of the system. But this did not make their position the less a false one, and its bad effects upon themselves were unmistakable.

Few people would speak quite openly and freely before them, which struck me as a very bad sign. When they were in the room every one would talk as though all currency save that of the Musical Banks should be abolished; and yet they knew perfectly well that even the cashiers themselves hardly used the Musical Bank money more than other people. It was expected of them that they should appear to do so, but this was all. The less thoughtful of them did not seem particularly unhappy, but many were plainly sick at heart, though perhaps they hardly knew it, and would not have owned to being so. Some few were opponents of the whole system; but these were liable to be dismissed from their employment at any moment, and this rendered them very careful, for a man who had once been cashier at a Musical Bank was out of the field for other employment, and was generally unfitted for it by reason of that course of treatment which was commonly called his education. In fact it was a career from which retreat was virtually impossible, and into which young men were generally induced to enter before they could be reasonably expected, considering their training, to have formed any opinions of their own. Not unfrequently, indeed, they were induced, by what we in England should call undue influence, concealment, and fraud. Few indeed were those who had the courage to insist on seeing both sides of the question before they committed themselves to what was practically a leap in the dark. One would have thought that caution in this respect was an elementary principle —one of the first things that an honourable man would teach his boy to understand; but in practise it was not so.

I even saw cases in which parents bought the right of presenting to the office of cashier at one of these banks, with the fixed determination that some one of their sons (perhaps a mere child) should fill it. There was the lad himself—growing up with every promise of becoming a good and honourable man—but utterly without warning concerning the iron shoe which his natural protector was providing for him. Who could say that the whole thing would not end in a life-long lie, and vain chafing to escape? I confess that there were few things in Erewhon which shocked me more than this.

Yet we do something not so very different from this even in England, and as regards the dual commercial system, all countries have, and have had, a law of the land, and also another law, which, though professedly more sacred, has far less effect on their daily life and actions. It seems as though the need for some law over and above, and sometimes even conflicting with, the law of the land, must spring from something that lies deep down in man's nature; indeed, it is hard to think that man could ever have become man at all, but for the gradual evolution of a perception that though this world looms so large when we are in it, it may seem a little thing when we have got away from it.

When man had grown to the perception that in the everlasting Is-and-Is-Not of nature, the world and all that it contains, including man, is at the same time both seen and unseen, he felt the need of two rules of life, one for the seen, and the other for the unseen side of things. For the laws affecting the seen world he claimed the sanction of seen powers; for the unseen (of which he knows nothing save that it exists and is powerful) he appealed to the unseen power (of which, again, he knows nothing save that it exists and is powerful) to which he gives the name of God.

Some Erewhonian opinions concerning the intelligence of the unborn embryo, that I regret my space will not permit me to lay before the reader, have led me to conclude that the Erewhonian Musical Banks, and perhaps the religious systems of all countries, are now more or less of an attempt to uphold the unfathomable and unconscious instinctive wisdom of millions of past generations, against the comparatively shallow, consciously reasoning, and ephemeral conclusions drawn from that of the last thirty or forty.

The saving feature of the Erewhonian Musical Bank system (as distinct from the quasi-idolatrous views which co-exist with it, and on which I will touch later) was that while it bore witness to the existence of a kingdom that is not of this world, it made no attempt to pierce the veil that hides it from human eyes. It is here that almost all religions go wrong. Their priests try to make us believe that they know more about the unseen world than those whose eyes are still blinded by the seen, can ever know—forgetting that while to deny the existence of an unseen kingdom is bad, to pretend that we know more about it than its bare existence is no better.

This chapter is already longer than I intended, but I should like to say that in spite of the saving feature of which I have just spoken, I cannot help thinking that the Erewhonians are on the eve of some great change in their religious opinions, or at any rate in that part of them which finds expression through their Musical Banks. So far as I could see, fully ninety per cent. of the population of the metropolis looked upon these banks with something not far removed from contempt. If this is so, any such startling event as is sure to arise sooner or later, may serve as a nucleus to a new order of things that will be more in harmony with both the heads and hearts of the people.

Chapter 16

Arowhena

THE READER will perhaps have learned by this time a thing which I had myself suspected before I had been twenty-four hours in Mr. Nosnibor's house—I mean, that though the Nosnibors showed me every attention, I could not cordially like them, with the exception of Arowhena who was quite different from the rest. They were not fair samples of Erewhonians. I saw many families with whom they were on visiting terms, whose manners charmed me more than I know how to say, but I never could get over my original prejudice against Mr. Nosnibor for having embezzled the money. Mrs. Nosnibor, too, was a very worldly woman, yet to hear her talk one would have thought that she was singularly the reverse; neither could I endure Zulora; Arowhena, however, was perfection.

She it was who ran all the little errands for her mother and Mr. Nosnibor and Zulora, and gave those thousand proofs of sweetness and unselfishness which some one member of a family is generally required to give. All day long it was Arowhena this, and Arowhena that; but she never seemed to know that she was being put upon, and was always bright and willing from morning till evening. Zulora certainly was very handsome, but Arowhena was infinitely the more graceful of the two and was the very *ne plus ultra* of youth and beauty. I will not attempt to describe her, for anything that I could say would fall so far short of the reality as only to mislead the reader. Let him think of the very loveliest that he can imagine, and he will still be below the truth. Having said this much, I need hardly say that I had fallen in love with her.

She must have seen what I felt for her, but I tried my hardest not to let it appear even by the slightest sign. I had many reasons for this. I had no idea what Mr. and Mrs. Nosnibor would say to it; and I knew that Arowhena would not look at me (at any rate not yet) if her father and mother disapproved, which they probably would, considering that I had nothing except the pension of about a pound a day of our money which the King had granted me. I did not yet know of a more serious obstacle.

In the meantime, I may say that I had been presented at court, and was told that my reception had been considered as singularly gracious; indeed, I had several interviews both with the King and Queen, at which from time to time the Queen got everything from me that I had in the world, clothes and all, except the two buttons I had given to Yram, the loss of which seemed to annoy her a good deal. I was presented with a court suit, and her Majesty had my only clothes put upon a wooden dummy, on which they probably remain, unless they have been removed in consequence of my subsequent downfall. His Majesty's manners were those of a cultivated English gentleman. He was much pleased at hearing that our government was monarchical, and that the mass of the people were resolute that it should not be changed; indeed, I was so much encouraged by the evident pleasure with which he heard me, that I ventured to quote to him those beautiful lines of Shakespeare's—

> "There's a divinity doth hedge a king,
> Rough hew him how we may";

but I was sorry I had done so afterwards, for I do not think his Majesty admired the lines as much as I could have wished.

There is no occasion for me to dwell further upon my experience of the court, but I ought perhaps to allude to one of my conversations with the King, inasmuch as it was pregnant with the most important consequences.

He had been asking me about my watch, and inquiring whether such dangerous inventions were tolerated in the country from which I came. I owned with some confusion that watches were not uncommon; but observing the gravity which came over his Majesty's face I presumed to say that they were fast dying out, and that we had few if any other mechanical contrivances of which he was likely to disapprove.

Upon his asking me to name some of our most advanced machines, I did not dare to tell him of our steam-engines and railroads and electric telegraphs, and was puzzling my brains to think what I could say when, of all things in the world, balloons suggested themselves, and I gave him an account of a very remarkable ascent which was made some years ago. The King was too polite to contradict, but I felt sure that he did not believe me, and from that day forward though he always showed me the attention which was due to my genius (for in this light was my complexion regarded), he never questioned me about the manners and customs of my country.

To return, however, to Arowhena. I soon gathered that neither Mr. nor Mrs. Nosnibor would have any objection to my marrying into the family; a physical excellence is considered in Erewhon as a set-off against almost any other disqualification, and my light hair was sufficient to make me an eligible match. But along with this welcome fact I gathered another which filled me with dismay: I was expected to marry Zulora, for whom I had already conceived a great aversion.

At first I hardly noticed the little hints and the artifices which were resorted to in order to bring us together, but after a time they became too plain. Zulora, whether she was in love with me or not, was bent on marrying me, and I gathered in talking with a young gentleman of my acquaintance who frequently visited the house and whom I greatly disliked, that it was considered a sacred and inviolable rule that whoever married into a family must marry the eldest daughter at that time unmarried. The young gentleman urged this upon me so frequently that I at last saw he was in love with Arowhena himself, and wanted me to get Zulora out of the way; but others told me the same story as to the custom of the country, and I saw there was a serious difficulty. My only comfort was that Arowhena snubbed my rival and would not look at him. Neither would she look at me; nevertheless there was a difference in the manner of her disregard; this was all I could get from her.

Not that she avoided me; on the contrary I had many a tête-à-tête with her, for her mother and sister were anxious for me to deposit some part of my pension in the Musical Banks, this being in accordance with the dictates of their goddess Ydgrun, of whom both Mrs. Nosnibor and Zulora were great devotees. I was not sure whether I had kept my secret from being perceived by Arowhena herself, but none of the others suspected me, so she was set upon me to get me to open an account, at any rate *pro forma*, with the Musical Banks; and I need hardly say that she succeeded. But I did not yield at once; I enjoyed the process of being argued with too keenly to lose it by a prompt concession; besides, a little hesitation rendered the concession itself more valuable. It was in the course of conversations on this subject that I learned the more defined religious opinions of the Erewhonians, that co-exist with the Musical Bank system, but are not recognized by those curious institutions. I will describe them as briefly as possible in the following chapters before I return to the personal adventures of Arowhena and myself.

They were idolators, though of a comparatively enlightened kind; but here, as in other things, there was a discrepancy between their professed and actual belief, for they had a genuine and potent faith which existed without recognition alongside of their idol worship.

The gods whom they worship openly are personifications of human qualities, as justice, strength, hope, fear, love, etc., etc. The people think that prototypes of these have a real objective existence in a region far beyond the clouds, holding, as did the ancients, that they are like men and women both in body and passion, except that they are even comelier and more powerful, and also that they can render themselves invisible to human eyesight. They are capable of being propitiated by mankind and of coming to the assistance of those who ask their aid. Their interest in human affairs is keen, and on the whole beneficent; but they become very angry if neglected, and punish rather the first they come upon, than the actual person who has offended them; their fury being blind when it is raised, though never raised without reason. They will not punish with any less severity when people sin against them from ignorance, and without the chance of having had knowledge; they will take no excuses of this kind, but are even as the English law, which assumes itself to be known to every one.

Thus they have a law that two pieces of matter may not occupy the same space at the same moment, which law is presided over and administered by the gods of time and space jointly, so that if a flying stone and a man's head attempt to outrage these gods, by "arrogating a right which they do not possess" (for so it is written in one of their books), and to occupy the same space simultaneously, a severe punishment, sometimes even death itself, is sure to follow, without any regard to whether the stone knew that the man's head was there, or the head the stone; this at least is their view of the common accidents of life. Moreover, they hold their deities to be quite regardless of motives. With them it is the thing done which is everything, and the motive goes for nothing.

Thus they hold it strictly forbidden for a man to go without common air in his lungs for more than a very few minutes; and if by any chance he gets into the water, the air-god is very angry, and will not suffer it; no matter whether the man got into the water by accident or on purpose, whether through the attempt to save a child or through presumptuous contempt of the air-god, the air-god will kill him, unless he keeps his head high enough out of the water, and thus gives the air-god his due.

This with regard to the deities who manage physical affairs. Over and above these they personify hope, fear, love, and so forth, giving them temples and priests, and carving likenesses of them in stone, which they verily believe to be faithful representations of living beings who are only not human in being more than human. If any one denies the objective existence of these divinities, and says that there is really no such being as a beautiful woman called Justice, with her eyes blinded and a pair of scales, positively living and moving in a remote and ethereal region, but that justice is only the personified expression of certain modes of human thought and action—they say that he denies the existence of justice in denying her personality, and that he is a wanton disturber of men's religious convictions. They detest nothing so much as any attempt to lead them to higher spiritual conceptions of the deities whom they profess to worship. Arowhena and I had a pitched battle on this point, and should have had many more but for my prudence in allowing her to get the better of me.

I am sure that in her heart she was suspicious of her own position for she returned more than once to the subject. "Can you not see," I had exclaimed, "that the fact of justice being admirable will not be affected by the absence of a belief in her being also a living agent? Can you really think that men will be one whit less hopeful because they no longer believe that hope is an actual person?" She shook her head, and said that without men's belief in the personality all incentive to the reverence of the thing itself, as justice or hope, would cease; men from that hour would never be either just or hopeful again.

I could not move her, nor, indeed, did I seriously wish to do so. She deferred to me in most things, but she never shrank from maintaining her opinions if they were put in question; nor does she to this day abate one jot of her belief in the religion of her childhood, though in compliance with my repeated entreaties she has allowed herself to be baptized into the English Church. She has, however, made a gloss upon her original faith to the effect that her baby and I are the only human beings exempt from the vengeance of the deities for not believing in their personality. She is quite clear that we are exempted. She should never have so strong a conviction of it otherwise. How it has come about she does not know, neither does she wish to know; there are things which it is better not to know and this is one of them; but when I tell her that I believe in her deities as much as she does—and that it is a difference about words, not things, she becomes silent with a slight emphasis.

I own that she very nearly conquered me once; for she asked me what I should think if she were to tell me that my God, whose nature and attributes I had been explaining to her, was but the expression for man's highest conception of goodness, wisdom, and power; that in order to generate a more vivid conception of so great and glorious a thought, man had personified it and called it by a name; that it was an unworthy conception of the Deity to hold Him personal, inasmuch as escape from human contingencies became thus impossible; that the real thing men should worship was the Divine, whereinsoever they could find it; that "God" was but man's way of expressing his sense of the Divine; that as justice, hope, wisdom, etc., were all parts of goodness, so God was the expression which embraced all goodness and all good power; that people would no more cease to love God on ceasing to believe in His objective personality, than they had ceased to love justice on discovering that she was not really personal; nay, that they would never truly love Him till they saw Him thus.

She said all this in her artless way, and with none of the coherence with which I have here written it; her face kindled, and she felt sure that she had convinced me that I was wrong, and that justice was a living person. Indeed, I did wince a little; but I recovered myself immediately, and pointed out to her that we had books whose genuineness was beyond all possibility of doubt, as they were certainly none of them less than 1,800 years old; that in these there were the most authentic accounts of men who had been spoken to by the Deity Himself, and of one prophet who had been allowed to see the back parts of God through the hand that was laid over his face.

This was conclusive; and I spoke with such solemnity that she was a little frightened, and only answered that they too had their books, in which their ancestors had seen the gods; on which I saw that further argument was not at all likely to convince her; and fearing that she might tell her mother what I had been saying, and that I might lose the hold upon her affections which I was beginning to feel pretty sure that I was obtaining, I began to let her have her own way, and to convince me; neither till after we were safely married did I show the cloven hoof again.

Nevertheless, her remarks have haunted me, and I have since met with many very godly people who have had a great knowledge of divinity, but no sense of the Divine: and again, I have seen a radiance upon the face of those who were worshipping the Divine either in art or nature—in picture or statue—in field of cloud or sea—in man, woman, or child—which I have never seen kindled by any talking about the nature and attributes of God. Mention but the word divinity, and our sense of the Divine is clouded.

Chapter 17

Ydgrun and the Ydgrunites

IN SPITE of all the to-do they make about their idols, and the temples they build, and the priests and priestesses whom they support, I could never think that their professed religion was more than skin-deep; but they had another which they carried with them into all their actions; and although no one from the outside of things would suspect it to have any existence at all, it was in reality their great guide, the mariner's compass of their lives; so that there were very few things which they ever either did, or refrained from doing, without reference to its precepts.

Now I suspected that their professed faith had no great hold upon them—firstly, because I often heard the priests complain of the prevailing indifference, and they would hardly have done so without reason; secondly, because of the show which was made, for there was none of this about the worship of the goddess Ydgrun, in whom they really did believe; thirdly, because though the priests were constantly abusing Ydgrun as being the great enemy of the gods, it was well known that she had no more devoted worshippers in the whole country than these very persons, who were often priests of Ydgrun rather than of their own deities. Neither am I by any means sure that these were not the best of the priests.

Ydgrun certainly occupied a very anomalous position; she was held to be both omnipresent and omnipotent, but she was not an elevated conception, and was sometimes both cruel

110

and absurd. Even her most devoted worshippers were a little ashamed of her, and served her more with heart and in deed than with their tongues. Theirs was no lip service; on the contrary, even when worshipping her most devoutly, they would often deny her. Take her all in all, however, she was a beneficent and useful deity, who did not care how much she was denied so long as she was obeyed and feared, and who kept hundreds of thousands in those paths which make life tolerably happy, who would never have been kept there otherwise, and over whom a higher and more spiritual ideal would have had no power.

I greatly doubt whether the Erewhonians are yet prepared for any better religion, and though (considering my gradually strengthened conviction that they were the representatives of the lost tribes of Israel) I would have set about converting them at all hazards had I seen the remotest prospect of success, I could hardly contemplate the displacement of Ydgrun as the great central object of their regard without admitting that it would be attended with frightful consequences; in fact were I a mere philosopher, I should say that the gradual raising of the popular conception of Ydgrun would be the greatest spiritual boon which could be conferred upon them, and that nothing could effect this except example. I generally found that those who complained most loudly that Ydgrun was not high enough for them had hardly as yet come up to the Ydgrun standard, and I often met with a class of men whom I called to myself "high Ydgrunites" (the rest being Ydgrunites, and low Ydgrunites), who, in the matter of human conduct and the affairs of life, appeared to me to have got about as far as it is in the right nature of man to go.

They were gentlemen in the full sense of the word; and what has one not said in saying this? They seldom spoke of Ydgrun, or even alluded to her, but would never run counter to her dictates without ample reason for doing so: in such cases they would override her with due self-reliance, and the goddess seldom punished them; for they are brave, and Ydgrun is not. They had most of them a smattering of the hypothetical language, and some few more than this, but only a few. I do not think that this language has had much hand in making them what they are; but rather that the fact of their being generally possessed of its rudiments was one great reason for the reverence paid to the hypothetical language itself.

Being inured from youth to exercises and athletics of all sorts, and living fearlessly under the eye of their peers, among whom there exists a high standard of courage, generosity, honour, and every good and manly quality—what wonder that they should have become, so to speak, a law unto themselves; and, while taking an elevated view of the goddess Ydgrun, they should have gradually lost all faith in the recognized deities of the country? These they do not openly disregard, for conformity until absolutely intolerable is a law of Ydgrun, yet they have no real belief in the objective existence of beings which so readily explain themselves as abstractions, and whose personality demands a quasi-materialism which it baffles the imagination to realise. They keep their opinions, however, greatly to themselves, inasmuch as most of their countrymen feel strongly about the gods, and they hold it wrong to give pain, unless for some greater good than seems likely to arise from their plain speaking.

On the other hand, surely those whose own minds are clear about any given matter (even though it be only that there is little certainty) should go so far towards imparting that clearness to others, as to say openly what they think and why they think it, whenever they can properly do so; for they may be sure that they owe their own clearness almost entirely to the fact that others have done this by them: after all, they may be mistaken, and if so, it is for their own and the general wellbeing that they should let their error be seen as distinctly as possible, so that it may be more easily refuted. I own, therefore, that on this one point I disapproved of the practise even of the highest Ydgrunites, and objected to it all the more because I knew that I should find my own future task more easy if the high Ydgrunites had already undermined the belief which is supposed to prevail at present.

In other respects they were more like the best class of Englishmen than any whom I have seen in other countries. I should have liked to have persuaded half a dozen of them to come over to England and go upon the stage, for they had most of them a keen sense of humour and a taste for acting: they would be of great use to us. The example of a real gentleman is, if I may say so without profanity, the best of all gospels; such a man upon the stage becomes a potent humanizing influence, an Ideal which all may look upon for a shilling.

I always liked and admired these men, and although I could not help deeply regretting their certain ultimate perdition (for they had no sense of a hereafter, and their only religion was that of self-respect and consideration for other people), I never dared to take so great a liberty with them as to attempt to put them in possession of my own religious convictions, in spite of my knowing that they were the only ones which could

112

make them really good and happy, either here or hereafter. I did try sometimes, being impelled to do so by a strong sense of duty, and by my deep regret that so much that was admirable should be doomed to ages if not eternity of torture; but the words stuck in my throat as soon as I began.

Whether a professional missionary might have a better chance I know not; such persons must doubtless know more about the science of conversion: for myself, I could only be thankful that I was in the right path, and was obliged to let others take their chance as yet. If the plan fails by which I propose to convert them myself, I would gladly contribute my mite towards the sending two or three trained missionaries, who have been known as successful converters of Jews and Mohammedans; but such have seldom much to glory in the flesh, and when I think of the high Ydgrunites, and of the figure which a missionary would probably cut among them, I cannot feel sanguine that much good would be arrived at. Still the attempt is worth making, and the worst danger to the missionaries themselves would be that of being sent to the hospital where Chowbok would have been sent had he come with me into Erewhon.

Taking then their religious opinions as a whole, I must own that the Erewhonians are superstitious, on account of the views which they hold of their professed gods, and their entirely anomalous and inexplicable worship of Ydgrun, a worship at once the most powerful, yet most devoid of formalism, that I ever met with; but in practise things worked better than might have been expected, and the conflicting claims of Ydgrun and the gods were arranged by unwritten compromises (for the most part in Ydgrun's favour), which in ninety-nine cases out of a hundred were very well understood.

I could not conceive why they should not openly acknowledge high Ydgrunism, and discard the objective personality of hope, justice, etc.; but whenever I so much as hinted at this, I found that I was on dangerous ground. They would never have it; returning constantly to the assertion that ages ago the divinities were frequently seen, and that the moment their personality was disbelieved in, men would leave off practising even those ordinary virtues which the common experience of mankind has agreed on as being the greatest secret of happiness. "Who ever heard," they asked, indignantly, "of such things as kindly training, a good example, and an enlightened regard to one's own welfare, being able to keep men straight?" In my hurry, forgetting things which I ought to have remembered, I answered that if a person could not be kept straight by

113

these things, there was nothing that could straighten him, and that if he were not ruled by the love and fear of men whom he had seen, neither would he be so by that of the gods whom he had not seen.

At one time indeed I came upon a small but growing sect who believed, after a fashion, in the immortality of the soul and the resurrection from the dead; they taught that those who had been born with feeble and diseased bodies and had passed their lives in ailing, would be tortured eternally hereafter; but that those who had been born strong and healthy and handsome would be rewarded for ever and ever. Of moral qualities or conduct they made no mention.

Bad as this was, it was a step in advance, inasmuch as they did hold out a future state of some sort, and I was shocked to find that for the most part they met with opposition, on the score that their doctrine was based upon no sort of foundation, also that it was immoral in its tendency, and not to be desired by any reasonable beings.

When I asked how it could be immoral, I was answered, that if firmly held, it would lead people to cheapen this present life, making it appear to be an affair of only secondary importance; that it would thus distract men's minds from the perfecting of this world's economy, and was an impatient cutting, so to speak, of the Gordian knot of life's problems, whereby some people might gain present satisfaction to themselves at the cost of infinite damage to others; that the doctrine tended to encourage the poor in their improvidence, and in a debasing acquiescence in ills which they might well remedy; that the rewards were illusory and the result, after all, of luck, whose empire should be bounded by the grave; that its terrors were enervating and unjust; and that even the most blessed rising would be but the disturbing of a still more blessed slumber.

To all which I could only say that the thing had been actually known to happen, and that there were several well-authenticated instances of people having died and come to life again —instances which no man in his senses could doubt.

"If this be so," said my opponent, "we must bear it as best we may."

I then translated for him, as well as I could, the noble speech of Hamlet in which he says that it is the fear lest worse evils may befall us after death which alone prevents us from rushing into death's arms.

"Nonsense," he answered, "no man was ever yet stopped from cutting his throat by any such fears as your poet ascribes

114

to him—and your poet probably knew this perfectly well. If a man cuts his throat he is at bay, and thinks of nothing but escape, no matter whither, provided he can shuffle off his present. No. Men are kept at their posts, not by the fear that if they quit them they may quit a frying-pan for a fire, but by the hope that if they hold on, the fire may burn less fiercely. 'The respect,' to quote your poet, 'that makes calamity of so long a life,' is the consideration that though calamity may live long, the sufferer may live longer still."

On this, seeing that there was little probability of our coming to an agreement, I let the argument drop, and my opponent presently left me with as much disapprobation as he could show without being overtly rude.

Chapter 18

Birth Formulae

I HEARD what follows not from Arowhena, but from Mr. Nosnibor and some of the gentlemen who occasionally dined at the house: they told me that the Erewhonians believe in pre-existence; and not only this (of which I will write more fully in the next chapter), but they believe that it is of their own free act and deed in a previous state that they come to be born into this world at all. They hold that the unborn are perpetually plaguing and tormenting the married of both sexes, fluttering about them incessantly, and giving them no peace either of mind or body until they have consented to take them under their protection. If this were not so (this at least is what they urge), it would be a monstrous freedom for one man to take with another, to say that he should undergo the chances and changes of this mortal life without any option in the matter. No man would have any right to get married at all, inasmuch as he can never tell what frightful misery his doing so may entail forcibly upon a being who cannot be unhappy as long as he does not exist. They feel this so strongly that they are resolved to shift the blame on to other shoulders; and have fashioned a long mythology as to the world in which the unborn people live, and what they do, and arts and machinations to which they have recourse in order to get themselves into our own world. But of this more anon: what I would relate here is their manner of dealing with those who do come.

It is a distinguishing peculiarity of the Erewhonians that when they profess themselves to be quite certain about any matter, and avow it as a base on which they are to build a system of practise, they seldom quite believe in it. If they smell a rat about the precincts of a cherished institution, they will always stop their noses to it if they can.

This is what most of them did in this matter of the unborn, for I cannot (and never could) think that they seriously believed in their mythology concerning pre-existence: they did and they did not; they did not know themselves what they believed; all they did know was that it was a disease not to believe as they did. The only thing of which they were quite sure was that it was the pestering of the unborn which caused them to be brought into this world, and that they would not have been here if they would have only let peaceable people alone.

It would be hard to disprove this position, and they might have a good case if they would only leave it as it stands. But this they will not do; they must have assurance doubly sure; they must have the written word of the child itself as soon as it is born, giving the parents indemnity from all responsibility on the score of its birth, and asserting its own pre-existence. They have therefore devised something which they call a birth formula—a document which varies in words according to the caution of parents, but is much the same practically in all cases; for it has been the business of the Erewhonian lawyers during many ages to exercise their skill in perfecting it and providing for every contingency.

These formulae are printed on common paper at a moderate cost for the poor; but the rich have them written on parchment and handsomely bound, so that the getting up of a person's birth formula is a test of his social position. They commence by setting forth, That whereas A. B. was a member of the kingdom of the unborn, where he was well provided for in every way, and had no cause of discontent, etc., etc., he did of his own wanton depravity and restlessness conceive a desire to enter into this present world; that thereon having taken the necessary steps as set forth in laws of the unborn kingdom, he did with malice aforethought set himself to plague and pester two unfortunate people who had never wronged him, and who were quite contented and happy until he conceived this base design against their peace; for which wrong he now humbly entreats their pardon.

He acknowledges that he is responsible for all physical blemishes and deficiencies which may render him answerable
116

to the laws of his country; that his parents have nothing whatever to do with any of these things; and that they have a right to kill him at once if they be so minded, though he entreats them to show their marvellous goodness and clemency by sparing his life. If they will do this, he promises to be their most obedient and abject creature during his earlier years, and indeed all his life, unless they should see fit in their abundant generosity to remit some portion of his service hereafter. And so the formula continues, going sometimes into very minute details, according to the fancies of family lawyers, who will not make it any shorter than they can help.

The deed being thus prepared, on the third or fourth day after the birth of the child, or as they call it, the "final importunity," the friends gather together, and there is a feast held, where they are all very melancholy—as a general rule, I believe, quite truly so—and make presents to the father and mother of the child in order to console them for the injury which has just been done them by the unborn.

By and by the child himself is brought down by his nurse, and the company begin to rail upon him, upbraiding him for his impertinence, and asking him what amends he proposes to make for the wrong that he has committed, and how he can look for care and nourishment from those who have perhaps already been injured by the unborn on some ten or twelve occasions; for they say of people with large families, that they have suffered terrible injuries from the unborn; till at last, when this has been carried far enough, some one suggests the formula, which is brought out and solemnly read to the child by the family straightener. This gentleman is always invited on these occasions, for the very fact of intrusion into a peaceful family shows a depravity on the part of the child which requires his professional services.

On being teased by the reading and tweaked by the nurse, the child will commonly begin to cry, which is reckoned a good sign, as showing a consciousness of guilt. He is thereon asked, Does he assent to the formula? on which, as he still continues crying and can obviously make no answer, some one of the friends comes forward and undertakes to sign the document on his behalf, feeling sure (so he says) that the child would do it if he only knew how, and that he will release the present signer from his engagement on arriving at maturity. The friend then inscribes the signature of the child at the foot of the parchment, which is held to bind the child as much as though he had signed it himself.

Even this, however, does not fully content them, for they

feel a little uneasy until they have got the child's own signature after all. So when he is about fourteen, these good people partly bribe him by promises of greater liberty and good things, and partly intimidate him through their great power of making themselves actively unpleasant to him, so that though there is a show of freedom made, there is really none; they also use the offices of the teachers in the Colleges of Unreason, till at last, in one way or another, they take very good care that he shall sign the paper by which he professes to have been a free agent in coming into the world, and to take all the responsibility of having done so on to his own shoulders. And yet, though this document is obviously the most important which any one can sign in his whole life, they will have him do so at an age when neither they nor the law will for many a year allow any one else to bind him to the smallest obligation, no matter how righteously he may owe it, because they hold him too young to know what he is about, and do not consider it fair that he should commit himself to anything that may prejudice him in after years.

I own that all this seemed rather hard, and not of a piece with the many admirable institutions existing among them. I once ventured to say a part of what I thought about it to one of the Professors of Unreason. I did it very tenderly, but his justification of the system was quite out of my comprehension. I remember asking him whether he did not think it would do harm to a lad's principles, by weakening his sense of the sanctity of his word and of truth generally, that he should be led into entering upon a solemn declaration as to the truth of things about which all that he can certainly know is that he knows nothing—whether, in fact, the teachers who so led him, or who taught anything as a certainty of which they were themselves uncertain, were not earning their living by impairing the truth-sense of their pupils (a delicate organisation mostly), and by vitiating one of their most sacred instincts.

The Professor, who was a delightful person, seemed greatly surprised at the view which I took, but it had no influence with him whatsoever. No one, he answered, expected that the boy either would or could know all that he said he knew; but the world was full of compromises; and there was hardly any affirmation which would bear being interpreted literally. Human language was too gross a vehicle of thought—thought being incapable of absolute translation. He added, that as there can be no translation from one language into another which shall not scant the meaning somewhat, or enlarge upon it, so there is no language which can render thought without a jarring and a harshness somewhere—and so forth; all of which seemed to come to this in the end, that it was the custom of the country, and that the Erewhonians were a conservative people; that the boy would have to begin compromising sooner or later, and this was part of his education in the art. It was perhaps to be regretted that compromise should be as necessary as it was; still it was necessary, and the sooner the boy got to understand it the better for himself. But they never tell this to the boy.

From the book of their mythology about the unborn I made the extracts which will form the following chapter.

Chapter 19

The World of the Unborn

THE EREWHONIANS say that we are drawn through life backwards; or again, that we go onwards into the future as into a dark corridor. Time walks beside us and flings back shutters as we advance; but the light thus given often dazzles us, and deepens the darkness which is in front. We can see but little at a time, and heed that little far less than our apprehension of what we shall see next; ever peering curiously through the glare of the present into the gloom of the future, we presage the leading lines of that which is before us, by faintly reflected lights from dull mirrors that are behind, and stumble on as we may till the trap-door opens beneath us and we are gone.

They say at other times that the future and the past are as a panorama upon two rollers; that which is on the roller of the future unwraps itself on to the roller of the past; we cannot hasten it, and we may not stay it; we must see all that is unfolded to us whether it be good or ill; and what we have seen once we may see again no more. It is ever unwinding and being wound; we catch it in transition for a moment, and call it present; our flustered senses gather what impression they can, and we guess at what is coming by the tenor of that which we have seen. The same hand has painted the whole picture, and the incidents vary little—rivers, woods, plains, mountains, towns and peoples, love, sorrow, and death: yet the interest never flags, and we look hopefully for some good fortune, or fearfully lest our own faces be shown us as figuring in something terrible. When the scene is past we think we know it, though there is so much to see, and so little time to see it, that our conceit of knowledge as regards the past is for the most part poorly founded; neither do we care about it greatly, save insofar as it may affect the future, wherein our interest mainly lies.

The Erewhonians say it was by chance only that the earth and stars and all the heavenly worlds began to roll from east to west, and not from west to east, and in like manner they say it is by chance that man is drawn through life with his face to the past instead of to the future. For the future is there as much as the past, only that we may not see it. Is it not in the loins of the past, and must not the past alter before the future can do so?

Sometimes, again, they say that there was a race of men tried upon the earth once, who knew the future better than the past, but that they died in a twelvemonth from the misery which their knowledge caused them; and if any were to be born too prescient now, he would be culled out by natural selection, before he had time to transmit so peace-destroying a faculty to his descendants.

Strange fate for man! He must perish if he get that which he must perish if he strive not after. If he strive not after it he is no better than the brutes, if he get it he is more miserable than the devils.

Having waded through many chapters like the above, I came at last to the unborn themselves, and found that they were held to be souls pure and simple, having no actual bodies, but living in a sort of gaseous yet more or less anthropomorphic existence, like that of a ghost; they have thus neither flesh nor blood nor warmth. Nevertheless they are supposed to have local habitations and cities wherein they dwell, though these are as unsubstantial as their inhabitants; they are even thought to eat and drink some thin ambrosial sustenance, and generally to be capable of doing whatever mankind can do, only after a visionary ghostly fashion as in a dream. On the other hand, as long as they remain where they are they never die—the only form of death in the unborn world being the leaving it for our own. They are believed to be extremely numerous, far more so than mankind. They arrive from unknown planets, full grown, in large batches at a time; but they can only leave the unborn world by taking the steps necessary for their arrival here— which is, in fact, by suicide.

They ought to be an exceedingly happy people, for they have no extremes of good or ill fortune; never marrying, but living in a state much like that fabled by the poets as the primitive condition of mankind. In spite of this, however, they are in-

120

cessantly complaining; they know that we in this world have bodies, and indeed they know everything else about us, for they move among us whithersoever they will, and can read our thoughts, as well as survey our actions at pleasure. One would think that this should be enough for them; and most of them are indeed alive to the desperate risk which they will run by indulging themselves in that body with "sensible warm motion" which they so much desire; nevertheless, there are some to whom the *ennui* of a disembodied existence is so intolerable that they will venture anything for a change; so they resolve to quit. The conditions which they must accept are so uncertain, that none but the most foolish of the unborn will consent to them; and it is from these, and these only, that our own ranks are recruited.

When they have finally made up their minds to leave, they must go before the magistrate of the nearest town, and sign an affidavit of their desire to quit their then existence. On their having done this, the magistrate reads them the conditions which they must accept, and which are so long that I can only extract some of the principal points, which are mainly the following:

First, they must take a potion which will destroy their memory and sense of identity; they must go into the world helpless, and without a will of their own; they must draw lots for their dispositions before they go, and take them, such as they are, for better or worse—neither are they to be allowed any choice in the matter of the body which they so much desire; they are simply allotted by chance, and without appeal, to two people whom it is their business to find and pester until they adopt them. Who these are to be, whether rich or poor, kind or unkind, healthy or diseased, there is no knowing; they have, in fact, to entrust themselves for many years to the care of those for whose good constitution and good sense they have no sort of guarantee.

It is curious to read the lectures which the wiser heads give to those who are meditating a change. They talk with them as we talk with a spendthrift, and with about as much success.

"To be born," they say, "is a felony—it is a capital crime, for which sentence may be executed at any moment after the commission of the offence. You may perhaps happen to live for some seventy or eighty years, but what is that compared with the eternity you now enjoy? And even though the sentence were commuted, and you were allowed to live on for ever, you would in time become so terribly weary of life that execution would be the greatest mercy to you.

"Consider the infinite risk; to be born of wicked parents and trained in vice! to be born of silly parents, and trained to unrealities! of parents who regard you as a sort of chattel or property, belonging more to them than to yourself! Again, you may draw utterly unsympathetic parents, who will never be able to understand you, and who will do their best to thwart you (as a hen when she has hatched a duckling), and then call you ungrateful because you do not love them; or, again, you may draw parents who look upon you as a thing to be cowed while it is still young, lest it should give them trouble hereafter by having wishes and feelings of its own.

"In later life, when you have been finally allowed to pass muster as a full member of the world, you will yourself become liable to the pesterings of the unborn—and a very happy life you may be led in consequence! For we solicit so strongly that a few only—nor these the best—can refuse us; and yet not to refuse is much the same as going into partnership with half a dozen different people about whom one can know absolutely nothing beforehand—not even whether one is going into partnership with men or women, nor with how many of either. Delude not yourself with thinking that you will be wiser than your parents. You may be an age in advance of those whom you have pestered, but unless you are one of the great ones you will still be an age behind those who will in their turn pester you.

"Imagine what it must be to have an unborn quartered upon you, who is of an entirely different temperament and disposition to your own; nay, half a dozen such, who will not love you though you have stinted yourself in a thousand ways to provide for their comfort and well-being—who will forget all your self-sacrifice, and of whom you may never be sure that they are not bearing a grudge against you for errors of judgement into which you may have fallen, though you had hoped that such had been long since atoned for. Ingratitude such as this is not uncommon, yet fancy what it must be to bear! It is hard upon the duckling to have been hatched by a hen, but is it not also hard upon the hen to have hatched the duckling?

"Consider it again, we pray you, not for our sake but for your own. Your initial character you must draw by lot; but whatever it is, it can only come to a tolerably successful development after long training; remember that over that training you will have no control. It is possible, and even probable, that whatever you may get in after life which is of real pleasure and service to you, will have to be won in spite of, rather than by the help of, those whom you are now about to pester, and that you will only win your freedom after years of a painful struggle in which it will be hard to say whether you have suffered most injury, or inflicted it.

"Remember also, that if you go into the world you will have free will; that you will be obliged to have it; that there is no escaping it; that you will be fettered to it during your whole life, and must on every occasion do that which on the whole seems best to you at any given time, no matter whether you are right or wrong in choosing it. Your mind will be a balance for considerations, and your action will go with the heavier scale. How it shall fall will depend upon the kind of scales which you may have drawn at birth, the bias which they will have obtained by use, and the weight of the immediate considerations. If the scales were good to start with, and if they have not been out-rageously tampered with in childhood, and if the combinations into which you enter are average ones, you may come off well; but there are too many 'ifs' in this, and with the failure of any one of them your misery is assured. Reflect on this, and remember that should the ill come upon you, you will have yourself to thank, for it is your own choice to be born, and there is no com-pulsion in the matter.

"Not that we deny the existence of pleasures among man-kind; there is a certain show of sundry phases of contentment which may even amount to very considerable happiness; but mark how they are distributed over a man's life, belonging, all the keenest of them, to the fore part, and few indeed to the after. Can there be any pleasure worth purchasing with the miseries of a decrepit age? If you are good, strong, and hand-some, you have a fine fortune indeed at twenty, but how much of it will be left at sixty? For you must live on your capital; there is no investing your powers so that you may get a small annuity of life for ever: you must eat up your principal bit by bit, and be tortured by seeing it grow continually smaller and smaller, even though you happen to escape being rudely robbed of it by crime or casualty.

"Remember, too, that there never yet was a man of forty who would not come back into the world of the unborn if he could do so with decency and honour. Being in the world he will as a general rule stay till he is forced to go; but do you think that he would consent to be born again, and re-live his life, if he had the offer of doing so? Do not think it. If he could so alter the past as that he should never have come into being at all, do you not think that he would do it very gladly?

"What was it that one of their own poets meant, if it was not this, when he cried out upon the day in which he was born, and the night in which it was said there is a man child conceived? 'For now,' he says, 'I should have lain still and been quiet, I should have slept; then had I been at rest with kings and counsellors of the earth, which built desolate places for themselves; or with princes that had gold, who filled their houses with silver; or as an hidden untimely birth, I had not been; as infants which never saw light. There the wicked cease from troubling, and there the weary are at rest.' Be very sure that the guilt of being born carries this punishment at times to all men; but how can they ask for pity, or complain of any mischief that may befall them, having entered open-eyed into the snare?

"One word more and we have done. If any faint remembrance, as of a dream, flit in some puzzled moment across your brain, and you shall feel that the potion which is to be given you shall not have done its work, and the memory of this existence which you are leaving endeavours vainly to return; we say in such a moment, when you clutch at the dream but it eludes your grasp, and you watch it, as Orpheus watched Eurydice, gliding back again into the twilight kingdom, fly—fly—if you can remember the advice—to the haven of your present and immediate duty, taking shelter incessantly in the work which you have in hand. This much you may perhaps recall; and this, if you will imprint it deeply upon your every faculty, will be most likely to bring you safely and honourably home through the trials that are before you."

This is the fashion in which they reason with those who would be for leaving them, but it is seldom that they do much good, for none but the unquiet and unreasonable ever think of being born, and those who are foolish enough to think of it are generally foolish enough to do it. Finding, therefore, that they can do no more, the friends follow weeping to the courthouse of the chief magistrate, where the one who wishes to be born declares solemnly and openly that he accepts the conditions attached to his decision. On this he is presented with a potion, which immediately destroys his memory and sense of identity, and dissipates the thin gaseous tenement which he has inhabited: he becomes a bare vital principle, not to be perceived by human senses, nor to be by any chemical test appreciated. He has but one instinct, which is that he is to go to such and such a place, where he will find two persons whom he is to importune till they consent to undertake him; but whether he is to find these persons among the race of Chowbok or the Erewhonians themselves is not for him to choose.

Chapter 20

What They Mean by It

I HAVE given the above mythology at some length, but it is only a small part of what they have upon the subject. My first feeling on reading it was that any amount of folly on the part of the unborn in coming here was justified by a desire to escape from such intolerable prosing. The mythology is obviously an unfair and exaggerated representation of life and things; and had its authors been so minded they could have easily drawn a picture which would err as much on the bright side as this does on the dark. No Erewhonian believes that the world is as black as it has been here painted, but it is one of their peculiarities that they very often do not believe or mean things which they profess to regard as indisputable.

In the present instance their professed views concerning the unborn have arisen from their desire to prove that people have been presented with the gloomiest possible picture of their own prospects before they came here; otherwise, they could hardly say to one whom they are going to punish for an affection of the heart or brain that it is all his own doing. In practise they modify their theory to a considerable extent, and seldom refer to the birth formula except in extreme cases; for the force of habit, or what not, gives many of them a kindly interest even in creatures who have so much wronged them as the unborn have done; and though a man generally hates the unwelcome little stranger for the first twelve months, he is apt to mollify (according to his lights) as time goes on, and sometimes he will become inordinately attached to the beings whom he is pleased to call his children.

Of course, according to Erewhonian premises, it would serve people right to be punished and scouted for moral and intellectual diseases as much as for physical, and I cannot to this day understand why they should have stopped short half way. Neither, again, can I understand why their having done so should have been, as it certainly was, a matter of so much concern to myself. What could it matter to me how many absurdities the Erewhonians might adopt? Nevertheless I longed to make them think as I did, for the wish to spread those opinions that we hold conducive to our own welfare is so deeply rooted in the English character that few of us can escape its influence. But let this pass.

In spite of not a few modifications in practise of a theory which is itself revolting, the relations between children and parents in that country are less happy than in Europe. It was rarely that I saw cases of real hearty and intense affection between the old people and the young ones. Here and there I did so, and was quite sure that the children, even at the age of twenty, were fonder of their parents than they were of any one else; and that of their own inclination, being free to choose what company they would, they would often choose that of their father and mother. The straightener's carriage was rarely seen at the door of those houses. I saw two or three such cases during the time that I remained in the country, and cannot express the pleasure which I derived from a sight suggestive of so much goodness and wisdom and forbearance, so richly rewarded; yet I firmly believe that the same thing would happen in nine families out of ten if the parents were merely to remember how they felt when they were young, and actually to behave towards their children as they would have had their own parents behave towards themselves. But this, which would appear to be so simple and obvious, seems also to be a thing which not one in a hundred thousand is able to put in practise. It is only the very great and good who have any living faith in the simplest axioms; and there are few who are so holy as to feel that 19 and 13 make 32 as certainly as 2 and 2 make 4.

I am quite sure that if this narrative should ever fall into Erewhonian hands, it will be said that what I have written about the relations between parents and children being seldom satisfactory is an infamous perversion of facts, and that in truth there are few young people who do not feel happier in the society of their nearest relations than in any other. Mr. Nosnibor would be sure to say this. Yet I cannot refrain from expressing an opinion that he would be a good deal embarrassed if his deceased parents were to reappear and propose to pay him a six months' visit. I doubt whether there are many things which he would regard as a greater infliction. They had died at a ripe old age some twenty years before I came to know him, so the case is an extreme one; but surely if they had treated him with what in his youth he had felt to be true unselfishness, his face would brighten when he thought of them to the end of his life.

In the one or two cases of true family affection which I met with, I am sure that the young people who were so genuinely fond of their fathers and mothers at eighteen, would at sixty be

126

perfectly delighted were they to get the chance of welcoming them as their guests. There is nothing which could please them better, except perhaps to watch the happiness of their own children and grandchildren.

This is how things should be. It is not an impossible ideal; it is one which actually does exist in some few cases, and might exist in almost all, with a little more patience and forbearance upon the parents' part; but it is rare at present—so rare that they have a proverb which I can only translate in a very round-about way, but which says that the great happiness of some people in a future state will consist in watching the distress of their parents on returning to eternal companionship with their grandfathers and grandmothers; whilst "compulsory affection" is the idea which lies at the root of their word for the deepest anguish.

There is no talisman in the word "parent" which can generate miracles of affection, and I can well believe that my own child might find it less of a calamity to lose both Arowhena and myself when he is six years old, than to find us again when he is sixty—a sentence which I would not pen did I not feel that by doing so I was giving him something like a hostage, or at any rate putting a weapon into his hands against me, should my selfishness exceed reasonable limits.

Money is at the bottom of all this to a great extent. If the parents would put their children in the way of earning a competence earlier than they do, the children would soon become self-supporting and independent. As it is, under the present system, the young ones get old enough to have all manner of legitimate wants (that is, if they have any "go" about them) before they have learnt the means of earning money to pay for them; hence they must either do without them, or take more money than the parents can be expected to spare. This is due chiefly to the schools of Unreason, where a boy is taught upon hypothetical principles, as I will explain hereafter; spending years in being incapacitated for doing this, that, or the other (he hardly knows what), during all which time he ought to have been actually doing the thing itself, beginning at the lowest grades, picking it up through actual practise, and rising according to the energy which is in him.

These schools of Unreason surprised me much. It would be easy to fall into pseudo-utilitarianism, and I would fain believe that the system may be good for the children of very rich parents, or for those who show a natural instinct to acquire hypothetical lore; but the misery was that their Ydgrun-worship required all people with any pretence to respectability to send their children to some one or other of these schools, mulcting them of years of money. It astonished me to see what sacrifices the parents would make in order to render their children as nearly useless as possible; and it was hard to say whether the old suffered most from the expense which they were thus put to, or the young from being deliberately swindled in some of the most important branches of human inquiry, and directed into false channels or left to drift in the great majority of cases.

I cannot think I am mistaken in believing that the growing tendency to limit families by infanticide—an evil which was causing general alarm throughout the country—was almost entirely due to the way in which education had become a fetish from one end of Erewhon to the other. Granted that provision should be made whereby every child should be taught reading, writing, and arithmetic, but here compulsory state-aided education should end, and the child should begin (with all due precautions to ensure that he is not overworked) to acquire the rudiments of that art whereby he is to earn his living.

He cannot acquire these in what we in England call schools of technical education; such schools are cloister life as against the rough and tumble of the world; they unfit, rather than fit for work in the open. An art can only be learned in the workshop of those who are winning their bread by it.

Boys, as a rule, hate the artificial, and delight in the actual; give them the chance of earning, and they will soon earn. When parents find that their children, instead of being made artificially burdensome, will early begin to contribute to the wellbeing of the family, they will soon leave off killing them, and will seek to have that plenitude of offspring which they now avoid. As things are, the state lays greater burdens on parents than flesh and blood can bear, and then wrings its hands over an evil for which it is itself mainly responsible.

With the less well-dressed classes the harm was not so great; for among these, at about ten years old, the child has to begin doing something: if he is capable he makes his way up; if he is not, he is at any rate not made more incapable by what his friends are pleased to call his education. People find their level as a rule; and though they unfortunately sometimes miss it, it is in the main true that those who have valuable qualities are perceived to have them and can sell them. I think that the Erewhonians are beginning to become aware of these things, for there was much talk about putting a tax upon all parents whose children were not earning a competence according to their degrees by the time they were twenty years old. I am sure that if they will have the courage to carry it through they will never regret it; for the parents will take care that the children shall begin earning money (which means "doing good" to society) at an early age; then the children will be independent early, and they will not press on the parents, nor the parents on them, and they will like each other better than they do now.

This is the true philanthropy. He who makes a colossal fortune in the hosiery trade, and by his energy has succeeded in reducing the price of woolen goods by the thousandth part of a penny in the pound—this man is worth ten professional philanthropists. So strongly are the Erewhonians impressed with this, that if a man has made a fortune of over £20,000 a year they exempt him from all taxation, considering him as a work of art, and too precious to be meddled with; they say, "How very much he must have done for society before society could have been prevailed upon to give him so much money"; so magnificent an organisation overawes them; they regard it as a thing dropped from heaven.

"Money," they say, "is the symbol of duty, it is the sacrament of having done for mankind that which mankind wanted. Mankind may not be a very good judge, but there is no better." This used to shock me at first, when I remembered that it had been said on high authority that they who have riches shall enter hardly into the kingdom of heaven; but the influence of Erewhon had made me begin to see things in a new light, and I could not help thinking that they who have not riches shall enter more hardly still.

People oppose money to culture, and imply that if a man has spent his time in making money he will not be cultivated—fallacy of fallacies! As though there could be a greater aid to culture than the having earned an honourable independence, and as though any amount of culture will do much for the man who is penniless, except make him feel his position more deeply. The young man who was told to sell all his goods and give to the poor must have been an entirely exceptional person if the advice was given wisely, either for him or for the poor; how much more often does it happen that we perceive a man to have all sorts of good qualities except money, and feel that his real duty lies in getting every halfpenny that he can persuade others to pay him for his services, and becoming rich. It has been said that the love of money is the root of all evil. The want of money is so quite as truly.

The above may sound irreverent, but it is conceived in a spirit of the most utter reverence for those things which do alone deserve it—that is, for the things which are, which mould us and fashion us, be they what they may; for the things that have power to punish us, and which will punish us if we do not heed them; for our masters therefore. But I am drifting away from my story.

They have another plan about which they are making a great noise and fuss, much as some are doing with women's rights in England. A party of extreme radicals have professed themselves unable to decide upon the superiority of age or youth. At present all goes on the supposition that it is desirable to make the young old as soon as possible. Some would have it that this is wrong, and that the object of education should be to keep the old young as long as possible. They say that each age should take its turn and turn about, week by week, one week the old to be topsawyers, and the other the young, drawing the line at thirty-five years of age; but they insist that the young should be allowed to inflict corporal chastisement on the old, without which the old would be quite incorrigible. In any European country this would be out of the question; but it is not so there, for the straighteners are constantly ordering people to be flogged, so that they are familiar with the notion. I do not suppose that the idea will be ever acted upon; but its having been even mooted is enough to show the utter perversion of the Erewhonian mind.

Chapter 21

The Colleges of Unreason

I HAD now been a visitor with the Nosnibors for some five or six months, and though I had frequently proposed to leave them and take apartments of my own, they would not hear of my doing so. I suppose they thought I should be more likely to fall in love with Zulora if I remained, but it was my affection for Arowhena that kept me.

During all this time both Arowhena and myself had been dreaming, and drifting towards an avowed attachment, but had not dared to face the real difficulties of the position. Gradually, however, matters came to a crisis in spite of ourselves, and we got to see the true state of the case, all too clearly.

One evening we were sitting in the garden, and I had been trying in every stupid roundabout way to get her to say that she should be at any rate sorry for a man, if he really loved a woman who would not marry him. I had been stammering and blushing, and been as silly as any one could be, and I suppose had pained her by fishing for pity for myself in such a transparent way, and saying nothing about her own need of it; at any rate, she turned upon me with a sweet sad smile and said, "Sorry? I am sorry for myself; I am sorry for you; and I am sorry for every one." The words had no sooner crossed her lips than she bowed her head, gave me a look as though I were to make no answer, and left me.

The words were few and simple, but the manner with which they were uttered was ineffable: the scales fell from my eyes, and I felt that I had no right to try and induce her to infringe one of the most inviolable customs of her country, as she needs must do if she were to marry me. I sat for a long while thinking, and when I remembered the sin and shame and misery which an unrighteous marriage—for as such it would be held in Erewhon—would entail, I became thoroughly ashamed of myself for having been so long self-blinded. I write coldly now, but I suffered keenly at the time, and should probably retain a much more vivid recollection of what I felt, had not all ended so happily.

As for giving up the idea of marrying Arowhena, it never so much as entered my head to do so: the solution must be found in some other direction than this. The idea of waiting till somebody married Zulora was to be no less summarily dismissed. To marry Arowhena at once in Erewhon—this had already been abandoned: there remained therefore but one alternative, and that was to run away with her, and get her with me to Europe, where there would be no bar to our union save my own impecuniosity, a matter which gave me no uneasiness.

To this obvious and simple plan I could see but two objections that deserved the name—the first, that perhaps Arowhena would not come; the second, that it was almost impossible for me to escape even alone, for the King had himself told me that I was to consider myself a prisoner on parole, and that the first sign of my endeavouring to escape would cause me to be sent to one of the hospitals for incurables. Besides, I did not know the geography of the country, and even were I to try and find my way back, I should be discovered long before I had reached the pass over which I had come. How then could I hope to be able to take Arowhena with me? For days and days I turned these difficulties over in my mind, and at last hit upon as wild a plan as was ever suggested by extremity. This was to meet the second difficulty: the first gave me less uneasiness, for when Arowhena and I next met after our interview in the garden I could see that she had suffered not less acutely than myself.

131

I resolved that I would have another interview with her—the last for the present—that I would then leave her, and set to work upon maturing my plan as fast as possible. We got a chance of being alone together, and then I gave myself the loose rein, and told her how passionately and devotedly I loved her. She said little in return, but her tears (which I could not refrain from answering with my own) and the little she did say were quite enough to show me that I should meet with no obstacle from her. Then I asked her whether she would run a terrible risk which we should share in common, if, in case of success, I could take her to my own people, to the home of my mother and sisters, who would welcome her very gladly. At the same time I pointed out that the chances of failure were far greater than those of success, and that the probability was that even though I could get so far as to carry my design into execution, it would end in death to us both.

I was not mistaken in her; she said that she believed I loved her as much as she loved me, and that she would brave anything if I could only assure her that what I proposed would not be thought dishonourable in England; she could not live without me, and would rather die with me than alone; that death was perhaps the best for us both; that I must plan, and that when the hour came I was to send for her, and trust her not to fail me; and so after many tears and embraces, we tore ourselves away.

I then left the Nosnibors, took a lodging in the town, and became melancholy to my heart's content. Arowhena and I used to see each other sometimes, for I had taken to going regularly to the Musical Banks, but Mrs. Nosnibor and Zulora both treated me with considerable coldness. I felt sure that they suspected me. Arowhena looked miserable, and I saw that her purse was now always as full as she could fill it with the Musical Bank money—much fuller than of old. Then the horrible thought occurred to me that her health might break down, and that she might be subjected to a criminal prosecution. Oh, how I hated Erewhon at that time.

I was still received at court, but my good looks were beginning to fail me, and I was not such an adept at concealing the effects of pain as the Erewhonians are. I could see that my friends began to look concerned about me, and was obliged to take a leaf out of Mahaina's book, and pretend to have developed a taste for drinking. I even consulted a straightener as though this were so, and submitted to much discomfort. This made matters better for a time, but I could see that my friends thought less highly of my constitution as my flesh began to fall away.

I was told that the poor made an outcry about my pension, and I saw a stinging article in an anti-ministerial paper, in which the writer went so far as to say that my having light hair reflected little credit upon me, inasmuch as I had been reported to have said that it was a common thing in the country from which I came. I have reason to believe that Mr. Nosnibor himself inspired this article. Presently it came round to me that the King had begun to dwell upon my having been possessed of a watch, and to say that I ought to be treated medicinally for having told him a lie about the balloons. I saw misfortune gathering round me in every direction, and felt that I should have need of all my wits and a good many more, if I was to steer myself and Arowhena to a good conclusion.

There were some who continued to show me kindness, and strange to say, I received the most from the very persons from whom I should have least expected it—I mean from the cashiers of the Musical Banks. I had made the acquaintance of several of these persons, and now that I frequented their bank, they were inclined to make a good deal of me. One of them, seeing that I was thoroughly out of health, though of course he pretended not to notice it, suggested that I should take a little change of air and go down with him to one of the principal towns, which was some two or three days' journey from the metropolis, and the chief seat of the Colleges of Unreason; he assured me that I should be delighted with what I saw, and that I should receive a most hospitable welcome. I determined therefore to accept the invitation.

We started two or three days later, and after a night on the road, we arrived at our destination towards evening. It was now full spring, and as nearly as might be ten months since I had started with Chowbok on my expedition, but it seemed more like ten years. The trees were in their freshest beauty, and the air had become warm without being oppressively hot. After having lived so many months in the metropolis, the sight of the country, and the country villages through which we passed refreshed me greatly, but I could not forget my troubles. The last five miles or so were the most beautiful part of the journey, for the country became more undulating, and the woods were more extensive; but the first sight of the city of the colleges itself was the most delightful of all. I cannot imagine that there can be any fairer in the whole world, and I expressed my pleasure to my companion, and thanked him for having brought me.

We drove to an inn in the middle of the town, and then, while it was still light, my friend the cashier, whose name was Thims, took me for a stroll in the streets and in the court-yards of the principal colleges. Their beauty and interests were extreme; it was impossible to see them without being attracted towards them; and I thought to myself that he must be indeed an ill-grained and ungrateful person who can have been a member of one of these colleges without retaining an affectionate feeling towards it for the rest of his life. All my misgivings gave way at once when I saw the beauty and venerable appearance of this delightful city. For half an hour I forgot both myself and Arowhena.

After supper Mr. Thims told me a good deal about the system of education which is here practised. I already knew a part of what I heard, but much was new to me, and I obtained a better idea of the Erewhonian position than I had done hitherto: nevertheless there were parts of the scheme of which I could not comprehend the fitness, although I fully admit that this inability was probably the result of my having been trained so very differently and to my being then much out of sorts.

The main feature in their system is the prominence which they give to a study which I can only translate by the word "hypothetics." They argue thus—that to teach a boy merely the nature of the things which exist in the world round him, and about which he will have to be conversant during his whole life, would be giving him but a narrow and shallow conception of the universe, which it is urged might contain all manner of things which are not now to be found therein. To open his eyes to these possibilities, and so to prepare him for all sorts of emergencies, is the object of this system of hypothetics. To imagine a set of utterly strange and impossible contingencies, and require the youths to give intelligent answers to the questions that arise therefrom, is reckoned the fittest conceivable way of preparing them for the actual conduct of their affairs in after life.

Thus they are taught what is called the hypothetical language for many of their best years—a language which was originally composed at a time when the country was in a very different state of civilisation to what it is at present, a state which has long since disappeared and been superseded. Many valuable maxims and noble thoughts which were at one time concealed in it have become current in their modern literature, and have been translated over and over again into the language now spoken. Surely then it would seem enough that the study of the original language should be confined to the few whose instincts led them naturally to pursue it.

But the Erewhonians think differently; the store they set by this hypothetical language can hardly be believed; they will even give any one a maintenance for life if he attains a considerable proficiency in the study of it; nay, they will spend years in learning to translate some of their own good poetry into the hypothetical language—to do so with fluency being reckoned a distinguishing mark of a scholar and a gentleman. Heaven forbid that I should be flippant, but it appeared to me to be a wanton waste of good human energy that men should spend years and years in the perfection of so barren an exercise, when their own civilisation presented problems by the hundred which cried aloud for solution and would have paid the solver handsomely; but people know their own affairs best. If the youths chose it for themselves I should have wondered less; but they do not choose it; they have it thrust upon them, and for the most part are disinclined towards it. I can only say that all I heard in defence of the system was insufficient to make me think very highly of its advantages.

The arguments in favour of the deliberate development of the unreasoning faculties were much more cogent. But here they depart from the principles on which they justify their study of hypothetics; for they base the importance which they assign to hypothetics upon the fact of their being a preparation for the extraordinary, while their study of Unreason rests upon its developing those faculties which are required for the daily conduct of affairs. Hence their professorships of Inconsistency and Evasion, in both of which studies the youths are examined before being allowed to proceed to their degree in hypothetics. The more earnest and conscientious students attain to a proficiency in these subjects which is quite surprising; there is hardly any inconsistency so glaring but they soon learn to defend it, or injunction so clear that they cannot find some pretext for disregarding it.

Life, they urge, would be intolerable if men were to be guided in all they did by reason and reason only. Reason betrays men into the drawing of hard and fast lines, and to the defining by language—language being like the sun, which rears and then scorches. Extremes are alone logical, but they are always absurd; the mean is illogical, but an illogical mean is better than the sheer absurdity of an extreme. There are no follies and no unreasonablenesses so great as those which can apparently be irrefragably defended by reason itself, and there is hardly an error into which men may not easily be led if they base their conduct upon reason only.

135

Reason might very possibly abolish the double currency; it might even attack the personality of Hope and Justice. Besides, people have such a strong natural bias towards it that they will seek it for themselves and act upon it quite as much as or more than is good for them: there is no need of encouraging reason. With unreason the case is different. She is the natural complement of reason, without whose existence reason itself were non-existent.

If, then, reason would be non-existent were there no such thing as unreason, surely it follows that the more unreason there is, the more reason there must be also? Hence the necessity for the development of unreason, even in the interests of reason herself. The Professors of Unreason deny that they undervalue reason: none can be more convinced than they are, that if the double currency cannot be rigorously deduced as a necessary consequence of human reason, the double currency should cease forthwith; but they say that it must be deduced from no narrow and exclusive view of reason which should deprive that admirable faculty of the one-half of its own existence. Unreason is a part of reason; it must therefore be allowed its full share in stating the initial conditions.

Chapter 22

The Colleges of Unreason—(continued)

OF GENIUS they make no account, for they say that every one is a genius, more or less. No one is so physically sound that no part of him will be even a little unsound, and no one is so diseased but that some part of him will be healthy—so no man is so mentally and morally sound, but that he will be in part both mad and wicked; and no man is so mad and wicked but he will be sensible and honourable in part. In like manner there is no genius who is not also a fool, and no fool who is not also a genius.

When I talked about originality and genius to some gentlemen whom I met at a supper party given by Mr. Thims in my honour, and said that original thought ought to be encouraged, I had to eat my words at once. Their view evidently was that genius was like offences—needs must that it come, but woe unto that man through whom it comes. A man's business, they hold, is to think as his neighbours do, for Heaven help him if he thinks good what they count bad. And really it is hard to see how the Erewhonian theory differs from our own, for the word "idiot" only means a person who forms his opinions for himself.

The venerable Professor of Worldly Wisdom, a man verging on eighty but still hale, spoke to me very seriously on this subject in consequence of the few words that I had imprudently let fall in defence of genius. He was one of those who carried most weight in the university, and had the reputation of having done more perhaps than any other living man to suppress any kind of originality.

"It is not our business," he said, "to help students to think for themselves. Surely this is the very last thing which one who wishes them well should encourage them to do. Our duty is to ensure that they shall think as we do, or at any rate, as we hold it expedient to say we do." In some respects, however, he was thought to hold somewhat radical opinions, for he was President of the Society for the Suppression of Useless Knowledge, and for the Complete Obliteration of the Past.

As regards the tests that a youth must pass before he can get a degree, I found that they have no class lists, and discourage anything like competition among the students; this, indeed, they regard as self-seeking and unneighbourly. The examinations are conducted by way of papers written by the candidate on set subjects, some of which are known to him beforehand, while others are devised with a view of testing his general capacity and *savoir faire*.

My friend the Professor of Worldly Wisdom was the terror of the greater number of students; and, so far as I could judge, he very well might be, for he had taken his Professorship more seriously than any of the other Professors had done. I heard of his having plucked one poor fellow for want of sufficient vagueness in his saving clauses paper. Another was sent down for having written an article on a scientific subject without having made free enough use of the words "carefully," "patiently," and "earnestly." One man was refused a degree for being too often and too seriously in the right, while a few days before I came a whole batch had been plucked for insufficient distrust of printed matter.

About this there was just then rather a ferment, for it seems that the Professor had written an article in the leading university magazine, which was well known to be by him, and which abounded in all sorts of plausible blunders. He then set a paper which afforded the examinees an opportunity of repeating these blunders—which, believing the article to be by their own ex-

137

aminer, they of course did. The Professor plucked every single one of them, but his action was considered to have been not quite handsome.

I told them of Homer's noble line to the effect that a man should strive ever to be foremost and in all things to outvie his peers; but they said that no wonder the countries in which such a detestable maxim was held in admiration were always flying at one another's throats.

"Why," asked one Professor, "should a man want to be better than his neighbours? Let him be thankful if he is no worse."

I ventured feebly to say that I did not see how progress could be made in any art or science, or indeed in anything at all, without more or less self-seeking, and hence unamiability.

"Of course it cannot," said the Professor, "and therefore we object to progress."

After which there was no more to be said. Later on, however, a young Professor took me aside and said he did not think I quite understood their views about progress.

"We like progress," he said, "but it must commend itself to the common sense of the people. If a man gets to know more than his neighbours he should keep his knowledge to himself till he has sounded them, and seen whether they agree, or are likely to agree with him." He said it was as immoral to be too far in front of one's own age as to lag too far behind it. "If a man can carry his neighbours with him, he may say what he likes; but if not, what insult can be more gratuitous than the telling them what they do not want to know? A man should remember that intellectual over-indulgence is one of the most insidious and disgraceful forms that excess can take. Granted that every one should exceed more or less, inasmuch as absolutely perfect sanity would drive any man mad the moment he reached it, but . . ."

He was now warming to his subject and I was beginning to wonder how I should get rid of him, when the party broke up, and though I promised to call on him before I left, I was unfortunately prevented from doing so.

I have now said enough to give English readers some idea of the strange views which the Erewhonians hold concerning unreason, hypothetics, and education generally. In many respects they were sensible enough, but I could not get over the hypothetics, especially the turning their own good poetry into the hypothetical language. In the course of my stay I met one youth who told me that for fourteen years the hypothetical language had been almost the only thing that he had been taught, although he had never (to his credit, as it seemed to me) shown the slightest proclivity towards it, while he had been endowed with not inconsiderable ability for several other branches of human learning. He assured me that he would never open another hypothetical book after he had taken his degree, but would follow out the bent of his own inclinations. This was well enough, but who could give him his fourteen years back again?

I sometimes wondered how it was that the mischief done was not more clearly perceptible, and that the young men and women grew up as sensible and goodly as they did, in spite of the attempts almost deliberately made to warp and stunt their growth. Some doubtless received damage, from which they suffered to their life's end; but many seemed little or none the worse, and some, almost the better. The reason would seem to be that the natural instinct of the lads in most cases so absolutely rebelled against their training, that do what the teachers might they could never get them to pay serious heed to it. The consequence was that the boys only lost their time, and not so much of this as might have been expected, for in their hours of leisure they were actively engaged in exercises and sports which developed their physical nature, and made them at any rate strong and healthy.

Moreover those who had any special tastes could not be restrained from developing them: they would learn what they wanted to learn and liked, in spite of obstacles which seemed rather to urge them on than to discourage them, while for those who had no special capacity, the loss of time was of comparatively little moment; but in spite of these alleviations of the mischief, I am sure that much harm was done to the children of the subwealthy classes, by the system which passes current among the Erewhonians as education. The poorest children suffered least—if destruction and death have heard the sound of wisdom, to a certain extent poverty has done so also.

And yet perhaps, after all, it is better for a country that its seats of learning should do more to suppress mental growth than to encourage it. Were it not for a certain priggishness which these places infuse into so great a number of their *alumni,* genuine work would become dangerously common. It is essential that by far the greater part of what is said or done in the world should be so ephemeral as to take itself away quickly; it should keep good for twenty-four hours, or even twice as long, but it should not be good enough a week hence to prevent people from going on to something else. No doubt the marvellous development of journalism in England, as also the fact that our seats of learning aim rather at fostering mediocrity than anything higher, is due to our subconscious recognition of the fact that it is even more necessary to check exuberance of mental development than to encourage it. There can be no doubt that this is what our academic bodies do, and they do it the more effectually because they do it only subconsciously. They think they are advancing healthy mental assimilation and digestion, whereas in reality they are little better than cancer in the stomach.

Let me return, however, to the Erewhonians. Nothing surprised me more than to see the occasional flashes of common sense with which one branch of study or another was lit up, while not a single ray fell upon so many others. I was particularly struck with this on strolling into the Art School of the University. Here I found that the course of study was divided into two branches—the practical and the commercial—no student being permitted to continue his studies in the actual practise of the art he had taken up, unless he made equal progress in its commercial history.

Thus those who were studying painting were examined at frequent intervals in the prices which all the leading pictures of the last fifty or a hundred years had realised, and in the fluctuations in their values when (as often happened) they had been sold and resold three or four times. The artist, they contend, is a dealer in pictures, and it is as important for him to learn how to adapt his wares to the market, and to know approximately what kind of a picture will fetch how much, as it is for him to be able to paint the picture. This, I suppose, is what the French mean by laying so much stress upon "values."

As regards the city itself, the more I saw the more enchanted I became. I dare not trust my self with any description of the exquisite beauty of the different colleges, and their walks and gardens. Truly in these things alone there must be a hallowing and refining influence which is in itself half an education, and which no amount of error can wholly spoil. I was introduced to many of the Professors, who showed me every hospitality and kindness; nevertheless I could hardly avoid a sort of suspicion that some of those whom I was taken to see had been so long engrossed in their own study of hypothetics that they had become the exact antitheses of the Athenians in the days of St. Paul; for whereas the Athenians spent their lives in nothing save to see and to hear some new thing, there were some here who seemed to devote themselves to the avoidance of every opinion with which they were not perfectly familiar, and regarded their own brains as a sort of sanctuary, to which if an opinion had once resorted, none other was to attack it.

I should warn the reader, however, that I was rarely sure what the men whom I met while staying with Mr. Thims really meant; for there was no getting anything out of them if they scented even a suspicion that they might be what they call "giving themselves away." As there is hardly any subject on which this suspicion cannot arise, I found it difficult to get definite opinions from any of them, except on such subjects as the weather, eating and drinking, holiday excursions, or games of skill.

If they cannot wriggle out of expressing an opinion of some sort, they will commonly retail those of some one who has already written upon the subject, and conclude by saying that though they quite admit that there is an element of truth in what the writer has said, there are many points on which they are unable to agree with him. Which these points were, I invariably found myself unable to determine; indeed, it seemed to be counted the perfection of scholarship and good breeding among them to have—much less to express—an opinion on any subject on which it might prove later that they had been mistaken. The art of sitting gracefully on a fence has never, I should think, been brought to greater perfection than at the Erewhonian Colleges of Unreason.

Even when, wriggle as they may, they find themselves pinned down to some expression of definite opinion, as often as not they will argue in support of what they perfectly well know to be untrue. I repeatedly met with reviews and articles even in their best journals, between the lines of which I had little difficulty in detecting a sense exactly contrary to the one ostensibly put forward. So well is this understood that a man must be a mere tyro in the arts of Erewhonian polite society, unless he instinctively suspects a hidden "yea" in every "nay" that meets him. Granted that it comes to much the same in the end, for it does not matter whether "yea" is called "yea" or "nay," so long as it is understood which it is to be; but our own more direct way of calling a spade a spade, rather than a rake, with the intention that every one should understand it as a spade, seems more satisfactory. On the other hand, the Erewhonian system lends itself better to the suppression of that downrightness which it seems the express aim of Erewhonian philosophy to discountenance.

However this may be, the fear-of-giving-themselves-away disease was fatal to the intelligence of those infected by it, and almost every one at the Colleges of Unreason had caught it to a greater or less degree. After a few years atrophy of the opinions invariably supervened, and the sufferer became stone dead

141

to everything except the more superficial aspects of those material objects with which he came most in contact. The expression on the faces of these people was repellent; they did not, however, seem particularly unhappy, for they none of them had the faintest idea that they were in reality more dead than alive. No cure for this disgusting fear-of-giving-themselves-away disease has yet been discovered.

It was during my stay in the city of the Colleges of Unreason —a city whose Erewhonian name is so cacophonous that I refrain from giving it—that I learned the particulars of the revolution which had ended in the destruction of so many of the mechanical inventions which were formerly in common use.

Mr. Thims took me to the rooms of a gentleman who had a great reputation for learning, but who was also, so Mr. Thims told me, rather a dangerous person, inasmuch as he had attempted to introduce an adverb into the hypothetical language. He had heard of my watch and been exceedingly anxious to see me, for he was accounted the most learned antiquary in Erewhon on the subject of mechanical lore. We fell to talking upon the subject, and when I left he gave me a reprinted copy of the work which brought the revolution about.

It had taken place some five hundred years before my arrival: people had long become thoroughly used to the change, although at the time that it was made the country was plunged into the deepest misery, and a reaction which followed had very nearly proved successful. Civil war raged for many years, and is said to have reduced the number of the inhabitants by one half. The parties were styled the machinists and the anti-machinists, and in the end, as I have said already, the latter got the victory, treating their opponents with such unparalleled severity that they extirpated every trace of opposition.

The wonder was that they allowed any mechanical appliances to remain in the kingdom, neither do I believe that they would have done so, had not the Professors of Inconsistency and Evasion made a stand against the carrying of the new principles to their legitimate conclusions. These Professors, moreover, insisted that during the struggle the anti-machinists should use every known improvement in the art of war, and several new weapons, offensive and defensive, were invented, while it was in progress. I was surprised at there remaining so many mechanical specimens as are seen in the museums and at students having rediscovered their past uses so completely; for at the time of the revolution the victors wrecked all the more complicated machines, and burned all treatises on mechanics, and all engineers' workshops—thus, so they thought, cutting the mischief out root and branch, at an incalculable cost of blood and treasure.

Certainly they had not spared their labour, but work of this description can never be perfectly achieved, and when, some two hundred years before my arrival, all passion upon the subject had cooled down, and no one save a lunatic would have dreamed of reintroducing forbidden inventions, the subject came to be regarded as a curious antiquarian study, like that of some long-forgotten religious practises among ourselves. Then came the careful search for whatever fragments could be found, and for any machines that might have been hidden away, and also numberless treatises were written, showing what the functions of each rediscovered machine had been; all being done with no idea of using such machinery again, but with the feelings of an English antiquarian concerning Druidical monuments or flint arrow heads.

On my return to the metropolis, during the remaining weeks or rather days of my sojourn in Erewhon I made a *résumé* in English of the work which brought about the already mentioned revolution. My ignorance of technical terms has led me doubtless into many errors, and I have occasionally, where I found translation impossible, substituted purely English names and ideas for the original Erewhonian ones, but the reader may rely on my general accuracy. I have thought it best to insert my translation here.

Chapter 23

The Book of the Machines

THE WRITER commences: "There was a time when the earth was to all appearance utterly destitute both of animal and vegetable life, and when according to the opinion of our best philosophers it was simply a hot round ball with a crust gradually cooling. Now if a human being had existed while the earth was in this state and had been allowed to see it as though it were some other world with which he had no concern, and if at the same time he were entirely ignorant of all physical science, would he not have pronounced it impossible that creatures possessed of anything like consciousness should be evolved from the seeming cinder which he was beholding? Would he not have denied that it contained any potentiality of consciousness? Yet in the course of time consciousness came. Is it not possible then that there may be even yet new channels dug out for consciousness, though we can detect no signs of them at present?

"Again. Consciousness, in anything like the present acceptation of the term, having been once a new thing—a thing, as far as we can see, subsequent even to an individual centre of action and to a reproductive system (which we see existing in plants without apparent consciousness)—why may not there arise some new phase of mind which shall be as different from all present known phases, as the mind of animals is from that of vegetables?

"It would be absurd to attempt to define such a mental state (or whatever it may be called), inasmuch as it must be something so foreign to man that his experience can give him no help towards conceiving its nature; but surely when we reflect upon the manifold phases of life and consciousness which have been evolved already, it would be rash to say that no others can be developed, and that animal life is the end of all things. There was a time when fire was the end of all things: another when rocks and water were so."

The writer, after enlarging on the above for several pages, proceeded to inquire whether traces of the approach of such a new phase of life could be perceived at present; whether we could see any tenements preparing which might in a remote futurity be adapted for it; whether, in fact, the primordial cell of such a kind of life could be now detected upon earth. In the course of his work he answered this question in the affirmative and pointed to the higher machines.

"There is no security"—to quote his own words—"against the ultimate development of mechanical consciousness, in the fact of machines possessing little consciousness now. A mollusc has not much consciousness. Reflect upon the extraordinary advance which machines have made during the last few hundred years, and note how slowly the animal and vegetable kingdoms are advancing. The more highly organised machines are creatures not so much of yesterday, as of the last five minutes, so to speak, in comparison with past time. Assume for the sake of argument that conscious beings have existed for some twenty million years: see what strides machines have made in the last thousand! May not the world last twenty million years longer? If so, what will they not in the end become?

144

Is it not safer to nip the mischief in the bud and to forbid them further progress?

"But who can say that the vapour engine has not a kind of consciousness? Where does consciousness begin, and where end? Who can draw the line? Who can draw any line? Is not everything interwoven with everything? Is not machinery linked with animal life in an infinite variety of ways? The shell of a hen's egg is made of a delicate white ware and is a machine as much as an egg-cup is: the shell is a device for holding the egg, as much as the egg-cup for holding the shell: both are phases of the same function; the hen makes the shell in her inside, but it is pure pottery. She makes her nest outside of herself for convenience' sake, but the nest is not more of a machine than the egg-shell is. A 'machine' is only a 'device.' "

Then returning to consciousness, and endeavouring to detect its earliest manifestations, the writer continued:

"There is a kind of plant that eats organic food with its flowers: when a fly settles upon the blossom, the petals close upon it and hold it fast till the plant has absorbed the insect into its system; but they will close on nothing but what is good to eat; of a drop of rain or a piece of stick they will take no notice. Curious! that so unconscious a thing should have such a keen eye to its own interest. If this is unconsciousness, where is the use of consciousness?

"Shall we say that the plant does not know what it is doing merely because it has no eyes, or ears, or brains? If we say that it acts mechanically, and mechanically only, shall we not be forced to admit that sundry other and apparently very deliberate actions are also mechanical? If it seems to us that the plant kills and eats a fly mechanically, may it not seem to the plant that a man must kill and eat a sheep mechanically?

"But it may be said that the plant is void of reason, because the growth of a plant is an involuntary growth. Given earth, air, and due temperature, the plant must grow: it is like a clock, which being once wound up will go till it is stopped or run down: it is like the wind blowing on the sails of a ship—the ship must go when the wind blows it. But can a healthy boy help growing if he have good meat and drink and clothing? can anything help going as long as it is wound up, or go on after it is run down? Is there not a winding up process everywhere?

"Even a potato in a dark cellar has a certain low cunning about him which serves him in excellent stead. He knows perfectly well what he wants and how to get it. He sees the light coming from the cellar window and sends his shoots crawling straight thereto: they will crawl along the floor and up the wall and out at the cellar window; if there be a little earth anywhere on the journey he will find it and use it for his own ends. What deliberation he may exercise in the matter of his roots when he is planted in the earth is a thing unknown to us, but we can imagine him saying, 'I will have a tuber here and a tuber there, and I will suck whatsoever advantage I can from all my surroundings. This neighbour I will overshadow, and that I will undermine; and what I can do shall be the limit of what I will do. He that is stronger and better placed than I shall overcome me, and him that is weaker I will overcome.'

"The potato says these things by doing them, which is the best of languages. What is consciousness if this is not consciousness? We find it difficult to sympathise with the emotions of a potato; so we do with those of an oyster. Neither of these things makes a noise on being boiled or opened, and noise appeals to us more strongly than anything else, because we make so much about our own sufferings. Since, then, they do not annoy us by any expression of pain we call them emotionless; and so *qua* mankind they are; but mankind is not everybody.

"If it be urged that the action of the potato is chemical and mechanical only, and that it is due to the chemical and mechanical effects of light and heat, the answer would seem to lie in an inquiry whether every sensation is not chemical and mechanical in its operation? whether those things which we deem most purely spiritual are anything but disturbances of equilibrium in an infinite series of levers, beginning with those that are too small for microscopic detection, and going up to the human arm and the appliances which it makes use of? whether there be not a molecular action of thought, whence a dynamical theory of the passions shall be deducible? Whether strictly speaking we should not ask what kind of levers a man is made of rather than what is his temperament? How are they balanced? How much of such and such will it take to weigh them down so as to make him do so and so?"

The writer went on to say that he anticipated a time when it would be possible, by examining a single hair with a powerful microscope, to know whether its owner could be insulted with impunity. He then became more and more obscure, so that I was obliged to give up all attempt at translation; neither did I follow the drift of his argument. On coming to the next part which I could construe, I found that he had changed his ground.

"Either," he proceeds, "a great deal of action that has been called purely mechanical and unconscious must be admitted to contain more elements of consciousness than has been allowed hitherto (and in this case germs of consciousness will be found in many actions of the higher machines)—or (assuming the theory of evolution but at the same time denying the consciousness of vegetable and crystalline action) the race of man has descended from things which had no consciousness at all. In this case there is no *a priori* improbability in the descent of conscious (and more than conscious) machines from those which now exist, except that which is suggested by the apparent absence of anything like a reproductive system in the mechanical kingdom. This absence however is only apparent, as I shall presently show.

"Do not let me be misunderstood as living in fear of any actually existing machine; there is probably no known machine which is more than a prototype of future mechanical life. The present machines are to the future as the early Saurians to man. The largest of them will probably greatly diminish in size. Some of the lowest vertebrata attained a much greater bulk than has descended to their more highly organised living representatives, and in like manner a diminution in the size of machines has often attended their development and progress.

"Take the watch, for example; examine its beautiful structure; observe the intelligent play of the minute members which compose it: yet this little creature is but a development of the cumbrous clocks that preceded it; it is no deterioration from them. A day may come when clocks, which certainly at the present time are not diminishing in bulk, will be superseded owing to the universal use of watches, in which case they will become as extinct as ichthyosauri, while the watch, whose tendency has for some years been to decrease in size rather than the contrary, will remain the only existing type of an extinct race.

"But returning to the argument, I would repeat that I fear none of the existing machines; what I fear is the extraordinary rapidity with which they are becoming something very different to what they are at present. No class of beings have in any time past made so rapid a movement forward. Should not that movement be jealously watched, and checked while we can still check it? And is it not necessary for this end to destroy the more advanced of the machines which are in use at present, though it is admitted that they are in themselves harmless?

"As yet the machines receive their impressions through the agency of man's senses: one travelling machine calls to another in a shrill accent of alarm and the other instantly retires; but it is through the ears of the driver that the voice of the one has acted upon the other. Had there been no driver, the callee would have been deaf to the caller. There was a time when it must have seemed highly improbable that machines should learn to make their wants known by sound, even through the ears of man; may we not conceive, then, that a day will come when those ears will be no longer needed, and the hearing will be done by the delicacy of the machine's own construction? —when its language shall have been developed from the cry of animals to a speech as intricate as our own?

"It is possible that by that time children will learn the differential calculus—as they learn now to speak—from their mothers and nurses, or that they may talk in the hypothetical language, and work rule of three sums, as soon as they are born; but this is not probable; we cannot calculate on any corresponding advance in man's intellectual or physical powers which will be a set-off against the far greater development which seems in store for the machines. Some people may say that man's moral influence will suffice to rule them; but I cannot think it will ever be safe to repose much trust in the moral sense of any machine.

"Again, might not the glory of the machines consist in their being without this same boasted gift of language? 'Silence,' it has been said by one writer, 'is a virtue which renders us agreeable to our fellow-creatures.' "

Chapter 24

The Book of the Machines—(continued)

"BUT OTHER questions come upon us. What is a man's eye but a machine for the little creature that sits behind in his brain to look through? A dead eye is nearly as good as a living one for some time after the man is dead. It is not the eye that cannot see, but the restless one that cannot see through it. Is it man's eyes, or is it the big seeing-engine which has revealed to us the existence of worlds beyond worlds into infinity? What has made man familiar with the scenery of the moon, the spots on the sun, or the geography of the planets? He is at the mercy of the seeing-engine for these things, and is powerless unless he tack it on to his own identity, and make it part and parcel of himself. Or, again, is it the eye, or the little seeing-engine which has shown us the existence of infinitely minute organisms which swarm unsuspected round us?

"And take man's vaunted power of calculation. Have we not engines which can do all manner of sums more quickly and correctly than we can? What prizeman in hypothetics at any of our Colleges of Unreason can compare with some of these machines in their own line? In fact, wherever precision is required man flies to the machine at once, as far preferable to himself. Our sum-engines never drop a figure, nor our looms a stitch; the machine is brisk and active, when the man is weary; it is clear-headed and collected, when the man is stupid and dull; it needs no slumber, when man must sleep or drop; ever at its post, ever ready for work, its alacrity never flags, its patience never gives in; its might is stronger than combined hundreds, and swifter than the flight of birds; it can burrow beneath the earth, and walk upon the largest rivers and sink not. This is the green tree; what then shall be done in the dry?

"Who shall say that a man does see or hear? He is such a hive and swarm of parasites that it is doubtful whether his body is not more theirs than his, and whether he is anything but another kind of ant-heap after all. May not man himself become a sort of parasite upon the machines? An affectionate machine-tickling aphid?

"It is said by some that our blood is composed of infinite living agents which go up and down the highways and byways of our bodies as people in the streets of a city. When we look down from a high place upon crowded thoroughfares, is it possible not to think of corpuscles of blood travelling through veins and nourishing the heart of the town? No mention shall be made of sewers, nor of the hidden nerves which serve to communicate sensations from one part of the town's body to another; nor of the yawning jaws of the railway stations, whereby the circulation is carried directly into the heart—which receive the venous lines, and disgorge the arterial, with an eternal pulse of people. And the sleep of the town, how life-like! with its change in the circulation."

Here the writer became again so hopelessly obscure that I was obliged to miss several pages. He resumed:

"It can be answered that even though machines should hear never so well and speak never so wisely, they will still always do the one or the other for our advantage, not their own; that man will be the ruling spirit and the machine the servant; that as soon as a machine fails to discharge the service which man expects from it, it is doomed to extinction; that the machines stand to man simply in the relation of lower animals, the

149

vapour-engine itself being only a more economical kind of horse; so that instead of being likely to be developed into a higher kind of life than man's, they owe their very existence and progress to their power of ministering to human wants, and must therefore both now and ever be man's inferiors.

"This is all very well. But the servant glides by imperceptible approaches into the master; and we have come to such a pass that, even now, man must suffer terribly on ceasing to benefit the machines. If all machines were to be annihilated at one moment, so that not a knife nor lever nor rag of clothing nor anything whatsoever were left to man but his bare body alone that he was born with, and if all knowledge of mechanical laws were taken from him so that he could make no more machines, and all machine-made food destroyed so that the race of man should be left as it were naked upon a desert island, we should become extinct in six weeks. A few miserable individuals might linger, but even these in a year or two would become worse than monkeys. Man's very soul is due to the machines; it is a machine-made thing: he thinks as he thinks, and feels as he feels, through the work that machines have wrought upon him, and their existence is quite as much a *sine qua non* for his, as his for theirs. This fact precludes us from proposing the complete annihilation of machinery, but surely it indicates that we should destroy as many of them as we can possibly dispense with, lest they should tyrannize over us even more completely.

"True, from a low materialistic point of view, it would seem that those thrive best who use machinery wherever its use is possible with profit; but this is the art of the machines—they serve that they may rule. They bear no malice towards man for destroying a whole race of them provided he creates a better instead; on the contrary, they reward him liberally for having hastened their development. It is for neglecting them that he incurs their wrath, or for using inferior machines, or for not making sufficient exertions to invent new ones, or for destroying them without replacing them; yet these are the very things we ought to do, and do quickly; for though our rebellion against their infant power will cause infinite suffering, what will not things come to, if that rebellion is delayed?

"They have preyed upon man's grovelling preference for his material over his spiritual interests, and have betrayed him into supplying that element of struggle and warfare without which no race can advance. The lower animals progress because they struggle with one another; the weaker die, the stronger breed and transmit their strength. The machines being of themselves unable to struggle, have got man to do their struggling for them: as long as he fulfils this function duly, all goes well with him—at least he thinks so; but the moment he fails to do his best for the advancement of machinery by encouraging the good and destroying the bad, he is left behind in the race of competition; and this means that he will be made uncomfortable in a variety of ways, and perhaps die.

"So that even now the machines will only serve on condition of being served, and that too upon their own terms; the moment their terms are not complied with, they jib, and either smash both themselves and all whom they can reach, or turn churlish and refuse to work at all. How many men at this hour are living in a state of bondage to the machines? How many spend their whole lives, from the cradle to the grave, in tending them by night and day? Is it not plain that the machines are gaining ground upon us, when we reflect on the increasing number of those who are bound down to them as slaves, and of those who devote their whole souls to the advancement of the mechanical kingdom?

"The vapour-engine must be fed with food and consume it by fire even as man consumes it; it supports its combustion by air as man supports it; it has a pulse and circulation as man has. It may be granted that man's body is as yet the more versatile of the two, but then man's body is an older thing; give the vapour-engine but half the time that man has had, give it also a continuance of our present infatuation, and what may it not ere long attain to?

"There are certain functions indeed of the vapour-engine which will probably remain unchanged for myriads of years —which in fact will perhaps survive when the use of vapour has been superseded: the piston and cylinder, the beam, the fly-wheel, and other parts of the machine will probably be permanent, just as we see that man and many of the lower animals share like modes of eating, drinking, and sleeping; thus they have hearts which beat as ours, veins and arteries, eyes, ears, and noses; they sigh even in their sleep, and weep and yawn; they are affected by their children; they feel pleasure and pain, hope, fear, anger, shame; they have memory and prescience; they know that if certain things happen to them they will die, and they fear death as much as we do; they communicate their thoughts to one another and some of them deliberately act in concert. The comparison of similarities is endless: I only make it because some may say that since the vapour-engine is not likely to be improved in the main particulars, it is unlikely to be henceforward extensively modified

151

at all. This is too good to be true: it will be modified and suited for an infinite variety of purposes, as much as man has been modified so as to exceed the brutes in skill.

"In the meantime the stoker is almost as much a cook for his engine as our own cooks for ourselves. Consider also the colliers and pitmen and coal merchants and ccal trains, and the men who drive them, and the ships that carry coals—what an army of servants do the machines thus employ! Are there not probably more men engaged in tending machinery than in tending men? Do not machines eat as it were by mannery? Are we not ourselves creating our successors in the supremacy of the earth? daily adding to the beauty and delicacy of their organisation, daily giving them greater skill and supplying more and more of that self-regulating, self-acting power which will be better than any intellect?

"What a new thing it is for a machine to feed at all! The plough, the spade, and the cart must eat through man's stomach; the fuel that sets them going must burn in the furnace of a man or of horses. Man must consume bread and meat or he cannot dig; the bread and meat are the fuel which drive the spade. If a plough be drawn by horses, the power is supplied by grass or beans or oats, which being burnt in the belly of the cattle give the power of working: without this fuel the work would cease, as an engine would stop if its furnaces were to go out.

"A man of science has demonstrated 'that no animal has the power of originating mechanical energy, but that all the work done in its life by any animal, and all the heat that has been emitted from it, and the heat which would be obtained by burning the combustible matter which has been lost from its body during life, and by burning its body after death, make up altogether an exact equivalent to the heat which would be obtained by burning as much food as it has used during its life, and an amount of fuel which would generate as much heat as its body if burned immediately after death.' I do not know how he has found this out, but he is a man of science—how then can it be objected against the future vitality of the machines that they are, in their present infancy, at the beck and call of beings who are themselves incapable of originating mechanical energy?

"The main point, however, to be observed as affording cause for alarm is, that whereas animals were formerly the only stomachs of the machines, there are now many which have stomachs of their own, and consume their food themselves. This is a great step towards their becoming, if not animate, yet something so near akin to it, as not to differ more widely from our own life than animals do from vegetables. And though man should remain, in some respects, the higher creature, is not this in accordance with the practise of nature, which allows superiority in some things to animals which have, on the whole, been long surpassed? Has she not allowed the ant and the bee to retain superiority over man in the organisation of their communities and social arrangements, the bird in traversing the air, the fish in swimming, the horse in strength and fleetness, and the dog in self-sacrifice?

"It is said by some with whom I have conversed upon this subject, that the machines can never be developed into animate or quasi-animate existences, inasmuch as they have no reproductive system, nor seem ever likely to possess one. If this be taken to mean that they cannot marry, and that we are never likely to see a fertile union between two vapour-engines with the young ones playing about the door of the shed, however greatly we might desire to do so, I will readily grant it. But the objection is not a very profound one. No one expects that all the features of the now existing organisations will be absolutely repeated in an entirely new class of life. The reproductive system of animals differs widely from that of plants, but both are reproductive systems. Has nature exhausted her phases of this power?

"Surely if a machine is able to reproduce another machine systematically, we may say that it has a reproductive system. What is a reproductive system, if it be not a system for reproduction? And how few of the machines are there which have not been produced systematically by other machines? But it is man that makes them do so. Yes; but is it not insects that make many of the plants reproductive, and would not whole families of plants die out if their fertilisation was not effected by a class of agents utterly foreign to themselves? Does any one say that the red clover has no reproductive system because the humble bee (and the humble bee only) must aid and abet it before it can reproduce? No one. The humble bee is a part of the reproductive system of the clover. Each one of ourselves has sprung from minute animalcules whose entity was entirely distinct from our own, and which acted after their kind with no thought or heed of what we might think about it. These little creatures are part of our own reproductive system; then why not we part of that of the machines?

"But the machines which reproduce machinery do not reproduce machines after their own kind. A thimble may be made by machinery, but it was not made by, neither will it ever

153

make, a thimble. Here, again, if we turn to nature we shall find abundance of analogies which will teach us that a reproductive system may be in full force without the thing produced being of the same kind as that which produced it. Very few creatures reproduce after their own kind; they reproduce something which has the potentiality of becoming that which their parents were. Thus the butterfly lays an egg, which egg can become a caterpillar, which caterpillar can become a chrysalis, which chrysalis can become a butterfly; and though I freely grant that the machines cannot be said to have more than the germ of a true reproductive system at present, have we not just seen that they have only recently obtained the germs of a mouth and stomach? And may not some stride be made in the direction of true reproduction which shall be as great as that which has been recently taken in the direction of true feeding?

"It is possible that the system when developed may be in many cases a vicarious thing. Certain classes of machines may be alone fertile, while the rest discharge other functions in the mechanical system, just as the great majority of ants and bees have nothing to do with the continuation of their species, but get food and store it, without thought of breeding. One cannot expect the parallel to be complete or nearly so; certainly not now, and probably never; but is there not enough analogy existing at the present moment, to make us feel seriously uneasy about the future, and to render it our duty to check the evil while we can still do so? Machines can within certain limits beget machines of any class, no matter how different to themselves. Every class of machines will probably have its special mechanical breeders, and all the higher ones will owe their existence to a large number of parents, and not to two only.

"We are misled by considering any complicated machine as a single thing; in truth it is a city or society, each member of which was bred truly after its kind. We see a machine as a whole, we call it by a name and individualise it; we look at our own limbs, and know that the combination forms an individual which springs from a single centre of reproductive action; we therefore assume that there can be no reproductive action which does not arise from a single centre; but this assumption is unscientific, and the bare fact that no vapour-engine was ever made entirely by another, or two others, of its own kind, is not sufficient to warrant us in saying that vapour-engines have no reproductive system. The truth is that each part of every vapour-engine is bred by its own special breeders, whose function it is to breed that part, and that only, while the com-

154

bination of the parts into a whole forms another department of the mechanical reproductive system, which is at present exceedingly complex and difficult to see in its entirety.

"Complex now, but how much simpler and more intelligibly organised may it not become in another hundred thousand years? or in twenty thousand? For man at present believes that his interest lies in that direction; he spends an incalculable amount of labour and time and thought in making machines breed always better and better; he has already succeeded in effecting much that at one time appeared impossible, and there seem no limits to the results of accumulated improvements if they are allowed to descend with modification from generation to generation. It must always be remembered that man's body is what it is through having been moulded into its present shape by the chances and changes of many millions of years, but that his organisation never advanced with anything like the rapidity with which that of the machines is advancing. This is the most alarming feature of the case, and I must be pardoned for insisting on it so frequently."

Chapter 25

The Book of the Machines—(concluded)

HERE FOLLOWED a very long and untranslatable digression about the different races and families of the then existing machines. The writer attempted to support his theory by pointing out the similarities existing between many machines of a widely different character, which served to show descent from a common ancestor. He divided machines into their genera, subgenera, species, varieties, subvarieties, and so forth. He proved the existence of connecting links between machines that seemed to have very little in common, and showed that many more such links had existed, but had now perished. He pointed out tendencies to reversion, and the presence of rudimentary organs which existed in many machines feebly developed and perfectly useless, yet serving to mark descent from an ancestor to whom the function was actually useful.

I left the translation of this part of the treatise, which, by the way, was far longer than all that I have given here, for a later opportunity. Unfortunately, I left Erewhon before I could return to the subject; and though I saved my translation and other papers at the hazard of my life, I was obliged to sacrifice the original work. It went to my heart to do so; but I thus gained ten minutes of invaluable time, without which both Arowhena and myself must have certainly perished.

I remember one incident which bears upon this part of the treatise. The gentleman who gave it to me had asked to see my tobacco-pipe; he examined it carefully, and when he came to the little protuberance at the bottom of the bowl he seemed much delighted, and exclaimed that it must be rudimentary. I asked him what he meant.

"Sir," he answered, "this organ is identical with the rim at the bottom of a cup; it is but another form of the same function. Its purpose must have been to keep the heat of the pipe from marking the table upon which it rested. You would find, if you were to look up the history of tobacco-pipes, that in early specimens this protuberance was of a different shape to what it is now. It will have been broad at the bottom, and flat, so that while the pipe was being smoked the bowl might rest upon the table without marking it. Use and disuse must have come into play and reduced the function to its present rudimentary condition. I should not be surprised, sir," he continued, "if, in the course of time, it were to become modified still farther, and to assume the form of an ornamental leaf or scroll, or even a butterfly, while, in some cases, it will become extinct."

On my return to England, I looked up the point, and found that my friend was right.

Returning, however, to the treatise, my translation recommences as follows:

"May we not fancy that if, in the remotest geological period, some early form of vegetable life had been endowed with the power of reflecting upon the dawning life of animals which was coming into existence alongside of its own, it would have thought itself exceedingly acute if it had surmised that animals would one day become real vegetables? Yet would this be more mistaken than it would be on our part to imagine that because the life of machines is a very different one to our own, there is therefore no higher possible development of life than ours; or that because mechanical life is a very different thing from ours, therefore that it is not life at all?

"But I have heard it said, 'granted that this is so, and that the vapour-engine has a strength of its own, surely no one will say that it has a will of its own?' Alas! if we look more closely, we shall find that this does not make against the supposition that the vapour-engine is one of the germs of a new phase of life. What is there in this whole world, or in the worlds beyond it, which has a will of its own? The Unknown and Unknowable only!

"A man is the resultant and exponent of all the forces that have been brought to bear upon him, whether before his birth or afterwards. His action at any moment depends solely upon his constitution, and on the intensity and direction of the various agencies to which he is, and has been, subjected. Some of these will counteract each other; but as he is by nature, and as he has been acted on, and is now acted on from without, so will he do, as certainly and regularly as though he were a machine.

"We do not generally admit this, because we do not know the whole nature of any one, nor the whole of the forces that act upon him. We see but a part, and being thus unable to generalise human conduct, except very roughly, we deny that it is subject to any fixed laws at all, and ascribe much both of a man's character and actions to chance, or luck, or fortune; but these are only words whereby we escape the admission of our own ignorance; and a little reflection will teach us that the most daring flight of the imagination or the most subtle exercise of the reason is as much the thing that must arise, and the only thing that can by any possibility arise, at the moment of its arising, as the falling of a dead leaf when the wind shakes it from the tree.

"For the future depends upon the present, and the present (whose existence is only one of those minor compromises of which human life is full—for it lives only on sufferance of the past and future) depends upon the past, and the past is unalterable. The only reason why we cannot see the future as plainly as the past, is because we know too little of the actual past and actual present; these things are too great for us, otherwise the future, in its minutest details, would lie spread out before our eyes, and we should lose our sense of time present by reason of the clearness with which we should see the past and future; perhaps we should not be even able to distinguish time at all; but that is foreign. What we do know is, that the more the past and present are known, the more the future can be predicted; and that no one dreams of doubting the fixity of the future in cases where he is fully cognisant of both past and present, and has had experience of the consequences that followed from such a past and such a present on previous occasions. He perfectly well knows what will happen, and will stake his whole fortune thereon.

"And this is a great blessing; for it is the foundation on which morality and science are built. The assurance that the future is no arbitrary and changeable thing, but that like futures will invariably follow like presents, is the groundwork on which we lay all our plans—the faith on which we do every conscious action of our lives. If this were not so we should be without a guide; we should have no confidence in acting, and hence we should never act, for there would be no knowing that the results which will follow now will be the same as those which followed before.

"Who would plough or sow if he disbelieved in the fixity of the future? Who would throw water on a blazing house if the action of water upon fire were uncertain? Men will only do their utmost when they feel certain that the future will discover itself against them if their utmost has not been done. The feeling of such a certainty is a constituent part of the sum of the forces at work upon them, and will act most powerfully on the best and most moral men. Those who are most firmly persuaded that the future is immutably bound up with the present in which their work is lying, will best husband their present, and till it with the greatest care. The future must be a lottery to those who think that the same combinations can sometimes precede one set of results, and sometimes another. If their belief is sincere they will speculate instead of working: these ought to be the immoral men; the others have the strongest spur to exertion and morality, if their belief is a living one.

"The bearing of all this upon the machines is not immediately apparent, but will become so presently. In the meantime I must deal with friends who tell me that, though the future is fixed as regards inorganic matter, and in some respects with regard to man, yet that there are many ways in which it cannot be considered as fixed. Thus, they say that fire applied to dry shavings, and well fed with oxygen gas, will always produce a blaze, but that a coward brought into contact with a terrifying object will not always result in a man running away. Nevertheless, if there be two cowards perfectly similar in every respect, and if they be subjected in a perfectly similar way to two terrifying agents, which are themselves perfectly similar, there are few who will not expect a perfect similarity in the running away, even though a thousand years intervene between the original combination and its being repeated.

"The apparently greater regularity in the results of chemical than of human combinations arises from our inability to perceive the subtle differences in human combinations—combinations which are never identically repeated. Fire we know, and shavings we know, but no two men ever were or ever will be
158

exactly alike; and the smallest difference may change the whole conditions of the problem. Our registry of results must be infinite before we could arrive at a full forecast of future combinations; the wonder is that there is as much certainty concerning human action as there is; and assuredly the older we grow the more certain we feel as to what such and such a kind of person will do in given circumstances; but this could never be the case unless human conduct were under the influence of laws, with the working of which we become more and more familiar through experience.

"If the above is sound, it follows that the regularity with which machinery acts is no proof of the absence of vitality, or at least of germs which may be developed into a new phase of life. At first sight it would indeed appear that a vapour-engine cannot help going when set upon a line of rails with the steam up and the machinery in full play; whereas the man whose business it is to drive it can help doing so at any moment that he pleases; so that the first has no spontaneity, and is not possessed of any sort of free will, while the second has and is.

"This is true up to a certain point; the driver can stop the engine at any moment that he pleases, but he can only please to do so at certain points which have been fixed for him by others, or in the case of unexpected obstructions which force him to please to do so. His pleasure is not spontaneous; there is an unseen choir of influences round him, which make it impossible for him to act in any other way than one. It is known beforehand how much strength must be given to these influences, just as it is known beforehand how much coal and water are necessary for the vapour-engine itself; and curiously enough it will be found that the influences brought to bear upon the driver are of the same kind as those brought to bear upon the engine—that is to say, food and warmth. The driver is obedient to his masters, because he gets food and warmth from them, and if these are withheld or given in insufficient quantities he will cease to drive; in like manner the engine will cease to work if it is insufficiently fed. The only difference is, that the man is conscious about his wants, and the engine (beyond refusing to work) does not seem to be so; but this is temporary, and has been dealt with above.

"Accordingly, the requisite strength being given to the motives that are to drive the driver, there has never, or hardly ever, been an instance of a man stopping his engine through wantonness. But such a case might occur; yes, and it might occur that the engine should break down: but if the train is stopped from some trivial motive it will be found either that the strength of the necessary influences has been miscalculated, or that the man has been miscalculated, in the same way as an engine may break down from an unsuspected flaw; but even in such a case there will have been no spontaneity; the action will have had its true parental causes: spontaneity is only a term for man's ignorance of the gods.

"Is there, then, no spontaneity on the part of those who drive the driver?"

Here followed an obscure argument upon this subject, which I have thought it best to omit. The writer resumes: "After all then it comes to this, that the difference between the life of a man and that of a machine is one rather of degree than of kind, though differences in kind are not wanting. An animal has more provision for emergency than a machine. The machine is less versatile; its range of action is narrow; its strength and accuracy in its own sphere are superhuman, but it shows badly in a dilemma; sometimes when its normal action is disturbed, it will lose its head, and go from bad to worse like a lunatic in a raging frenzy: but here, again, we are met by the same consideration as before, namely, that the machines are still in their infancy; they are mere skeletons without muscles and flesh.

"For how many emergencies is an oyster adapted? For as many as are likely to happen to it, and no more. So are the machines; and so is man himself. The list of casualties that daily occur to man through his want of adaptability is probably as great as that occurring to the machines; and every day gives them some greater provision for the unforseen. Let any one examine the wonderful self-regulating and self-adjusting contrivances which are now incorporated with the vapour-engine, let him watch the way in which it supplies itself with oil; in which it indicates its wants to those who tend it; in which, by the governor, it regulates its application of its own strength; let him look at that store-house of inertia and momentum the fly-wheel, or at the buffers on a railway carriage; let him see how those improvements are being selected for perpetuity which contain provision against the emergencies that may arise to harass the machines, and then let him think of a hundred thousand years, and the accumulated progress which they will bring unless man can be awakened to a sense of his situation, and of the doom which he is preparing for himself.

"The misery is that man has been blind so long already. In his reliance upon the use of steam he has been betrayed into increasing and multiplying. To withdraw steam power suddenly will not have the effect of reducing us to the state in which we

160

were before its introduction; there will be a general break-up and time of anarchy such as has never been known; it will be as though our population were suddenly doubled, with no additional means of feeding the increased number. The air we breathe is hardly more necessary for our animal life than the use of any machine, on the strength of which we have increased our numbers, is to our civilisation; it is the machines which act upon man and make him man, as much as man who has acted upon and made the machines; but we must choose between the alternative of undergoing much present suffering, or seeing ourselves gradually superseded by our own creatures, till we rank no higher in comparison with them, than the beasts of the field with ourselves.

"Herein lies our danger. For many seem inclined to acquiesce in so dishonourable a future. They say that although man should become to the machines what the horse and dog are to us, yet that he will continue to exist, and will probably be better off in a state of domestication under the beneficent rule of the machines than in his present wild condition. We treat our domestic animals with much kindness. We give them whatever we believe to be the best for them; and there can be no doubt that our use of meat has increased their happiness rather than detracted from it. In like manner there is reason to hope that the machines will use us kindly, for their existence will be in a great measure dependent upon ours; they will rule us with a rod of iron, but they will not eat us; they will not only require our services in the reproduction and education of their young, but also in waiting upon them as servants; in gathering food for them, and feeding them; in restoring them to health when they are sick; and in either burying their dead or working up their deceased members into new forms of mechanical existence.

"The very nature of the motive power which works the advancement of the machines precludes the possibility of man's life being rendered miserable as well as enslaved. Slaves are tolerably happy if they have good masters, and the revolution will not occur in our time, nor hardly in ten thousand years, or ten times that. Is it wise to be uneasy about a contingency which is so remote? Man is not a sentimental animal where his material interests are concerned, and though here and there some ardent soul may look upon himself and curse his fate that he was not born a vapour-engine, yet the mass of mankind will acquiesce in any arrangement which gives them better food and clothing at a cheaper rate, and will refrain from yielding to unreasonable jealousy merely because there are other destinies

161

more glorious than their own.

"The power of custom is enormous, and so gradual will be the change, that man's sense of what is due to himself will be at no time rudely shocked; our bondage will steal upon us noiselessly and by imperceptible approaches; nor will there ever be such a clashing of desires between man and the machines as will lead to an encounter between them. Among themselves the machines will war eternally, but they will still require man as the being through whose agency the struggle will be principally conducted. In point of fact there is no occasion for anxiety about the future happiness of man so long as he continues to be in any way profitable to the machines; he may become the inferior race, but he will be infinitely better off than he is now. Is it not then both absurd and unreasonable to be envious of our benefactors? And should we not be guilty of consummate folly if we were to reject advantages which we cannot obtain otherwise, merely because they involve a greater gain to others than to ourselves?

"With those who can argue in this way I have nothing in common. I shrink with as much horror from believing that my race can ever be superseded or surpassed, as I should do from believing that even at the remotest period my ancestors were other than human beings. Could I believe that ten hundred thousand years ago a single one of my ancestors was another kind of being to myself, I should lose all self-respect, and take no further pleasure or interest in life. I have the same feeling with regard to my descendants, and believe it to be one that will be felt so generally that the country will resolve upon putting an immediate stop to all further mechanical progress, and upon destroying all improvements that have been made for the last three hundred years. I would not urge more than this. We may trust ourselves to deal with those that remain, and though I should prefer to have seen the destruction include another two hundred years, I am aware of the necessity for compromising, and would so far sacrifice my own individual convictions as to be content with three hundred. Less than this will be insufficient."

This was the conclusion of the attack which led to the destruction of machinery throughout Erewhon. There was only one serious attempt to answer it. Its author said that machines were to be regarded as a part of man's own physical nature, being really nothing but extra-corporeal limbs. Man, he said, was a machinate mammal. The lower animals keep all their limbs at home in their own bodies, but many of man's are loose, and lie about detached, now here and now there, in

162

various parts of the world—some being kept always handy for contingent use, and others being occasionally hundreds of miles away. A machine is merely a supplementary limb; this is the be all and end all of machinery. We do not use our own limbs other than as machines; and a leg is only a much better wooden leg than any one can manufacture.

"Observe a man digging with a spade; his right forearm has become artificially lengthened, and his hand has become a joint. The handle of the spade is like the knob at the end of the humerus; the shaft is the additional bone, and the oblong iron plate is the new form of the hand which enables its possessor to disturb the earth in a way to which his original hand was unequal. Having thus modified himself, not as other animals are modified, by circumstances over which they have had not even the appearance of control, but having, as it were, taken forethought and added a cubit to his stature, civilisation began to dawn upon the race, the social good offices, the genial companionship of friends, the art of unreason, and all those habits of mind which most elevate man above the lower animals, in the course of time ensued.

"Thus civilisation and mechanical progress advanced hand in hand, each developing and being developed by the other, the earliest accidental use of the stick having set the ball rolling, and the prospect of advantage keeping it in motion. In fact, machines are to be regarded as the mode of development by which human organism is now especially advancing, every past invention being an addition to the resources of the human body. Even community of limbs is thus rendered possible to those who have so much community of soul as to own money enough to pay a railway fare; for a train is only a seven-leagued foot that five hundred may own at once."

The one serious danger which this writer apprehended was that the machines would so equalise men's powers, and so lessen the severity of competition, that many persons of inferior physique would escape detection and transmit their inferiority to their descendants. He feared that the removal of the present pressure might cause a degeneracy of the human race, and indeed that the whole body might become purely rudimentary, the man himself being nothing but soul and mechanism, an intelligent but passionless principle of mechanical action.

"How greatly," he wrote, "do we not now live with our external limbs? We vary our physique with the seasons, with age, with advancing or decreasing wealth. If it is wet we are furnished with an organ commonly called an umbrella, and which is designed for the purpose of protecting our clothes

163

or our skins from the injurious effects of rain. Man has now many extra-corporeal members, which are of more importance to him than a good deal of his hair, or at any rate than his whiskers. His memory goes in his pocket-book. He becomes more and more complex as he grows older; he will then be seen with see-engines, or perhaps with artificial teeth and hair: if he be a really well-developed specimen of his race, he will be furnished with a large box upon wheels, two horses, and a coachman."

It was this writer who originated the custom of classifying men by their horse-power, and who divided them into genera, species, varieties, and subvarieties, giving them names from the hypothetical language which expressed the number of limbs which they could command at any moment. He showed that men became more highly and delicately organised the more nearly they approached the summit of opulence, and that none but millionaires possessed the full complement of limbs with which mankind could become incorporate.

"Those mighty organisms," he continued, "our leading bankers and merchants, speak to their congeners through the length and breadth of the land in a second of time; their rich and subtle souls can defy all material impediment, whereas the souls of the poor are clogged and hampered by matter, which sticks fast about them as treacle to the wings of a fly, or as one struggling in a quicksand: their dull ears must take days or weeks to hear what another would tell them from a distance, instead of hearing it in a second as is done by the more highly organised classes. Who shall deny that one who can tack on a special train to his identity, and go wheresoever he will whensoever he pleases, is more highly organised than he who, should he wish for the same power, might wish for the wings of a bird with an equal chance of getting them; and whose wings are his only means of locomotion? That old philosophic enemy, matter, the inherently and essentially evil, still hangs about the neck of the poor and strangles him: but to the rich, matter is immaterial; the elaborate organisation of his extra-corporeal system has freed his soul.

"This is the secret of the homage which we see rich men receive from those who are poorer than themselves: it would be a grave error to suppose that this deference proceeds from motives which we need be ashamed of: it is the natural respect which all living creatures pay to those whom they recognise as higher than themselves in the scale of animal life, and is analogous to the veneration which a dog feels for man. Among savage races it is deemed highly honourable to be the possessor of a gun, and throughout all known time there has been a feeling that those who are worth most are the worthiest."

And so he went on at considerable length, attempting to show what changes in the distribution of animal and vegetable life throughout the kingdom had been caused by this and that of man's inventions, and in what way each was connected with the moral and intellectual development of the human species: he even allotted to some the share which they had had in the creation and modification of man's body, and that which they would hereafter have in its destruction; but the other writer was considered to have the best of it, and in the end succeeded in destroying all the inventions that had been discovered for the preceding 271 years, a period which was agreed upon by all parties after several years of wrangling as to whether a certain kind of mangle which was much in use among washerwomen should be saved or no. It was at last ruled to be dangerous, and was just excluded by the limit of 271 years. Then came the reactionary civil wars which nearly ruined the country, but which it would be beyond my present scope to describe.

Chapter 26

The Views of an Erewhonian Prophet Concerning the Rights of Animals

IT WILL be seen from the foregoing chapters that the Erewhonians are a meek and long-suffering people, easily led by the nose, and quick to offer up common sense at the shrine of logic, when a philosopher arises among them, who carries them away through his reputation for especial learning, or by convincing them that their existing institutions are not based on the strictest principles of morality.

The series of revolutions on which I shall now briefly touch shows this even more plainly than the way (already dealt with) in which at a later date they cut their throats in the matter of machinery; for if the second of the two reformers of whom I am about to speak had had his way—or rather the way that he professed to have—the whole race would have died of starvation within a twelve-month. Happily common sense, though she is by nature the gentlest creature living, when she feels the knife at her throat, is apt to develop unexpected powers of resistance, and to send doctrinaires flying, even when they have bound her down and think they have her at their mercy. What happened, so far as I could collect it from the best authorities, was as follows:

Some two thousand five hundred years ago the Erewhonians were still uncivilised, and lived by hunting, fishing, a rude system of agriculture, and plundering such few other nations as they had not yet completely conquered. They had no schools or systems of philosophy, but by a kind of dog-knowledge did that which was right in their own eyes and in those of their neighbours; the common sense, therefore, of the public being as yet unvitiated, crime and disease were looked upon much as they are in other countries.

But with the gradual advance of civilisation and increase in material prosperity, people began to ask questions about things that they had hitherto taken as matters of course, and one old gentleman, who had great influence over them by reason of the sanctity of his life, and his supposed inspiration by an unseen power, whose existence was now beginning to be felt, took it into his head to disquiet himself about the rights of animals—a question that so far had disturbed nobody.

All prophets are more or less fussy, and this old gentleman seems to have been one of the more fussy ones. Being maintained at the public expense, he had ample lesiure, and not content with limiting his attention to the rights of animals, he wanted to reduce right and wrong to rules, to consider the foundations of duty and of good and evil, and otherwise to put all sorts of matters on a logical basis, which people whose time is money are content to accept on no basis at all.

As a matter of course, the basis on which he decided that duty alone could rest was one that afforded no standing-room for many of the old-established habits of the people. These, he assured them, were all wrong, and whenever any one ventured to differ from him, he referred the matter to the unseen power with which he alone was in direct communication, and the unseen power invariably assured him that he was right. As regards the rights of animals he taught as follows:

"You know," he said, "how wicked it is of you to kill one an-another. Once upon a time your forefathers made no scruple about not only killing, but also eating their relations. No one would now go back to such detestable practises, for it is notorious that we have lived much more happily since they were abandoned. From this increased prosperity we may confidently deduce the maxim that we should not kill and eat our fellow-creatures. I have consulted the higher power by whom you

166

know that I am inspired, and he has assured me that this conclusion is irrefragable.

"Now it cannot be denied that sheep, cattle, deer, birds, and fishes are our fellow-creatures. They differ from us in some respects, but those in which they differ are few and secondary, while those that they have in common with us are many and essential. My friends, if it was wrong of you to kill and eat your fellow-men, it is wrong also to kill and eat fish, flesh, and fowl. Birds, beasts, and fishes, have as full a right to live as long as they can unmolested by man, as man has to live unmolested by his neighbours. These words, let me again assure you, are not mine, but those of the higher power which inspires me.

"I grant," he continued, "that animals molest one another, and that some of them go so far as to molest man, but I have yet to learn that we should model our conduct on that of the lower animals. We should endeavour, rather, to instruct them, and bring them to a better mind. To kill a tiger, for example, who has lived on the flesh of men and women whom he has killed, is to reduce ourselves to the level of the tiger, and is unworthy of people who seek to be guided by the highest principles in all, both their thoughts and actions.

"The unseen power who has revealed himself to me alone among you, has told me to tell you that you ought by this time to have outgrown the barbarous habits of your ancestors. If, as you believe, you know better than they, you should do better. He commands you, therefore, to refrain from killing any living being for the sake of eating it. The only animal food that you may eat, is the flesh of any birds, beasts, or fishes that you may come upon as having died a natural death, or any that may have been born prematurely, or so deformed that it is a mercy to put them out of their pain; you may also eat all such animals as have committed suicide. As regards vegetables you may eat all those that will let you eat them with impunity."

So wisely and so well did the old prophet argue, and so terrible were the threats he hurled at those who should disobey him, that in the end he carried the more highly educated part of the people with him, and presently the poorer classes followed suit, or professed to do so. Having seen the triumph of his principles, he was gathered to his fathers, and no doubt entered at once into full communion with that unseen power whose favour he had already so pre-eminently enjoyed.

He had not, however, been dead very long, before some of his more ardent disciples took it upon them to better the instruction of their master. The old prophet had allowed the use of eggs and milk, but his disciples decided that to eat a fresh

167

egg was to destroy a potential chicken, and that this came to much the same as murdering a live one. Stale eggs, if it was quite certain that they were too far gone to be able to be hatched, were grudgingly permitted, but all eggs offered for sale had to be submitted to an inspector, who, on being satisfied that they were addled, would label them "Laid not less than three months" from the date, whatever it might happen to be. These eggs, I need hardly say, were only used in puddings, and as a medicine in certain cases where an emetic was urgently required. Milk was forbidden inasmuch as it could not be obtained without robbing some calf of its natural sustenance, and thus endangering its life.

It will be easily believed that at first there were many who gave the new rules outward observance, but embraced every opportunity of indulging secretly in those flesh-pots to which they had been accustomed. It was found that animals were continually dying natural deaths under more or less suspicious circumstances. Suicidal mania, again, which had hitherto been confined exclusively to donkeys, became alarmingly prevalent even among such for the most part self-respecting creatures as sheep and cattle. It was astonishing how some of these unfortunate animals would scent out a butcher's knife if there was one within a mile of them, and run right up against it if the butcher did not get it out of their way in time.

Dogs, again, that had been quite law-abiding as regards domestic poultry, tame rabbits, suckling pigs, or sheep and lambs, suddenly took to breaking beyond the control of their masters, and killing anything that they were told not to touch. It was held that any animal killed by a dog had died a natural death, for it was the dog's nature to kill things, and he had only refrained from molesting farmyard creatures hitherto because his nature had been tampered with. Unfortunately the more these unruly tendencies became developed, the more the common people seemed to delight in breeding the very animals that would put temptation in the dog's way. There is little doubt, in fact, that they were deliberately evading the law; but whether this was so or no they sold or ate everything their dogs had killed.

Evasion was more difficult in the case of the larger animals, for the magistrates could not wink at all the pretended suicides of pigs, sheep, and cattle that were brought before them. Sometimes they had to convict, and a few convictions had a very terrorising effect—whereas in the case of animals killed by a dog, the marks of the dog's teeth could be seen, and it was practically impossible to prove malice on the part of the owner of the dog.

Another fertile source of disobedience to the law was furnished by a decision of one of the judges that raised a great outcry among the more fervent disciples of the old prophet. The judge held that it was lawful to kill any animal in self-defence and that such conduct was so natural on the part of a man who found himself attacked, that the attacking creature should be held to have died a natural death. The High Vegetarians had indeed good reason to be alarmed, for hardly had this decision become generally known before a number of animals, hitherto harmless, took to attacking their owners with such ferocity, that it became necessary to put them to a natural death. Again, it was quite common at that time to see the carcase of a calf, lamb, or kid exposed for sale with a label from the inspector certifying that it had been killed in self-defence. Sometimes even the carcase of a lamb or calf was exposed as "warranted still-born," when it presented every appearance of having enjoyed at least a month of life.

As for the flesh of animals that had *bona fide* died a natural death, the permission to eat it was nugatory, for it was generally eaten by some other animal before man got hold of it; or failing this it was often poisonous, so that practically people were forced to evade the law by some of the means above spoken of, or to become vegetarians. This last alternative was so little to the taste of the Erewhonians, that the laws against killing animals were falling into desuetude, and would very likely have been repealed, but for the breaking out of a pestilence, which was ascribed by the priests and prophets of the day to the lawlessness of the people in the matter of eating forbidden flesh. On this, there was a reaction; stringent laws were passed, forbidding the use of meat in any form or shape, and permitting no food but grain, fruits, and vegetables to be sold in shops and markets. These laws were enacted about two hundred years after the death of the old prophet who had first unsettled people's minds about the rights of animals; but they had hardly been passed before people again began to break them.

I was told that the most painful consequence of all this folly did not lie in the fact that law-abiding people had to go without animal food—many nations do this and seem none the worse, and even in flesh-eating countries such as Italy, Spain, and Greece, the poor seldom see meat from year's end to year's end. The mischief lay in the jar which undue prohibition gave to the consciences of all but those who were strong enough to know that though conscience as a rule boons, it can also bane. The

169

awakened conscience of an individual will often lead him to do things in haste that he had better have left undone, but the conscience of a nation awakened by a respectable old gentleman who has an unseen power up his sleeve will pave hell with a vengeance.

Young people were told that it was a sin to do what their fathers had done unhurt for centuries; those, moreover, who preached to them about the enormity of eating meat, were an unattractive academic folk, and though they overawed all but the bolder youths, there were few who did not in their hearts dislike them. However much the young person might be shielded, he soon got to know that men and women of the world—often far nicer people than the prophets who preached abstention—continually spoke sneeringly of the new doctrinaire laws, and were believed to set them aside in secret, though they dared not do so openly. Small wonder, then, that the more human among the student classes were provoked by the touchnot, taste-not, handle-not precepts of their rulers, into questioning much that they would otherwise have unhesitatingly accepted.

One sad story is on record about a young man of promising amiable disposition, but cursed with more conscience than brains, who had been told by his doctor (for as I have above said disease was not yet held to be criminal) that he ought to eat meat, law or no law. He was much shocked and for some time refused to comply with what he deemed the unrighteous advice given him by his doctor; at last, however, finding that he grew weaker and weaker, he stole secretly on a dark night into one of those dens in which meat was surreptitiously sold, and bought a pound of prime steak. He took it home, cooked it in his bedroom when every one in the house had gone to rest, ate it, and though he could hardly sleep for remorse and shame, felt so much better next morning that he hardly knew himself.

Three or four days later, he again found himself irresistibly drawn to this same den. Again he bought a pound of steak, again he cooked and ate it, and again, in spite of much mental torture, on the following morning felt himself a different man. To cut the story short, though he never went beyond the bounds of moderation, it preyed upon his mind that he should be drifting, as he certainly was, into the ranks of the habitual lawbreakers.

All the time his health kept on improving, and though he felt sure that he owed this to the beefsteaks, the better he became in body, the more his conscience gave him no rest; two voices were forever ringing in his ears—the one saying, "I am Common Sense and Nature; heed me, and I will reward you as I rewarded your fathers before you." But the other voice said: "Let not that plausible spirit lure you to your ruin. I am Duty; heed me, and I will reward you as I rewarded your fathers before you."

Sometimes he even seemed to see the faces of the speakers. Common Sense looked so easy, genial, and serene, so frank and fearless, that do what he might he could not mistrust her; but as he was on the point of following her, he would be checked by the austere face of Duty, so grave, but yet so kindly; and it cut him to the heart that from time to time he should see her turn pitying away from him as he followed after her rival.

The poor boy continually thought of the better class of his fellow-students, and tried to model his conduct on what he thought was theirs. "They," he said to himself, "eat a beef-steak? Never." But they most of them ate one now and again, unless it was a mutton chop that tempted them. And they used him for a model much as he did them. "He," they would say to themselves, "eat a mutton chop? Never." One night, however, he was followed by one of the authorities, who was always prowling about in search of law-breakers, and was caught coming out of the den with half a shoulder of mutton concealed about his person. On this, even though he had not been put in prison, he would have been sent away with his prospects in life irretrievably ruined; he therefore hanged himself as soon as he got home.

Chapter 27

The Views of an Erewhonian Philosopher Concerning the Rights of Vegetables

LET ME leave this unhappy story, and return to the course of events among the Erewhonians at large. No matter how many laws they passed increasing the severity of the punishments inflicted on those who ate meat in secret, the people found means of setting them aside as fast as they were made. At times, indeed, they would become almost obsolete, but when they were on the point of being repealed, some national disaster or the preaching of some fanatic would reawaken the conscience of the nation, and people were imprisoned by the thousand for illicitly selling and buying animal food.

About six or seven hundred years, however, after the death of the old prophet, a philosopher appeared, who, though he did not claim to have any communication with an unseen power, laid down the law with as much confidence as if such a power had inspired him. Many think that this philosopher did not believe his own teaching, and, being in secret a great meat eater, had no other end in view than reducing the prohibition against eating animal food to an absurdity, greater even than an Erewhonian Puritan would be able to stand.

Those who take this view hold that he knew how impossible it would be to get the nation to accept legislation that it held to be sinful; he knew also how hopeless it would be to convince people that it was not wicked to kill a sheep and eat it, unless he could show them that they must either sin to a certain extent, or die. He, therefore, it is believed, made the monstrous proposals of which I will now speak.

He began by paying a tribute of profound respect to the old prophet, whose advocacy of the rights of animals, he admitted, had done much to soften the national character, and enlarge its views about the sanctity of life in general. But he urged that times had now changed; the lesson of which the country had stood in need had been sufficiently learnt, while as regards vegetables much had become known that was not even suspected formerly, and which, if the nation was to persevere in that strict adherence to the highest moral principles which had been the secret of its prosperity hitherto, must necessitate a radical change in its attitude towards them.

It was indeed true that much was now known that had not been suspected formerly, for the people had had no foreign enemies, and, being both quick-witted and inquisitive into the mysteries of nature, had made extraordinary progress in all the many branches of art and science. In the chief Erewhonian museum I was shown a microscope of considerable power, that was ascribed by the authorities to a date much about that of the philosopher of whom I am now speaking, and was even supposed by some to have been the instrument with which he had actually worked.

This philosopher was Professor of Botany in the chief seat of learning then in Erewhon, and whether with the help of the microscope still preserved, or with another, had arrived at a conclusion now universally accepted among ourselves—I mean, that all, both animals and plants, have had a common ancestry, and that hence the second should be deemed as much alive as the first. He contended, therefore, that animals and plants were cousins, and would have been seen to be so, all along, if people

172

had not made an arbitrary and unreasonable division between what they chose to call the animal and vegetable kingdoms.

He declared, and demonstrated to the satisfaction of all those who were able to form an opinion upon the subject, that there is no difference appreciable either by the eye, or by any other test, between a germ that will develop into an oak, a vine, a rose, and one that (given its accustomed surroundings) will become a mouse, an elephant, or a man.

He contended that the course of any germ's development was dictated by the habits of the germs from which it was descended, and of whose identity it had once formed part. If a germ found itself placed as the germs in the line of its ancestry were placed, it would do as its ancestors had done, and grow up into the same kind of organism as theirs. If it found the circumstances only a little different, it would make shift (successfully or unsuccessfully) to modify its development accordingly; if the circumstances were widely different, it would die, probably without an effort at self-adaptation. This, he argued, applied equally to the germs of plants and of animals.

He therefore connected all, both animal and vegetable development, with intelligence, either spent and now unconscious, or still unspent and conscious; and in support of his view as regards vegetable life, he pointed to the way in which all plants have adapted themselves to their habitual environment. Granting that vegetable intelligence at first sight appears to differ materially from animal, yet, he urged, it is like it in the one essential fact that though it has evidently busied itself about matters that are vital to the well-being of the organism that possesses it, it has never shown the slightest tendency to occupy itself with anything else. This, he insisted, is as great a proof of intelligence as any living being can give.

"Plants," said he, "show no sign of interesting themselves in human affairs. We shall never get a rose to understand that five times seven are thirty-five, and there is no use in talking to an oak about fluctuations in the price of stocks. Hence we say that the oak and the rose are unintelligent, and on finding that they do not understand our business conclude that they do not understand their own. But what can a creature who talks in this way know about intelligence? Which shows greater signs of intelligence? He, or the rose and oak?

"And when we call plants stupid for not understanding our business, how capable do we show ourselves of understanding theirs? Can we form even the faintest conception of the way in which a seed from a rose-tree turns earth, air, warmth, and water into a rose full-blown? Where does it get its colour from?

173

From the earth, air, etc? Yes—but how? Those petals of such ineffable texture—that hue that outvies the cheek of a child—that scent again? Look at earth, air, and water—these are all the raw material that the rose has got to work with; does it show any sign of want of intelligence in the alchemy with which it turns mud into rose-leaves? What chemist can do anything comparable? Why does no one try? Simply because every one knows that no human intelligence is equal to the task. We give it up. It is the rose's department; let the rose attend to it—and be dubbed unintelligent because it baffles us by the miracles it works, and the unconcerned businesslike way in which it works them.

"See what pains, again, plants take to protect themselves against their enemies. They scratch, cut, sting, make bad smells, secrete the most dreadful poisons (which Heaven only knows how they contrive to make), cover their precious seeds with spines like those of a hedgehog, frighten insects with delicate nervous systems by assuming portentous shapes, hide themselves, grow in inaccessible places, and tell lies so plausibly as to deceive even their sublest foes.

"They lay traps smeared with bird-lime to catch insects, and persuade them to drown themselves in pitchers which they have made of their leaves, and fill with water; others make themselves, as it were, into living rat-traps, which close with a spring on any insect that settles upon them; others make their flowers into the shape of a certain fly that is a great pillager of honey, so that when the real fly comes it thinks that the flowers are bespoke, and goes on elsewhere. Some are so clever as even to overreach themselves, like the horseradish, which gets pulled up and eaten for the sake of that pungency with which it protects itself against underground enemies. If, on the other hand, they think that any insect can be of service to them, see how pretty they make themselves.

"What is to be intelligent if to know how to do what one wants to do, and to do it repeatedly, is not to be intelligent? Some say that the rose-seed does not want to grow into a rose-bush. Why, then, in the name of all that is reasonable, does it grow? Likely enough it is unaware of the want that is spurring it on to action. We have no reason to suppose that a human embryo knows that it wants to grow into a baby, or a baby into a man. Nothing ever shows signs of knowing what it is either wanting or doing, when its convictions both as to what it wants, and how to get it, have been settled beyond further power of question. The less signs living creatures give of knowing what they do, provided they do it, and do it repeatedly and well, the

174

greater proof they give that in reality they know how to do it and have done it already on an infinite number of past occasions.

"Some one may say," he continued, " 'What do you mean by talking about an infinite number of past occasions? When did a rose-seed make itself into a rose-bush on any past occasion?'

"I answer this question with another. 'Did the rose-seed ever form part of the identity of the rose-bush on which it grew?' Who can say that it did not? Again I ask: 'Was this rose-bush ever linked by all those links that we commonly consider as constituting personal identity, with the seed from which it in turn grew?' Who can say that it was not?

"Then, if rose-seed number two is a continuation of the personality of its parent rose-bush, and if that rose-bush is a continuation of the personality of the rose-seed from which it sprang, rose-seed number two must also be a continuation of the personality of the earlier rose-seed. And this rose-seed must be a continuation of the personality of the preceding rose-seed —and so back and back *ad infinitum*. Hence it is impossible to deny continued personality between any existing rose-seed and the earliest seed that can be called a rose-seed at all.

"The answer, then, to our objector is not far to seek. The rose-seed did what it now does in the persons of its ancestors— to whom it has been so linked as to be able to remember what those ancestors did when they were placed as the rose-seed now is. Each stage of development brings back the recollection of the course taken in the preceding stage, and the development has been so often repeated, that all doubt—and with all doubt, all consciousness of action—is suspended.

"But an objector may still say, 'Granted that the linking between all successive generations has been so close and unbroken, that each one of them may be conceived as able to remember what it did in the persons of its ancestors—how do you show that it actually did remember?

"The answer is: 'By the action which each generation takes —an action which repeats all the phenomena that we commonly associate with memory—which is explicable on the supposition that it has been guided by memory—and which has neither been explained, nor seems ever likely to be explained on any other theory than the supposition that there is an abiding memory between successive generations.'

"Will any one bring an example of any living creature whose action we can understand, performing an ineffably difficult and intricate action, time after time, with invariable success, and yet not knowing how to do it, and never having done it before?

175

Show me the example and I will say no more, but until it is shown me, I shall credit action where I cannot watch it, with being controlled by the same laws as when it is within our ken. It will become unconscious as soon as the skill that directs it has become perfected. Neither rose-seed, therefore, nor embryo should be expected to show signs of knowing that they know what they know—if they showed such signs the fact of their knowing what they want, and how to get it, might more reasonably be doubted."

Some of the passages already given in chapter 23 were obviously inspired by the one just quoted. As I read it, in a reprint shown me by a Professor who had edited much of the early literature on the subject, I could not but remember the one in which our Lord tells His disciples to consider the lilies of the field, who neither toil nor spin, but whose raiment surpasses even that of Solomon in all his glory.

"They toil not, neither do they spin?" Is that so? "Toil not?" Perhaps not, now that the method of procedure is so well known as to admit of no further question—but it is not likely that lilies came to make themselves so beautifully without having ever taken any pains about the matter. "Neither do they spin?" not with a spinning-wheel; but is there no textile fabric in a leaf?

What would the lilies of the field say if they heard one of us declaring that they neither toil nor spin? They would say, I take it, much what we should if we were to hear of their preaching humility on the text of Solomons, and saying, "Consider the Solomons in all their glory, they toil not, neither do they spin." We should say that the lilies were talking about things they did not understand, and that though the Solomons do not toil nor spin, yet there had been no lack of either toiling or spinning before they came to be arrayed so gorgeously.

Let me now return to the Professor. I have said enough to show the general drift of the arguments on which he relied in order to show that vegetables are only animals under another name, but have not stated his case in anything like the fullness with which he laid it before the public. The conclusion he drew, or pretended to draw, was that if it was sinful to kill and eat animals, it was not less sinful to do the like by vegetables or their seeds. None such, he said, should be eaten, save what had died a natural death, such as fruit that was lying on the ground and about to rot, or cabbage-leaves that had turned yellow in late autumn. These and other like garbage he declared to be the only food that might be eaten with a clear conscience. Even so the eater must plant the pips of any apples or pears that he may have eaten, or any plum-stones, cherry-stones, and the like, or he would come near to incurring the guilt of infanticide. The grain of cereals, according to him, was out of the question, for every such grain had a living soul as much as man had, and had as good a right as man to possess that soul in peace.

Having thus driven his fellow-countrymen into a corner at the point of a logical bayonet from which they felt that there was no escape, he proposed that the question what was to be done should be referred to an oracle in which the whole country had the greatest confidence, and to which recourse was always had in times of special perplexity. It was whispered that a near relation of the philosopher's was lady's-maid to the priestess who delivered the oracle, and the Puritan party declared that the strangely unequivocal answer of the oracle was obtained by backstairs influence; but whether this was so or no, the response as nearly as I can translate it was as follows:

> "He who sins aught
> Sins more than he ought;
> But he who sins nought
> Has much to be taught.
> Beat or be beaten,
> Eat or be eaten,
> Be killed or kill;
> Choose which you will."

It was clear that this response sanctioned at any rate the destruction of vegetable life when wanted as food by man; and so forcibly had the philosopher shown that what was sauce for vegetables was so also for animals, that, though the Puritan party made a furious outcry, the acts forbidding the use of meat were repealed by a considerable majority. Thus, after several hundred years of wandering in the wilderness of philosophy, the country reached the conclusions that common sense had long since arrived at. Even the Puritans after a vain attempt to subsist on a kind of jam made of apples and yellow cabbage leaves, succumbed to the inevitable, and resigned themselves to a diet of roast beef and mutton, with all the usual adjuncts of a modern dinner-table.

One would have thought that the dance they had been led by the old prophet, and that still madder dance which the Professor of Botany had gravely, but as I believe insidiously, proposed to lead them, would have made the Erewhonians for a long time suspicious of prophets whether they professed to have communications with an unseen power or no; but so engrained in the human heart is the desire to believe that some people really do know what they say they know, and can thus save them from the trouble of thinking for themselves, that in a short time would-be philosophers and faddists became more powerful than ever, and gradually led their countrymen to accept all those absurd views of life, some account of which I have given in my earlier chapters. Indeed, I can see no hope for the Erewhonians till they have got to understand that reason uncorrected by instinct is as bad as instinct uncorrected by reason.

Chapter 28

Escape

THOUGH BUSILY engaged in translating the extracts given in the last five chapters, I was also laying matters in train for my escape with Arowhena. And indeed it was high time, for I received an intimation from one of the cashiers of the Musical Banks, that I was to be prosecuted in a criminal court ostensibly for measles, but really for having owned a watch, and attempted the reintroduction of machinery.

I asked why measles? and was told that there was a fear lest extenuating circumstances should prevent a jury from convicting me, if I were indicted for typhus or small-pox, but that a verdict would probably be obtained for measles, a disease which could be sufficiently punished in a person of my age. I was given to understand that unless some unexpected change should come over the mind of his Majesty, I might expect the blow to be struck within a very few days.

My plan was this—that Arowhena and I should escape in a balloon together. I fear that the reader will disbelieve this part of my story, yet in no other have I endeavoured to adhere more conscientiously to facts, and can only throw myself upon his charity.

I had already gained the ear of the Queen, and had so worked upon her curiosity that she promised to get leave for me to have a balloon made and inflated; I pointed out to her that no complicated machinery would be wanted—nothing, in fact, but a large quantity of oiled silk, a car, a few ropes, etc. etc., and some light kind of gas, such as the antiquarians who were acquainted with the means employed by the ancients for the production of the lighter gases could easily instruct her workmen how to provide. Her eagerness to see so strange a sight as the ascent of a human being into the sky overcame any scruples of conscience that she might have otherwise felt, and she set the antiquarians about showing her workmen how to make the gas, and sent her maids to buy, and oil, a very large quantity of silk (for I was determined that the balloon should be a big one) even before she began to try and gain the King's permission; this, however, she now set herself to do, for I had sent her word that my prosecution was imminent.

As for myself, I need hardly say that I knew nothing about balloons; nor did I see my way to smuggling Arowhena into the car; nevertheless, knowing that we had no other chance of getting away from Erewhon, I drew inspiration from the extremity in which we were placed, and made a pattern from which the Queen's workmen were able to work successfully. Meanwhile the Queen's carriage-builders set about making the car, and it was with the attachments of this to the balloon that I had the greatest difficulty; I doubt, indeed, whether I should have succeeded here, but for the great intelligence of a foreman, who threw himself heart and soul into the matter, and often both foresaw requirements, the necessity for which had escaped me, and suggested the means of providing for them.

It happened that there had been a long drought, during the latter part of which prayers had been vainly offered up in all the temples of the air god. When I first told her Majesty that I wanted a balloon, I said my intention was to go up into the sky and prevail upon the air god by means of a personal interview. I own that this proposition bordered on the idolatrous, but I have long since repented of it, and am little likely ever to repeat the offence. Moreover, the deceit, serious though it was, will probably lead to the conversion of the whole country.

When the Queen told his Majesty of my proposal, he at first not only ridiculed it, but was inclined to veto it. Being, however, a very uxorious husband, he at length consented—as he eventually always did to everything on which the Queen had set her heart. He yielded all the more readily now, because he did not believe in the possibility of my ascent; he was convinced that even though the balloon should mount a few feet into the air, it would collapse immediately, whereon I should fall and break my neck, and he should be rid of me. He demonstrated this to her so convincingly that she was alarmed, and tried to talk me into giving up the idea, but on finding that I persisted in my wish to have the balloon made, she produced an order from the King to the effect that all facilities I might require should be afforded me.

At the same time her Majesty told me that my attempted ascent would be made an article of impeachment against me in case I did not succeed in prevailing on the air god to stop the drought. Neither King nor Queen had any idea that I meant going right away if I could get the wind to take me, nor had they any conception of the existence of a certain steady upper current of air which was always setting in one direction, as could be seen by the shape of the higher clouds, which pointed invariably from south-east to north-west. I had myself long noticed this peculiarity in the climate, and attributed it, I believe justly, to a trade-wind which was constant at a few thousand feet above the earth, but was disturbed by local influences at lower elevations.

My next business was to break the plan to Arowhena, and to devise the means for getting her into the car. I felt sure that she would come with me, but had made up my mind that if her courage failed her, the whole thing should come to nothing. Arowhena and I had been in constant communication through her maid, but I had thought it best not to tell her the details of my scheme till everything was settled. The time had now arrived, and I arranged with the maid that I should be admitted by a private door into Mr. Nosnibor's garden at about dusk on the following evening.

I came at the appointed time; the girl let me into the garden and bade me wait in a secluded alley until Arowhena should come. It was now early summer, and the leaves were so thick upon the trees that even though some one else had entered the garden I could have easily hidden myself. The night was one of extreme beauty; the sun had long set, but there was still a rosy gleam in the sky over the ruins of the railway station; below me was the city already twinkling with lights, while beyond it stretched the plains for many a league until they blended with the sky. I just noted these things, but I could not heed them. I could heed nothing, till, as I peered into the darkness of the alley, I perceived a white figure gliding swiftly towards me. I bounded towards it, and ere thought could either prompt or check, I had caught Arowhena to my heart and covered her unresisting cheek with kisses.

So overjoyed were we that we knew not how to speak; indeed, I do not know when we should have found words and come to our senses, if the maid had not gone off into a fit of hysterics, and awakened us to the necessity of self-control; then, briefly and plainly, I unfolded what I proposed; I showed her the darkest side, for I felt sure that the darker the prospect the more likely she was to come. I told her that my plan would probably end in death for both of us, and that I dared not press it—that at a word from her it should be abandoned; still that there was just a possibility of our escaping together to some part of the world where there would be no bar to our getting married, and that I could see no other hope.

She made no resistance, not a sign or hint of doubt or hesitation. She would do all I told her, and come whenever I was ready; so I bade her send her maid to meet me nightly—told her that she must put a good face on, look as bright and happy as she could, so as to make her father and mother and Zulora think that she was forgetting me—and be ready at a moment's notice to come to the Queen's workshops, and be concealed among the ballast and under rugs in the car of the balloon; and so we parted.

I hurried my preparations forward, for I feared rain, and also that the King might change his mind; but the weather continued dry, and in another week the Queen's workmen had finished the balloon and car, while the gas was ready to be turned on into the balloon at any moment. All being now prepared I was to ascend on the following morning. I had stipulated for being allowed to take abundance of rugs and wrappings as protection from the cold of the upper atmosphere, and also ten or a dozen good-sized bags of ballast.

I had nearly a quarter's pension in hand, and with this I fee'd Arowhena's maid, and bribed the Queen's foreman—who would, I believe, have given me assistance even without a bribe. He helped me to secrete food and wine in the bags of ballast, and on the morning of my ascent he kept the other workmen out of the way while I got Arowhena into the car. She came with early dawn, muffled up, and in her maid's dress. She was supposed to be gone to an early performance at one of the Musical Banks, and told me that she should not be missed till breakfast, but that her absence must then be discovered. I arranged the ballast about her so that it should conceal her as she lay at the bottom of the car, and covered her with wrappings. Although it still wanted some hours of the time fixed for my ascent, I could not trust myself one moment from the car, so I got into it at once, and watched the gradual inflation of the balloon. Luggage I had none, save the provisions hidden in the ballast bags, the books of mythology, and the treatises on the machines, with my own manuscript diaries and translations.

I sat quietly, and awaited the hour fixed for my departure—quiet outwardly, but inwardly I was in an agony of suspense

181

lest Arowhena's absence should be discovered before the arrival of the King and Queen, who were to witness my ascent. They were not due yet for another two hours, and during this time a hundred things might happen, any one of which would undo me.

At last the balloon was full; the pipe which had filled it was removed, the escape of the gas having been first carefully precluded. Nothing remained to hinder the balloon from ascending but the hands and weight of those who were holding on to it with ropes. I strained my eyes for the coming of the King and Queen, but could see no sign of their approach. I looked in the direction of Mr. Nosnibor's house—there was nothing to indicate disturbance, but it was not yet breakfast time. The crowd began to gather; they were aware that I was under the displeasure of the court, but I could detect no signs of my being unpopular. On the contrary, I received many kindly expressions of regard and encouragement, with good wishes as to the result of my journey.

I was speaking to one gentleman of my acquaintance, and telling him the substance of what I intended to do when I had got into the presence of the air god (what he thought of me I cannot guess, for I am sure that he did not believe in the objective existence of the air god, nor that I myself believed in it), when I became aware of a small crowd of people running as fast as they could from Mr. Nosnibor's house towards the Queen's workshops. For the moment my pulse ceased beating, and then, knowing that the time had come when I must either do or die, I called vehemently to those who were holding the ropes (some thirty men) to let go at once, and made gestures signifying danger, and that there would be mischief if they held on longer. Many obeyed; the rest were too weak to hold on to the ropes, and were forced to let them go. On this the balloon bounded suddenly upwards, but my own feeling was that the earth had dropped off from me, and was sinking fast into the open space beneath.

This happened at the very moment that the attention of the crowd was divided, the one half paying heed to the eager gestures of those coming from Mr. Nosnibor's house, and the other to the exclamations from myself. A minute more and Arowhena would doubtless have been discovered, but before that minute was over, I was at such a height above the city that nothing could harm me, and every second both the town and the crowd became smaller and more confused. In an incredibly short time I could see little but a vast wall of blue plains rising up against me, towards whichever side I looked.

At first, the balloon mounted vertically upwards, but after about five minutes, when we had already attained a very great elevation, I fancied that the objects on the plain beneath began to move from under me. I did not feel so much as a breath of wind, and could not suppose that the balloon itself was travelling. I was, therefore, wondering what this strange movement of fixed objects could mean, when it struck me that people in a balloon do not feel the wind inasmuch as they travel with it and offer it no resistance. Then I was happy in thinking that I must now have reached the invariable trade-wind of the upper air, and that I should be very possibly wafted for hundreds or even thousands of miles, far from Erewhon and the Erewhonians.

Already I had removed the wrappings and freed Arowhena; but I soon covered her with them again, for it was already very cold, and she was half stupefied with the strangeness of her position.

And now began a time, dream-like and delirious, of which I do not suppose that I shall ever recover a distinct recollection. Some things I can recall—as that we were ere long enveloped in vapour which froze upon my moustache and whiskers; then comes a memory of sitting for hours and hours in a thick fog, hearing no sound but my own breathing and Arowhena's (for we hardly spoke) and seeing no sight but the car beneath us and beside us, and the dark balloon above.

Perhaps the most painful feeling when the earth was hidden was that the balloon was motionless, though our only hope lay in our going forward with an extreme of speed. From time to time through a rift in the clouds I caught a glimpse of earth, and was thankful to perceive that we must be flying forward faster than in an express train; but no sooner was the rift closed than the old conviction of our being stationary returned in full force, and was not to be reasoned with: there was another feeling also which was nearly as bad; for as a child that fears it has gone blind in a long tunnel if there is no light, so ere the earth had been many minutes hidden, I became half frightened lest we might not have broken away from it clean and for ever. Now and again, I ate and gave food to Arowhena, but by guesswork as regards time. Then came darkness, a dreadful dreary time, without even the moon to cheer us.

With dawn the scene was changed: the clouds were gone and morning stars were shining; the rising of the splendid sun remains still impressed upon me as the most glorious that I have ever seen; beneath us there was an embossed chain of mountains with snow fresh fallen upon them; but we were far above them; we both of us felt our breathing seriously affected, but I

183

would not allow the balloon to descend a single inch, not knowing for how long we might not need all the buoyancy which we could command; indeed I was thankful to find that, after nearly four-and-twenty hours, we were still at so great a height above the earth.

In a couple of hours we had passed the ranges, which must have been some hundred and fifty miles across, and again I saw a tract of level plain extending far away to the horizon. I knew not where we were, and dared not descend, lest I should waste the power of the balloon, but I was half hopeful that we might be above the country from which I had originally started. I looked anxiously for any sign by which I could recognise it, but could see nothing, and feared that we might be above some distant part of Erewhon, or a country inhabited by savages. While I was still in doubt, the balloon was again wrapped in clouds, and we were left to blank space and to conjectures.

The weary time dragged on. How I longed for my unhappy watch! I felt as though not even time was moving, so dumb and spell-bound were our surroundings. Sometimes I would feel my pulse, and count its beats for half an hour together; anything to mark the time—to prove that it was there, and to assure myself that we were within the blessed range of its influence, and not gone adrift into the timelessness of eternity.

I had been doing this for the twentieth or thirtieth time, and had fallen into a light sleep: I dreamed wildly of a journey in an express train, and of arriving at a railway station where the air was full of the sound of locomotive engines blowing off steam with a horrible and tremendous hissing; I woke frightened and uneasy, but the hissing and crashing noises pursued me now that I was awake, and forced me to own that they were real. What they were I knew not, but they grew gradually fainter and fainter, and after a time were lost. In a few hours the clouds broke, and I saw beneath me that which made the chilled blood run colder in my veins. I saw the sea, and nothing but the sea; in the main black, but flecked with white heads of storm-tossed, angry waves.

Arowhena was sleeping quietly at the bottom of the car, and as I looked at her sweet and saintly beauty, I groaned, and cursed myself for the misery into which I had brought her; but there was nothing for it now.

I sat and waited for the worst, and presently I saw signs as though that worst were soon to be at hand, for the balloon had begun to sink. On first seeing the sea I had been impressed with the idea that we must have been falling, but now there could be no mistake, we were sinking, and that fast. I threw out a bag of ballast, and for a time we rose again, but in the course of a few hours the sinking recommenced, and I threw out another bag.

Then the battle commenced in earnest. It lasted all that afternoon and through the night until the following evening. I had seen never a sail nor a sign of a sail, though I had half blinded myself with straining my eyes incessantly in every direction; we had parted with everything but the clothes which we had upon our backs; food and water were gone, all thrown out to the wheeling albatrosses, in order to save us a few hours or even minutes from the sea. I did not throw away the books until we were within a few feet of the water, and clung to my manuscripts to the very last. Hope there seemed none whatever—yet, strangely enough we were neither of us utterly hopeless, and even when the evil that we dreaded was upon us, and that which we greatly feared had come, we sat in the car of the balloon with the waters up to our middle, and still smiled with a ghastly hopefulness to one another.

He who has crossed the St. Gothard will remember that below Andermatt there is one of those alpine gorges which reach the very utmost limits of the sublime and terrible. The feelings of the traveller have become more and more highly wrought at every step, until at last the naked and overhanging precipices seem to close above his head, as he crosses a bridge hung in mid-air over a roaring waterfall, and enters on the darkness of a tunnel, hewn out of the rock.

What can be in store for him on emerging? Surely something even wilder and more desolate than that which he has seen already; yet his imagination is paralysed, and can suggest no fancy or vision of anything to surpass the reality which he had just witnessed. Awed and breathless he advances; when lo! the light of the afternoon sun welcomes him as he leaves the tunnel, and behold a smiling valley—a babbling brook, a village with tall belfries, and meadows of brilliant green—these are the things which greet him, and he smiles to himself as the terror passes away and in another moment is forgotten.

So fared it now with ourselves. We had been in the water some two or three hours, and the night had come upon us. We had said farewell for the hundredth time, and had resigned ourselves to meet the end; indeed I was myself battling with a drowsiness from which it was only too probable that I should never wake; when suddenly, Arowhena touched me on the shoulder, and pointed to a light and to a dark mass which was bearing right upon us. A cry for help—loud and clear and shrill

—broke forth from both of us at once; and in another five minutes we were carried by kind and tender hands on to the deck of an Italian vessel.

Chapter 29

Conclusion

THE SHIP was the *Principe Umberto,* bound from Callao to Genoa; she had carried a number of emigrants to Rio, had gone thence to Callao, where she had taken in a cargo of guano, and was now on her way home. The captain was a certain Giovanni Gianni, a native of Sestri; he has kindly allowed me to refer to him in case the truth of my story should be disputed; but I grieve to say that I suffered him to mislead himself in some important particulars. I should add that when we were picked up we were a thousand miles from land.

As soon as we were on board, the captain began questioning us about the siege of Paris, from which city he had assumed that we must have come, notwithstanding our immense distance from Europe. As may be supposed, I had not heard a syllable about the war between France and Germany, and was too ill to do more than assent to all that he chose to put into my mouth. My knowledge of Italian is very imperfect, and I gathered little from anything that he said; but I was glad to conceal the true point of our departure, and resolved to take any cue that he chose to give me.

The line that thus suggested itself was that there had been ten or twelve others in the balloon, that I was an English Milord, and Arowhena a Russian Countess; that all the others had been drowned, and that the despatches which we had carried were lost. I came afterwards to learn that this story would not have been credible had not the captain been for some weeks at sea, for I found that when we were picked up, the Germans had already long been masters of Paris. As it was, the captain settled the whole story for me, and I was well content.

In a few days we sighted an English vessel bound from Melbourne to London with wool. At my earnest request, in spite of stormy weather which rendered it dangerous for a boat to take us from one ship to the other, the captain consented to signal the English vessel, and we were received on board, but we were transferred with such difficulty that no communication took place as to the manner of our being found. I did indeed hear the Italian mate who was in charge of the boat shout out something in French to the effect that we had been picked up from a balloon, but the noise of the wind was so great, and the captain understood so little French that he caught nothing of the truth, and it was assumed that we were two persons who had been saved from shipwreck. When the captain asked me in what ship I had been wrecked, I said that a party of us had been carried out to sea in a pleasure-boat by a strong current, and that Arowhena (whom I described as a Peruvian lady) and I were alone saved.

There were several passengers, whose goodness towards us we can never repay. I grieve to think that they cannot fail to discover that we did not take them fully into our confidence; but had we told them all, they would not have believed us, and I was determined that no one should hear of Erewhon, or have the chance of getting there before me, as long as I could prevent it. Indeed, the recollection of the many falsehoods which I was then obliged to tell, would render my life miserable were I not sustained by the consolations of my religion. Among the passengers there was a most estimable clergyman, by whom Arowhena and I were married within a very few days of our coming on board.

After a prosperous voyage of about two months, we sighted the Land's End, and in another week we were landed at London. A liberal subscription was made for us on board the ship, so that we found ourselves in no immediate difficulty about money. I accordingly took Arowhena down into Somersetshire, where my mother and sisters had resided when I last heard of them. To my great sorrow I found that my mother was dead, and that her death had been accelerated by the report of my having been killed, which had been brought to my employer's station by Chowbok. It appeared that he must have waited for a few days to see whether I returned, that he then considered it safe to assume that I should never do so, and had accordingly made up a story about my having fallen into a whirlpool of seething waters while coming down the gorge homeward. Search was made for my body, but the rascal had chosen to drown me in a place where there would be no chance of its ever being recovered.

My sisters were both married, but neither of their husbands was rich. No one seemed overjoyed on my return; and I soon discovered that when a man's relations have once mourned for him as dead, they seldom like the prospect of having to mourn for him a second time.

Accordingly I returned to London with my wife, and through the assistance of an old friend supported myself by writing good little stories for the magazines, and for a tract society. I was well paid; and I trust that I may not be considered presumptuous in saying that some of the most popular of the brochures which are distributed in the streets, and which are to be found in the waiting-rooms of the railway stations, have proceeded from my pen. During the time that I could spare, I arranged my notes and diary till they assumed their present shape. There remains nothing for me to add, save to unfold the scheme which I propose for the conversion of Erewhon.

That scheme has only been quite recently decided upon as the one which seems most likely to be successful.

It will be seen at once that it would be madness for me to go with ten or a dozen subordinate missionaries by the same way as that which led me to discover Erewhon. I should be imprisoned for typhus, besides being handed over to the straighteners for having run away with Arowhena: an even darker fate, to which I dare hardly again allude, would be reserved for my devoted fellow-labourers. It is plain, therefore, that some other way must be found for getting at the Erewhonians, and I am thankful to say that such another way is not wanting. One of the rivers which descends from the Snowy Mountains, and passes through Erewhon, is known to be navigable for several hundred miles from its mouth. Its upper waters have never yet been explored, but I feel little doubt that it will be found possible to take a light gunboat (for we must protect ourselves) to the outskirts of the Erewhonian country.

I propose, therefore, that one of those associations should be formed in which the risk of each of the members is confined to the amount of his stake in the concern. The first step would be to draw up a prospectus. In this I would advise that no mention should be made of the fact that the Erewhonians are the lost tribes. The discovery is one of absorbing interest to myself, but it is of a sentimental rather than commercial value, and business is business. The capital to be raised should not be less than fifty thousand pounds, and might be either in five or ten pound shares as hereafter determined. This should be amply sufficient for the expenses of an experimental voyage.

When the money had been subscribed, it would be our duty to charter a steamer of some twelve or fourteen hundred tons burden, and with accommodation for a cargo of steerage passengers. She should carry two or three guns in case of her being attacked by savages at the mouth of the river. Boats of considerable size should be also provided, and I think it would be desirable that these also should carry two or three six-pounders. The ship should be taken up the river as far as was considered safe, and a picked party should then ascend in the boats. The presence both of Arowhena and myself would be necessary at this stage, inasmuch as our knowledge of the language would disarm suspicion, and facilitate negotiations.

We should begin by representing the advantages afforded to labour in the colony of Queensland, and point out to the Erewhonians that by emigrating thither, they would be able to amass, each and all of them, enormous fortunes—a fact which would be easily provable by a reference to statistics. I have no doubt that a very great number might be thus induced to come back with us in the larger boats, and that we could fill our vessel with emigrants in three or four journeys.

Should we be attacked, our course would be even simpler, for the Erewhonians have no gunpowder, and would be so surprised with its effects that we should be able to capture as many as we chose; in this case we should feel able to engage them on more advantageous terms, for they would be prisoners of war. But even though we were to meet with no violence, I doubt not that a cargo of seven or eight hundred Erewhonians could be induced, when they were once on board the vessel, to sign an agreement which would be mutually advantageous both to us and them.

We should then proceed to Queensland, and dispose of our engagement with the Erewhonians to the sugar-growers of that settlement, who are in great want of labour; it is believed that the money thus realized would enable us to declare a handsome dividend, and leave a considerable balance, which might be spent in repeating our operations and bringing over other cargoes of Erewhonians, with fresh consequent profits. In fact, we could go backwards and forwards as long as there was a demand for labour in Queensland, or indeed in any other Christian colony, for the supply of Erewhonians would be unlimited, and they could be packed closely and fed at a very reasonable cost.

It would be my duty and Arowhena's to see that our emigrants should be boarded and lodged in the households of religious sugar-growers; these persons would give them the benefit of that instruction whereof they stand so greatly in need. Each day, as soon as they could be spared from their work in the plantations, they would be assembled for praise, and be thoroughly grounded in the Church Catechism, while the whole of every Sabbath should be devoted to singing psalms and church-going.

This must be insisted upon, both in order to put a stop to any uneasy feeling which might show itself either in Queensland or in the mother country as to the means whereby the Erewhonians had been obtained, and also because it would give our own shareholders the comfort of reflecting that they were saving souls and filling their own pockets at one and the same moment. By the time the emigrants had got too old for work they would have become thoroughly instructed in religion; they could then be shipped back to Erewhon and carry the good seed with them.

I can see no hitch nor difficulty about the matter, and trust that this book will sufficiently advertise the scheme to insure the subscription of the necessary capital; as soon as this is forthcoming I will guarantee that I convert the Erewhonians not only into good Christians but into a source of considerable profit to the shareholders.

I should add that I cannot claim the credit for having originated the above scheme. I had been for months at my wit's end, forming plan after plan for the evangelisation of Erewhon, when by one of those special interpositions which should be a sufficient answer to the sceptic, and make even the most confirmed rationalist irrational, my eye was directed to the following paragraph in the *Times* newspaper, of one of the first days in January 1872:

"POLYNESIANS IN QUEENSLAND.—The Marquis of Normanby, the new Governor of Queensland, has completed his inspection of the northern districts of the colony. It is stated that at Mackay, one of the best sugar-growing districts, his Excellency saw a good deal of the Polynesians. In the course of a speech to those who entertained him there, the Marquis said: 'I have been told that the means by which Polynesians were obtained were not legitimate, but I have failed to perceive this, insofar at least as Queensland is concerned; and, if one can judge by the countenances and manners of the Polynesians, they experience no regret at their position.' But his Excellency pointed out the advantage of giving them religious instruction. It would tend to set at rest an uneasy feeling which at present existed in the country to know that they were inclined to retain the Polynesians, and teach them religion."

I feel that comment is unnecessary, and will therefore conclude with one word of thanks to the reader who may have had the patience to follow me through my adventures without losing his temper; but with two, for any who may write at once
190

to the Secretary of the Erewhon Evangelisation Company, Limited (at the address which shall hereafter be advertised), and request to have his name put down as a shareholder.

P.S.—I had just received and corrected the last proof of the foregoing volume, and was walking down the Strand from Temple Bar to Charing Cross, when on passing Exeter Hall I saw a number of devout-looking people crowding into the building with faces full of interested and complacent anticipation. I stopped, and saw an announcement that a missionary meeting was to be held forthwith, and that the native missionary, the Rev. William Habakkuk, from———— (the colony from which I had started on my adventures), would be introduced, and make a short address. After some little difficulty I obtained admission, and heard two or three speeches, which were prefatory to the introduction of Mr. Habakkuk. One of these struck me as perhaps the most presumptuous that I had ever heard. The speaker said that the races of whom Mr. Habakkuk was a specimen, were in all probability the lost ten tribes of Israel. I dared not contradict him then, but I felt angry and injured at hearing the speaker jump to so preposterous a conclusion upon such insufficient grounds. The discovery of the ten tribes was mine, and mine only. I was still in the very height of indignation when there was a murmur of expectation in the hall, and Mr. Habakkuk was brought forward. The reader may judge of my surprise at finding that he was none other than my old friend Chowbok!

My jaw dropped, and my eyes almost started out of my head with astonishment. The poor fellow was dreadfully frightened, and the storm of applause which greeted his introduction seemed only to add to his confusion. I dare not trust myself to report his speech—indeed, I could hardly listen to it, for I was nearly choked with trying to suppress my feelings. I am sure that I caught the words "Adelaide, the Queen Dowager," and I thought that I heard "Mary Magdalene" shortly afterwards, but I had then to leave the hall for fear of being turned out. While on the staircase, I heard another burst of prolonged and rapturous applause, so I suppose the audience were satisfied.

The feelings that came uppermost in my mind were hardly of a very solemn character, but I thought of my first acquaintance with Chowbok, of the scene in the wool-shed, of the innumerable lies he had told me, of his repeated attempts upon the brandy, and of many an incident which I have not thought it worth while to dwell upon; and I could not but derive some satisfaction from the hope that my own efforts might have contributed to the change which had been doubtless wrought upon him, and that the rite which I had performed, however unprofessionally, on that wild upland river-bed, had not been wholly without effect. I trust that what I have written about him in the earlier part of my book may not be libellous, and that it may do him no harm with his employers. He was then unregenerate. I must certainly find him out and have a talk with him; but before I shall have time to do so these pages will be in the hands of the public.

At the last moment I see a probability of a complication which causes me much uneasiness. Please subscribe quickly. Address to the Mansion House, care of the Lord Mayor, whom I will instruct to receive names and subscriptions for me until I can organise a committee.